NEVER

John Mair

Written by John Mair (1913-1942)

First published in 1941

This edition published in 2016 by Pontiflunk Press,
an imprint of Prepare to Publish Ltd, UK

Design © Prepare to Publish Ltd

Cover image:
Ewald Grabenbauer/iStock

ISBN 978 1 905315 63 5
Also available for Kindle

www.pontiflunk.com

Non-fiction titles available at:
www.heritagehunter.co.uk

ABOUT THE AUTHOR

John Mair (1913-1942) was born in London in 1913, to journalist G H Mair and actress Marie O'Neill. He became a literary journalist and book reviewer writing for, among others, the *New Statesman* and *News Chronicle*. *Never Come Back* was his only novel, written in 1940 and published in October 1941. He joined the RAF during the Second World War, and was killed in an airborne training accident off the coast of Yorkshire in April 1942. He was also the author of a book about the Shakespeare forgeries by William Ireland, *The Fourth Forger* (1938).

Never Come Back inspired the film *Tiger by the Tail* (also known as *Cross-Up*) in 1955, with the main character and plot changed considerably to feature an American journalist seeking to expose a gang of counterfeiters. *Never Come Back* was more faithfully adapted for British television in 1989, starring Nathaniel Parker and James Fox.

Var. And what say these Magi or Wise Men concerning the furious sprites that dwell in the waste places?

Luc. Of them they relate nothing, saying only: "That those who do visit them, whether it be of accident or intent, never come back."

NICHOLAS RYAM
A Brief Discourse upon the History,
Polity and Religion of the Golden Tartars,
London, 1697

CHAPTER I

A. phalloides, commonly called the "white" or deadly Amanita, and the allied species Amanita verna ("the destroying angel" of Bulliard) (poetic old Bulliard!) *is the cause of the great majority of cases of poisoning by mushrooms. The plant is pure white in colour with the exception of the pileus which varies in shade to the colour of amber. It receives its specific name from the general resemblance to a phallus, though the analogy is nothing like so striking as in the case of Phallus inpudicus* (really!). *The toxicity is very high, and death may ensue from quite small quantities* (good).

Symptoms. A prodromal stage of 6-15 hours in which there are no manifest symptoms ushers in an attack of extreme abdominal pain accompanied by vomiting and diarrhoea, the vomit containing blood and mucus. Remissions alternate with paroxysms of pain and vomiting, the suffering producing a characteristic expression which has been called by the French "la face voltueuse" (sounds like one of Bulliard's mots). *Loss of strength, prostration, cyanosis, jaundice, and coldness of the skin* (she's got that already) *supervene rapidly, and death with coma takes place within a few days* (too slow). *The prognosis is bad* (good), *the mortality being 60 to 100 per cent* (excellent).

Poisoning by Opium: There is nothing characteristic in the post-mortem appearances, unless it be the smell of opium in the stomach contents. There is often engorgement (look this up) *of the lungs and great lividity of the skin. The stomach is usually found in a healthy state. There are no means of detecting opium itself except by its smell and other physical properties, which may easily become disguised* (good). *Toxicity: Five grains would be fatal dose to most persons.* (This seems very promising. Follow up.)

But even as he laboriously made his notes at a corner desk in the Reading Room, he knew perfectly well that he would never murder Anna Raven. It was not that conscience restrained him (unless, in his case, morality disguised itself as sloth), but that he lacked the will to enter an undertaking requiring so much planning, preparation and careful execution, as he wanted the stamina to face the recurring fear of slow detection and sordid punishment. His resolve to kill Anna had been the last refuge of his feebleness, his last attempt to escape from his boring and ceaseless unhappiness.

With a depressing insight he saw that his careful researches into criminal chemistry were as fatuous and escapist as the burrowings of the other readers. He was brother to the old fellow at Desk E. 17, whose straggling, eager, grey beard forever brushed a vast facsimile of the *Codex Vatic anus* which he was reputed to be translating into vulgar Aramaic, as a prelude to an accurate rendering into Old High Hebrew. Worse, he was cousin to the dumpy little woman at K. 11, who invoked a no doubt imaginary thesis as excuse to pore endlessly over mildly indecent eighteenth- century French novels. In years to come he would probably go quite mad, and be pointed out to visitors with respectful mockery as the old man who was planning to poison a woman who had died of senility fifteen years before.

Two-fifteen. International Features called him. "Of course," as Mr. Poole had so often observed, putting his head on one side and stroking his neat little beard like a benevolent, slightly coy Trotsky, "I do not demand from my Editorial Staff the strict routine the House expects from the juniors, and I know, Thane, how much you prize your, eh, democratic liberties, tee-hee!" (He always giggled at his shy excursions into what he regarded as cultivated humour.) "But, as you are aware, the Directors, not I, make the rules, and should they see us, eh, arriving late, they might conduct an inquisition into our—tee-hee!—unholy office!"

No, he could face Mr. Poole's iron hand in its frilly glove to-day; and as he hurried through the railway terminus of a hall, down the steps and towards New Oxford Street, he shuffled and arranged in his mind the work of the afternoon. But beneath it all his thoughts plodded on their perpetual obsession, and moved wearily from one point to another of his three-horned dilemma— how to get over, get possession of, get rid of Anna Raven.

He was never quite sure how far his first interest in her was purely fortuitous. The Cafe Royal was crowded, but not so full that the empty chair at her table was the only vacant seat. Nor was her appearance strikingly attractive. A dark, strongly built woman in the early thirties, whose best features were her slender fingers and quick mouth, she made a gradual rather than an immediate impression, and the longer Desmond knew her, the less he could have described her physical characteristics. All he subsequently remembered of his first reaction to her was an approving surprise that a woman sitting alone should be drinking a really good Burgundy.

After two circuits of the room he stopped by her table. "May I sit here? Or are you expecting a friend?"

"I am not expecting anyone. I have no friends." Then for the first time he really noticed her.

It was at the beginning of the war, when one could address strangers without suspicion of drunkenness, monomania, or evil intentions. Desmond was a little intrigued by this direct-spoken woman who later introduced herself as Anna Raven, and drew her into conversation. Besides her name he learnt very little about her. She had been born, she said, in the south of England; and although she spoke with the unnaturally meticulous accuracy of the well-educated foreigner, he was unable, other than intuitively, to disprove her English origin. She talked well and was clearly unusually intelligent, but she lacked or concealed any particular interests, and gave the impression of a self-assured person with unlimited competence in a single specialised employment. She was strong. She was unusual. She attracted him.

Desmond for his part was quite aware that he was making a very good impression. His fluency made him seem cleverer than he in fact was, he could adapt himself rapidly to any audience, and he was adept at the difficult art of flattery by seeming detachment. In spite of his vanity he was far more acute than most people believed (though less so than he thought himself), and when, this evening, he turned at right angles ostensibly to look for acquaintances but really to display his fine late Roman profile, he was not only perfectly aware of what he was doing, but was fully conscious that Anna was aware of it also, and would take such crude showing-off as the most sincere of compliments. Desmond, in fact, was usually in command of such casual encounters. He lost control only when his feelings began to regard them as worth commanding.

For an hour they talked impersonally and at random. Suddenly looking him directly in the eyes, she said:

"It is late. I must go."

"Perhaps I may see you home?"

There was a pause. "Yes," she said slowly in her pedantic English, "I should be most grateful to you." Desmond felt a sudden flicker of doubt: not the momentary taste of boredom and tired self-condemnation he had often felt on similar occasions, but a sudden premonition of future trouble, like the headache that warns the approach of thunder. He pushed back his chair noisily and helped her into her coat.

In the taxi they were silent. She neither moved against him nor leant away in a corner, but sat upright and at ease a few inches from him. Her hand lay on the seat between them, and after a moment he laid his own over it and stroked her fingers. She remained so detached and uninterested that Desmond, who had sometimes himself adopted this line of passive resistance but was unused to it in women, became a little annoyed and then faintly embarrassed. Anna was not cold, but calm; not distant, but remotely thoughtful. It was like making improper advances to a Buddha. He cleared his throat and said: "I suppose the clock of a taxi is the only one really proving that time is money. If Big Ben worked on the same principle and ticked off the budget thousand by thousand, the electorate might take more interest in government." Not unnaturally she made no answer, and he felt more gauche and silly than he had done for nearly ten years.

They stopped in a Bloomsbury Square at a great house converted into flats. The wine Desmond had drunk during the evening had now completely deserted him, and as he fumbled to pay the driver he felt sick of what half an hour earlier had seemed a promising adventure, and hoped and resolved to say good-bye on the steps. But when he turned

he saw that Anna had already opened the door and was waiting for him in the blue dimness at the end of the hall. He made a face at himself in the darkness, and followed her upstairs.

Her flat was small but conventionally luxurious. It might have been ordered by telephone from an expensive shop, and was attractively furnished without revealing the least trace of individual character. Its relation to genuine good taste was about the same as that of a big hotel's set dinner to a good meal: it was plainly designed for a person of high material standards but quite undomestic interests. The room's only distinctive feature was a great black desk by the window, contrasting strangely with the well-planned Vogue Regency femininity of the other furnishings. It had the disturbing incongruity of a stage prop strayed into the wrong set, or of a carpenter's hammer left lying in an arranged shop-window.

Anna turned to him. "Would you care for some brandy?"

"Thanks, I should love some."

She gave him a glass and sank down on a couch by the fire, lighting a cigarette.

"Aren't you having some yourself?"

"No, I never drink here. I keep it for my guests."

He was puzzled, but her tone did not invite questions. After a moment's hesitation he sat down beside her, put an arm round her shoulder and kissed her on the mouth. Her lips were so cold that the warmth of her tongue seemed almost indecent; and as she lay back, neither repulsing him nor kissing in return, she might have been drugged or asleep. He gently slid his hand down the neck of her dress and touched her small breast. The nipple hardened under his fingers, but she did not move or vary

her steady breathing. As he took his mouth away from hers she drew again at her cigarette.

He glimpsed himself as a puzzled expert warily circling a new type of mine and wondering which was the detonator. Perhaps it was a dud, he thought, and suppressed an impulse to giggle. His arm was cramped and uncomfortable, and from a shift in Anna's position it was difficult to withdraw his hand without pushing her roughly forward. For the second time that evening he began to feel stupidly embarrassed, and did not like it. Neither of them said anything, and at last he got quickly to his feet.

"Where did I put my glass?"

As he turned to the mantelpiece he glanced in the mirror and saw Anna looking at him with a curious smile, but when he turned she was leaning back with her old abstracted expression.

So it was a game, was it? Or perhaps an emotional perversion, a higher masochism that passively inhibited pleasure? He was flooded with a surprising affection for her: he had become confident again. The next move was up to her: if she wanted to play she must offer a gambit. He stood looking down at her in bland and determined silence.

She stood up.

"I'm tired. I must go to bed," she said, and drawing back the curtains from what had appeared to be an alcove, walked into a large bedroom.

Desmond was once again uncertain, and moved doubtfully towards the door.

"Yes, it is quite late. I'm tired myself, I've got to work in the morning."

She made no answer, but turned her back to him and slipped off her dress. Desmond strode forward and caught

her by the shoulders. As he touched her she swung to face him, threw an arm round his neck, and dragged his mouth violently down to hers. With her free hand she wrenched at the buttons of his shirt.

"Detonator," he said.

They both laughed.

For the first few months their relationship was as satisfactory as a cool-hearted epicurean could desire. Their tastes seemed in common, they made no demands on each other, and Anna was mistress of a sensitive and ingenious perversity that kept sensuality interesting without the need for passion. But Desmond, in spite of his intellectual appreciation of such an affaire, found himself rapidly tiring of their cold if accomplished love-making, and would much have preferred a little of the emotionalism he pretended to despise. What he wished to find he soon provided; as lust declined his affections increased; and he began to fall in love with a woman who was ceasing to excite him physically. He grew curious about Anna's life and personality, and although what he learnt made him begin to dislike her, it in no way blunted his desire completely to possess her. If the man in the cliche kills the thing he loves, there are also those who seem compelled to love that which they would willingly destroy.

Anna was very reserved, in spite of a superficial frankness, and betrayed her feelings only for rare, puzzling instants.

One evening soon after they met she had remarked the dark-haired, unexpected thickness of his wrists and forearms. Flattered by her evident interest in his one notable animal attribute, Desmond had boasted of his localised strength: his power of pulling up his whole weight on one hand, his skill at tearing packs of cards. He had even, after encouragement, offered a demonstration, and with little apparent effort appreciably bent quite a formidable poker.

Anna seemed fascinated by this pointless display, caught his hands between her own, and drew them against her breasts. "I adore strength," she said, and kissed his wrists.

He was obscurely annoyed and snatched his hands away from her.

She laughed. "Poor darling! Would you rather I kissed your pericranium?"

"Well, why not?"

"Life belongs to the strong."

"Silly sentimental nonsense! It belongs to the mentally and psychologically strong if you like: not to stupid toughs."

She laid her hand over his mouth and drew him half-unwillingly towards her. She was more ardent than she had been since the first time they slept together.

For some reason he failed to understand, this little incident stayed like an angry spot in the back of Desmond's mind. Another actively disturbed him. They had been talking of death in the generalised way they enjoyed when Anna said:

"I've never seen a dead body close, though I've always wanted to."

"If I were a chivalrous medieval knight I should stop the next passer-by and make one for you. Anyway, with things as they are there'll soon be a great many corpses lying about all over Europe, so I shouldn't worry yourself —just wait for the air raids to start."

"But I am serious. I truly want to see one."

"Well, that's easy enough. Just look at the notice board outside police stations until you see a notice of some unknown person found dead. Then go in and say it answers the description of your missing Uncle Ben, and ask to see the body. There'd probably be a few formalities, but one shouldn't have much trouble."

"Clever Desmond, he always thinks of these things! Let's find a police station."

"I believe there's one just round the corner."

They were strolling through Covent Garden, and stopped under the blue lamp in Bow Street. Desmond bent to the notice board.

"Yes, they've had a quite good harvest lately. I think we're too proud to claim acquaintance with 'Body (Man); aged about sixty; three gold teeth in upper jaw; double- breasted blue suit, trilby hat, dark blue shirt, red spotted tie, patent leather shoes, no underclothing.' What about 'Body (Woman): about forty; birthmark extending down left side of face and neck, cataract of right eye; green coat, brown cloche hat?' There's something rather sad and appealing about the cloche hat—perhaps it's our elder sister who went wrong in the twenties."

He rambled on in this way for some time, until Anna interrupted him. "Well, make up your mind and we'll go in and ask them." She moved towards the steps. "Anna! Where are you going?"

"I'm going to see a body! What have we been talking about for the last ten minutes? Come along and stop gaping."

Desmond was taken aback. He had not for a moment imagined that she was serious, and thought even now that she might be playing one of her unpredictable jokes.

"Oh, come away and don't be ridiculous!"

She looked at him coldly.

"My dear Desmond, I am not like you. I don't waste my time making clever plans I never intend to carry out, but say what I mean and do what I wish. I have not asked you to accompany me: if you are squeamish, you can go home."

There was enough truth in her rebuke momentarily to silence him, and he did not answer. Without looking round she went up the steps of the police station. Desmond hesitated for a moment, and then walked on down the street, angry equally with her and with himself.

When next they met, several days later, he asked, "Well, did you see your corpse?"

"Yes. It was more difficult than you said, but I succeeded in the end. But it did not satisfy me," she added thoughtfully. "It was too old and must have died too peacefully."

He stared at her and saw that she was perfectly sincere.

"You disgusting little bitch," he said, and, not very lightly, slapped her face. He expected and would have welcomed a scene, but she only said,

"Why am I not like other people?" and, without covering her face, began to cry quietly and bitterly. He tried to put his arm round her, but she pushed it aside.

"Go away now," she said in a muffled voice, "and don't come back until I phone you."

He went. She did not phone him for three weeks. Neither of them mentioned the incident again.

Such glimpses of an odd and unpleasant side to her character disturbed him considerably; but it was his jealous suspicions that made him begin to hate her.

From the start he had realised that he was only an isolated part of her life, and at first had been glad of the freedom from responsibility such a position gave him. He had probably assumed, too, that he would easily find out everything about her, and place her, like all the women he had met previously, in one of a few uninteresting categories. In fact, however, he seemed to understand her less the longer he knew her; and what began as curiosity developed into an obsession. She was like no one he had ever met; and the thought that she must have another and broader life than the one he knew filled him with an unceasing discontent. He began to entertain the delusion, common in most men but unique in him, that there was no one else like her in the world; and that if he lost Anna he would, for good or ill, never find a substitute. He did not want her but could not get on without her, and felt all the emotions of the jealous lover except that of love itself. He had, in short, become possessed by her, and at once loathed and needed her as an addict does his drug.

He had discovered very little about her. She had never, directly or indirectly, mentioned any of her friends to him, and might, for all he knew, have hibernated when he was away from her. She would meet him only at irregular intervals, and then invariably at a time and place of her own choosing. Once he called on her without an appointment, but although he was sure he glimpsed her face at the window she had not answered his persistent knocking. Another time he had tried to follow her after a lunch together, but she had vanished into the crowd with the astonishing and unpleasant swiftness of a .snake into long grass. An hour later she had telephoned him and said, "This afternoon you tried to follow me. If you repeat the attempt I shall never see you again." She had rung off without listening to his apologies, and her voice told him that she would keep her word.

She appeared to have a great deal of money which she spent with a cold and careless extravagance, but she always refused to go with him to expensive restaurants or West End theatres. From the beginning she had declined to meet any of his friends (a refusal of which his own secretiveness approved), and their time together was spent in a curious mixture of places, from Kew and Box Hill, to Trust Houses, enormous commercial hotels, for which both of them had a perverse taste, and dog tracks where she proved herself a ruthless and successful gambler.

She had work of some kind, and he noticed that the leather of her desk was worn, as if she did a great deal of writing. But to hints and questions she would give no satisfaction, and something in her manner warned Desmond that if he pressed her too far she would immediately leave him. As he grew more jealous, discretion was harder, and he began to suspect that she was the mistress of some wealthy man, or even a very high-class prostitute. At last he managed to provoke a scene and taunted her with some of his suspicions. For the first time he saw her roused, and she turned furiously on him, her throat working and a speck of saliva at the corner of her mouth.

"How dare you suggest I am someone's paid mistress! I am no one's whore! I have work too important for you to understand! I have never inquired into your life—how dare you pry into mine! You appear to think you have some right over me because I have chosen you to sleep with. Understand then that you are a very small part of me, which I shall leave as soon as I will. I do not think that day is very far off, and when it comes I shall go from you and never see or think of you again!"

"For God's sake don't shout and show your ill-breeding," he had retorted feebly, and stumbled angrily downstairs, swearing to himself that this time he would not return. He had crawled back, of course; and Anna had seemed shamed and distressed by her outburst. But their relationship had never returned to its old easy footing. It was all over.

But although their intimacy was effectively dead, it petered on stubbornly and miserably, like a victim of inoperable cancer who, hacked and doped by the doctors, drags on his horrid life for a few more useless months. Anna, enjoying Desmond as a lover and genuinely liking him as a person, was self-satisfied and insensitive enough to forgive his continual moodiness; and seemed happily prepared to postpone the dreary finale to her own convenience.

Desmond's case was different. He knew now he would never possess or even really understand Anna, and realised that her death would give him unmixed satisfaction. But to think of her alive and out of his reach, loving another person, and, still worse, forgetting him and moving in some alien and delightful society he could never reach, was a continual ulcer in his peace of mind; a sore that would neither heal nor be forgotten, but which must be cut out.

So the affaire had drivelled on until just over a week ago. Then, as he left Anna early one morning, she had told him that she would be leaving London within ten days and that they had better not meet again. She had been very kind and gentle, and he had behaved with great courtesy and good humour. He had kissed her hand, smilingly quoted "Quoth the Raven 'Nevermore'," wished her good fortune, gently closed the door, and strolled slowly round the corner of the Square. Then, safely out of sight, he had leant sickly against a wall and plotted murder.

He had three days more. He must stop her going. He couldn't, and didn't want to if he could. He wanted to kill her. He was a fool; he hadn't the temperament for murder. He'd get over her in a few weeks. He must see her again. If only she were dead. He must be a little mad.

Two-thirty. International Features swallowed him.

There was a good deal of work to be done that afternoon. Captain McCulloch, D.S.O., who, since his success in placing a two hundred word short on Peat Fires of the Hebrides, had bombarded the office with forty thousand word reminiscences of his experiences in the Yogi country, had written threatening a personal call and would have tactfully but finally to be choked off; one of Mr. Poole's friends had submitted an illiterate article that would have to be rewritten because it could not be rejected; and Mr. Poole himself had, for the third time that day, been struck with a brilliant inspiration, and demanded Desmond's immediate attendance.

"Ah, Thane, here you are! What do you think of a series of articles entitled, eh, perhaps, 'Why I Love My Man'—that's just a provisional title, of course," he added hastily, going a little pink. Mr. Poole always seemed embarrassed by the lowbrow nature of the articles his firm supplied, but passionately obstructed any suggestions for improvement.

Desmond assured him that he thought it a very fine title.

"I thought the articles might be by, eh, a number of young women engaged to be married to different types of our readers—say, a doctor, an architect, an estate agent. . . He paused and rubbed his moustache, momentarily unable to think of anyone else who might conceivably read the endless chain of journals his agency supplied with features.

"What about having one of them engaged to a journalist?"

"No, no, we must keep it clean." Mr. Poole chuckled delightedly at his own doggishness.

"But who'll we get to write them?" asked Desmond, with a sinking certainty that he already knew the answer.

Mr. Poole waved his hand with a guilty airiness. "Oh, I thought you might have time for that, Thane; it's just your line—I can't think of anyone who'd do them better. There's no hurry about those proofs—you can easily do them over the week-end. I'd take the galleys home myself, but I've got the work of ten men on my hands as it is."

Desmond knew those ten men. They recurred constantly in

his superior's conversation, and must have been the ten laziest and most incompetent in the profession. Mr. Poole prattled on:

"I'll leave you a free hand with the articles, of course, but remember to bring a good deal of, eh, human interest into them."

"You mean some mild dirt? Okay, leave it to me."

"No, no, nothing of the sort," exclaimed Mr. Poole hastily, "you remember the trouble there was when the *Johannesburg Family Journal* used that ' Is Abortion a Sin ' article we sent them, at your suggestion, I may add. They say they lost five hundred subscriptions."

"Ah, but I expect every member of the families that cancelled their subscription buys them at a bookstall on the sly. They must have gained hundreds of readers on balance."

Mr. Poole was not sure how he ought to take this. Then he brightened. "You're a wag, Thane, and a cynic! You've shocked Miss Prestwood. Hasn't he, Miss Prest- wood?" The secretary giggled, Desmond smiled dutifully, and Mr. Poole bustled him out of the room, chuckling with pleasure at the happy, democratic informality of it all.

Back in his own office, Desmond sighed and sat down to write.

"My lover is a doctor, and he makes me happy because he understands my body as well as my heart. (?? Will P. like this?) *I don't think many girls can have met their man as strangely as I did. I was taking my kid sister to the Out-patients' of St. Margaret's, and I remember being surprised and a bit distrustful that the doctor should be so young. . .*

(It was no use; he'd have to see Anna again and make her change her mind, or at least say where she was going. Blast the cold-hearted bitch. No, blast his own stupid interest in her. It wasn't as if he cared for her in the least, really. . . .)

"'I didn't come here to see your father's piles,' he said, softly, 'I came for something much more interesting—to talk to you ! ' My heart thudded so that I thought he must hear it, but when I spoke my voice was so calm and mocking that I scarcely knew it was my own. 'Oh,

doctor,' I said, turning towards the mirror and patting my hair, as I'd seen Claudette Colbert do it on the films. 'Isn't this rather unprofessional ? . .

At a quarter past four Desmond could bear it no longer. He could not bring himself to phone Anna, and had a childish hope that a telegram might impress her with his urgent sincerity. Feeling at once foolish and desperate he phoned a wire: CALLING SEVENTHIRTY THIS EVENING IT IS IN YOUR OWN INTEREST TO

SEE ME DT. Directly he put down the receiver he knew the wording was stupidly melodramatic and wondered how he would justify it to her. But in the cold type of the telegraph it would probably impress even Anna a little, and what to say when he saw her would have to be left to the moment. There must be *something* that would move her. Love might, but he didn't feel it: hate and resolution would have to take its place. Suppose she phoned and put him off? He turned to his secretary. "Miss Hedley. If anyone—anyone at all—rings me this afternoon I've gone out and shan't be back. Be quite firm whoever it claims to be, and however urgent their business."

He felt instantly easier in mind, and was irrationally certain that his fluency, which had never yet failed him, could talk Anna round into some sort of compromise. He did not want to keep her now, but merely to leave her gradually in his own time. He returned to his work almost with enthusiasm.

"'But you mustn't, darling! It's—it's Disgraceful Conduct.' He laughed and held me closer. 'You adorable little creature,' he whispered. 'I'm never going to leave you, whatever the bearded old gentlemen of the Medical Council say. Don't worry your sweet wee head about me; it's true that love can always find a way, and you know that for an hour in your arms I'd tell off old Hippocrates himself' His kisses swept through me like liquid fire, and the grey walls of the Dispensary melted away until the coloured medicine bottles seemed like tropic fruit, and we might have been alone together on an atoll in the Pacific..."

CHAPTER II

When he saw Anna that evening he found he had nothing to say to her. This did not surprise him—he was used to her power of silencing him as effectively as the footlights dry up a nervous actor. It was his own indifference to her that seemed unusual; and as he sat on the edge of the desk swinging his legs, he felt as detached and superior as a biologist watching his specimens' natural processes. After a first casual greeting he said nothing, but quietly hummed an outmoded dance tune in smug self-satisfaction.

It was Anna who broke the silence.

"Why have you come here?"

"Oh, just a social call. As some people have religious calls, so I have social ones, and obey them with proper humility."

"What did you mean by your telegram?"

"Nothing, nothing at all. Don't you think the post office should have Bad News telegraph forms, like the Greetings ones? Then the Fatal Message from the War Office could arrive on black and silver paper garlanded with skulls, crosses, urns and broken pillars. I'm sure widows and orphans would love an artistic memento of their sacrifice to frame and hang in the front parlour."

Anna broke in impatiently.

"If you have anything to say to me, please say it now. I am going abroad in a few days and shall probably not return."

"Going abroad? How very nice for you. Don't go on a conducted tour: I did once, but found that too many Cooks spoiled the brothel." He gave an irritating titter.

Anna answered sharply.

"If you refuse to be sensible, do as you please. In a short time I have an appointment to keep. Please excuse me while I change."

He waved his hand graciously as she went abruptly into the bedroom. Through a gap in the curtain over the door she could see him smiling to himself and examining his nails. She began to feel faintly disturbed. She knew most types of men and thought she understood Desmond, but had never seen him quite in his present mood. She noticed that his gestures were slightly but perceptibly out of control, as if he were drunk. He swung his legs rather too vigorously, talked loudly, and continually moved his head or his hands. But she knew he was quite sober, for his eyes were cold and distant and a little strained, as though he was peering at something a great way off. She glanced at him again, and now, for the first time that evening, he was staring straight at her as if he was trying to memorise her face or guess her weight. As he stared he continued to turn his hand and go through the gestures of studying his nails. It was unnatural and suggested unpleasantly that his body was a sentient animal with a life of its own quite separate from that of his brain.

Desmond looked at Anna with the rude curiosity usually reserved for natives. Sitting half naked at her dressing table, she looked far older than he had originally supposed, and the texture of her throat and face seemed coarse against the smoothness of her shoulders. Her neck was going to fat, and he fancied a conscious effort in the straightness of her back. It was hard to remember that she had mind and personality: she might have been a cleverly constructed doll topped by a beautiful glossy wig. His thoughts grew spiteful and he wondered how to anger her.

It was eight o'clock and growing dark. Anna came in, patting her hair, and said:

"I must go soon. For the last time, have you anything to say to me?"

"Nothing that would interest you."

She raised her voice. "Say what you wish to now; I shall not ask you again."

"Don't speak so loudly. Go if you want to: I'm not stopping you."

His heel caught the edge of the desk and flicked off a splinter of polished wood, but he did not seem to notice. Outlined against the window in the fading light his humped shoulders and out-thrust head were like the silhouette of some fabulous bird.

Anna again felt a tremor of uncertainty and decided to leave at once, earlier than she had intended. She went over to the desk and pushed him aside.

"Excuse me, there is something I must get."

Unlocking one of the drawers she took out a small leather book with a metal clasp and lock. Desmond snatched it and slipped from the desk.

"Ah, a diary! Who'd have thought you kept a thing like that!"

He put it in his pocket and pretended to make for the door. Anna turned pale with anger and almost hissed at him.

"Stop this foolishness! Give it to me immediately!" "Not till I've seen what you've said about me. I'll send it back tomorrow."

He knew he was being childish but was not in the least ashamed of it. Anna was trembling with rage, and he enjoyed the rare feeling, where she was concerned, of being master of the situation. Then, unexpectedly, she reached for her handbag, drew out a little automatic pistol and pointed it at him.

"Now give that book back to me!"

Desmond's first impulse was to laugh. The whole scene was as ludicrous and improbable as a bad film, and the gun had no more threat in it than a stone axe in a museum. He mockingly raised his hands above his head and strolled towards her.

"My dear Anna, you do look stupid! The part of a gun- moll doesn't suit you in the least. Are you sure you've remembered to load it?"

"Give me that book or I shall shoot."

He was seized with sudden fury at her melodramatics, knocked the gun from her hand with a swift blow, and caught the silk scarf round her neck. He jerked it violently and snarled:

"Don't be such a bloody fool!"

She pushed against him and brought up her knee hard into his groin. He stumbled forward and they went over together on to the floor. Quite possessed with rage he twisted the scarf and tugged with all his strength. Again her knee caught him, and to drown the pain he wrenched at the silk until the veins on his wrists stood out. As her body writhed beneath him a detached corner of his mind wondered how long she would go on struggling. He lay there twisting the scarf for some time after she ceased to move. He knew perfectly well that she was dead.

When he stood up it was quite dark. He felt no emotions of any sort, but picked up the pistol and sat again on the edge of the desk, this time without moving. After a while he began to feel proud of his own detachment, and wandered round the room, stumbling into the furniture and talking to himself. He avoided the corner where the body lay.

"Well, well, who'd have thought it! I expect they'll hang me for this. I'm lucky it's not in America: the electric chair takes half an hour and you only die of the autopsy, or so they say. Who was it said that the head stays alive and sees several minutes after decapitation? They say people can be tickled to death or die of sneezing. A tyrant might try it out on his enemies and let their ludicrous death throes bring public contempt on their opinions. If you hang a person with too long a drop the head comes off— it's said that several people have had a drop too far when the hangman's had a drop too much. Poor old Anna! Anna who? Annabell to toll her knell. Perhaps I look different now I'm a murderer? Let's see."

He drew the curtains, turned on a reading lamp and stared at himself in the mirror, twisting and posturing like a mannequin.

"Same as ever, I'm afraid—I haven't the face of a tough guy. If I stick out my chin I'm a bit like a Roman— the ignoblest Roman of them all: the one who was borne home face downwards on his shield with all his wounds behind, except for a few cuts on the side he got as he tried to zigzag."

He began to strike attitudes and make appropriate faces, pointing Anna's gun at imaginary enemies, and aiming it through his pocket like an American gangster. All at once reality returned with a rush and he saw a pale, dishevelled figure grimacing grotesquely at itself in the mirror of a dimly-lit room, while a stiffening body lay half-hidden behind the sofa.

"Oh, my God!" he said, and felt really frightened.

He turned up all the lights, sat slowly down and tried to review his position. He felt no sort of conscience or pity for Anna—as he had imagined, death had killed his interest in her—but he was very afraid of the squalid and slow- moving consequences if the police began to suspect him. For a few minutes he breathed deeply to calm himself, and his mind began to run more normally.

In the first place, no one had seen him come in, and in the darkness it was practically certain that no one would see him leave. Actually, he had never met anyone in the house, and for all he knew Anna's might have been the only inhabited floor in the whole building. So far as he was aware there was no known connection between Anna and himself. He had never mentioned her to any of his friends, disapproving of people who boasted about their amours, and believing, in any case, that complete silence on that subject brought a far greater reputation for licentiousness, if one was so stupid as to desire such a thing, than did continual self-congratulatory anecdotes.

Anna, he was sure, had been equally discreet; and even had she an especial confidant, it was very unlikely that she had had time to mention his intended call that night. He had never written to her, given her signed or traceable presents, or been introduced by her to anyone. Scotland Yard could not conceivably trace him. The best thing he could do was to leave at once.

He got up briskly, wiped with his handkerchief the door-knobs and everything else he remembered touching, went softly out on to the landing and gently pulled the door shut. As the lock clicked he stopped dead with a horrible feeling in his stomach as if he had been shot. The telegram!

He pushed stupidly at the door, but it was unyielding. Desperately he tried his keys one after the other, but the lock was a Yale and none of them even fitted the keyhole. He searched his pockets for something to force the door, but found only Anna's automatic. He weighed it doubtfully in his hand. He had read that you could shoot doors open, and thought that, small as the gun was, it would no doubt blow in the lock if he fired a shot or two between the keyhole and the crack. But the house was dark and alarmingly still: the report would sound like a thunderbolt to anyone in the flat beneath. If he fired, people might well stream from every door like a city crowd to an accident : if he fled quietly, the police would find the telegram, trace the number from which it was sent, track him down and question him until he confessed. There might be no one in the house, and at the worst he could try to shoot his way out and be hanged for a lion instead of a sheep. He took off his coat and held it over the gun to muffle the explosion, then pressed the muzzle an inch to the left of the keyhole and fired twice.

The shot sounded like an earthquake, and before the echo died away he flung his full weight against the door. At his first charge the wood splintered; at the second, it gave, and he pitched forward into the flat. As he picked himself up, he heard a door open on the landing below, and the light clicked on. He slipped silently out and lay down on the floor, pointing his pistol through the banisters at the turn of the stairs. Unless anyone came up he was out of sight, and if they did he would see them first.

There was a pause, and a nervous middle-aged voice called:

"Er, I say, is anything the matter up there?"

Silence. Then a woman spoke querulously.

"Oh, do come in, Jack, and shut the door. It's none of our business *what* happens upstairs."

"I'm *sure* I heard a bang, dear. I think I ought to go up and see what it is."

"So you want to see if Miss Raven's safe, do you? I know you! Do you think I haven't noticed you making eyes at her on the stairs these last months? Come back at once and remember you're an elderly married man."

"I'm not elderly! I'm in my prime!"

"Prime or no prime, come back here and shut the door; there's a horrible draught."

"I shan't be a minute, dear, but I do think I ought to see if everything's all right."

Desmond could hear slippers moving towards the stairs. He tensed himself and thrust the gun forward. The woman's voice broke in decisively.

"Very well, if you're going upstairs, I'm coming too! We can *both* ask Miss Raven how she's feeling!"

The slippers stopped abruptly, and then the male voice said resignedly:

"Oh, very well, dear, I expect you're right. I'm sure there's nothing the matter; the News will be on in a few minutes and we don't want to miss it."

The door shut. Desmond crept back to the flat, pushed its door to, and shot the bolt. Then a shocking realisation of the danger he had passed came over him and he felt physically sick. He blundered into the lavatory and hung retching over the bowl for several minutes. When he felt better, he went to the sitting-room, and drawing on his gloves, began a systematic search. The waste-paper basket? Empty. The desk? It was locked, but the keys lay on the top where Anna had dropped them. He opened the drawers and went rapidly through them, throwing their contents on the floor. Everything was extremely neat—bundles of letters tied together in different coloured strings, files of receipted bills, notebooks filled with figures, apparently accounts of expenses. Some of the items were a little surprising—Anna had an American passport; and must have been a versatile linguist, for there were papers in several languages—but Desmond had no time for curiosity. He did pause for an instant at a drawer full of booksellers' catalogues, and was faintly surprised that a woman whose only books were half a dozen works of reference should apparently have gone through them carefully and marked several items. But he did not find his telegram.

He looked for fresh hiding places and remembered her bag. In it were a lipstick, a mirror, a gold compact, and a huge wad of dirty one-pound notes. There must have been several hundred of them, and as far as he could see in a hasty thumbing no two belonged to the same numerical series; they might have been carefully chosen to make their theft untraceable. He thrust the treasure into his pockets and felt enormously encouraged. He had never before had so much actual cash in his possession, and it gave him the same feeling of power and security that a savage must feel when he grasps a well-wrought weapon. He thought: "I wonder what Anna was doing with all this? She must have been a bookie."

He felt unreasonably cheerful, and continued his search humming happily to himself. He remembered having read somewhere that women hid their most secret possessions amongst their underclothing, and rifled Anna's bedroom with especial thoroughness. Under her quiet exterior she had concealed exotic tastes, and although he had always been secretly amused at her predilection for extraordinary and expensive undergarments that belonged in a Paris shop-window rather than on a human body, he was astonished at the contrast between the austerity of her dresses and the luxuriant profusion beneath. At last he touched something hard at the back of a drawer and eagerly pulled it out. It was a book: a cheap Latin edition of the Aeneid, with some of the lines marked as though they had been scanned. With an undefined idea that there must be some important secret here, he wrenched off the binding and tore out the end-papers to see what they concealed. He found nothing.

He walked back to the sitting-room and stood by the mantelpiece biting his fingers. All at once relief flooded him and he laughed hysterically.

"I must have a fine conceit of myself," he thought; "why the hell should she bother to keep my telegram at all, let alone lock it in her desk or hide it amongst her underclothing? She must have thrown it in the fire as soon as it came."

He knelt down and poked at the dying coals, and found no trace of paper but much ash. Anything thrown in had been consumed long ago. He stood up, resolved to make a last quick survey and then leave as quietly as possible.

With a long irregular buzz the phone rang.

He stood still, his heart beating and a vein pounding in his head, hoping that the noise would stop; but it went urgently on. He had the horrible fancy that if it rang long enough, Anna would get up to answer it. He felt an irresistible urge to pick up the receiver himself just to stop the ringing, and was moving as if hypnotised towards the table when abruptly the sound ceased.

There was no time to waste now. He knew that on the Museum exchange an irregular ring meant a local call: the ringer might well be in a call-box just outside, and getting no answer might come up to see what had happened to Anna.

He turned out the lights, pulled the front door to and crept downstairs holding the pistol in front of him. As he reached the first landing, the ringing began again. Out in the street and plunging into the darkness he imagined he could still hear it faintly, going on and on.

CHAPTER III

Out in the darkness Desmond felt extraordinarily alone. Behind him, a memory he did not wish to dwell on: ahead, a fear, a waiting and a self-justification. If he went home he would find a comfortable chair, and books that between them offered all the comforts of reason, beauty and philosophy. After only the briefest hesitation he pushed between the swing doors of The Jolly Conscript.

The saloon bar was as cheery as ever. In one corner a young corporal was defending Purity against the raucous humour of an old tart, and having much the worst of it. In another, three men with black overcoats that reached to their ankles were drinking whisky and talking importantly out of the corner of their mouths. By the pin-table an Indian student and his very pregnant blonde wife were eagerly explaining to a dense Czech refugee that Freud, Marx, and Einstein were but different aspects of the Life Force, and that an Italian peasant was wiser than all three put together. A bald man played the piano. Two Lesbians talked coldly through a miserable clerk who had tried to buy them a drink. A conscientious objector won the war by advancing through central China to the world's only source of some mumbled but indispensable mineral. For all of them the bar was home, truth and beauty. It was something worth fighting for.

As soon as he entered Desmond was sucked into a small whirlpool of acquaintances.

"Hallo, Thane, where have you been lately?"

"Oh, I've been working. How's everyone? Let's hear the latest slander."

Such a request was well calculated to give the asker a rest and the others a great deal of simple pleasure. The storm of gossip broke with all its customary verve.

It seemed that Milly had left Peter and Tony had joined Susan; Matthew was in the Ministry of Supply and Paul had been translated into French; John had been killed in the Air Force, and

Nancy was alleged to be in love with a taxi driver at her Ambulance Station; Mark said he would object on the grounds that the Germans were brute beasts and he was a member of the R.S.P.G.A.; and someone's cousin had apparently really run before a Tribunal crying: "I'm a Pillar of Fire." They went on and on, and Desmond, who usually enjoyed their chatter, thought that if he owned an angel with a flaming sword he would keep the creature thoroughly overworked. But when in the end they paused and began to talk more generally he found himself practically tongue-tied, and searched for an excuse to get away.

At the far end of the bar he noticed a tall, fair girl whose shrill voice and flashy clothes could not take the attractiveness from her loosely built figure, any more than the perfection of her features could hide the vacuousness of their expression. She was a little drunk and plainly becoming a problem to her dark, intense friend and the tooth-brush moustached young subaltern who had probably picked them up. "Down, down to the bottom," thought Desmond. "A person who has no conscience has no right to good taste," and, abruptly excusing himself, walked over and slapped the officer on the shoulder.

"Well, well, well! Fancy meeting you here! I don't expect you remember me—we met at Cowes before the war. Won't you and your friends have a drink?"

He had calculated that snob-appeal would certainly get Moustache, who had clearly never been to Cowes and had equally clearly been showing off to the women; and knew that any fears of a "touch" would be stilled by immediate lavishness.

"Oh, er, yes, thanks," stammered Moustache hesitatingly.

Desmond followed up.

"Leave what you're drinking now and let's have some champagne. I believe this place keeps some quite reasonable stuff though you mightn't expect it."

"Ooh, yes, let's," said Fair-Hair.

"That would be very nice," said Dark.

"Oh, I say," said Moustache.

The trick was done. As Desmond grandly flicked his fingers at the barman he could feel the astonished and reproachful eyes of his friends, and hear their disapproving whispers. He didn't care in the least; he was beginning to enjoy himself.

The man who had been kneeling by the body got up. "She can't have been dead for more than three hours," he said, "probably less." He made an entry in his notebook. One of the others began to search the room with unhurried expertness, while the third tested doorknobs and smooth surfaces for fingerprints.

He soon found out all he cared to know about his new acquaintances. Fair-Hair, whose conversation consisted largely of giggles, was, Dark assured him, "in a vurry responsible position— confidential secretary to a Big Advertising Executive." Desmond thought that she might be confidential from the Executive's wife, but that was about all. Dark was Canadian and worked in the same firm, but was really interested in higher things—"You've no *idea*, Mr. Tisket" (Desmond's *nom de jeu* for the evening) "what a wonderful *peace* you get if you think Astrally." Moustache was on week-end leave from his regiment ("Can't say where we're stationed, oh, no, no! Enemy ears and all that, you know, old man!") and very anxious to impress as an officer and a gentleman—roles that he found increasingly incompatible as he got more drunk.

Desmond's original idea had been to detach Fair-Hair from the party, but soon, seeing that this would be very difficult, decided it would be better to lose Moustache. The easiest method was to help him drink himself unconscious; a feat that should, from the look of his already glazed eyes, have been comparatively simple. Unfortunately, he had a stomach even if he lacked a head, and the only effect of Desmond's hospitality was to make him quarrelsome and suspicious.

Fair-Hair grew happier and happier.

"Tisky, darling, I think I'm getting tiddly! Don't you think I'm a naughty girl!"

"I'll spank you!" belched Moustache, and made a clumsy grab at her. Desmond pushed him back.

"Now, now, remember you're fighting for Liberty— not for licence. Why don't you have another drink?" Moustache rocked up to him.

"I'm fighting for my country, everyone's fighting for their country. What you doing, uh?"

"Well, I really oughtn't to tell you, but I'm in the propaganda section of the Ministry of Munitions."

"Oh, do tell me an official secret," screamed Fair-Hair, and spilt her glass over his sleeve.

"Well, I shouldn't really, I suppose, but I know I can trust you all." He leant forward confidentially. "I've been working recently on a device of my own, a Propaganda Shell."

Moustache blinked doubtfully.

"Wassat?"

"You'll know soon enough. It's quite a simple device, actually: based on the principle of the wind-organ. We make a shell of metal so perforated that when it's fired the air rushes through the holes and gives out a propagandist sound. Thus we've just made ten million which go 'Freeeeeeeeeeeeeeedom' as they plunge into the enemy lines. Imagine the demoralisation of the Nazis when they have to die to the sound of our glorious slogan!"

Dark thought intensively about this. "But oughtn't it to say it in German, so they'd understand it?"

"You're absolutely right. You've put your finger on the weakness of the whole scheme. It's all the fault of red tape and bureaucracy—no one in the Ministry thought of that point till we'd made the shells, and now they're trying to sell them to the Japanese to use against America. It's brains like yours that we need; I'll get you a job in my department."

Moustache was thinking. You could almost hear the caterpillar tracks as his train of thought rattled over an idea.

"But I say ..." he began.

Desmond went on hastily.

"Another device we've perfected recently is a poison gas cylinder which squirts out the gas in the shape of words— like sky-writing. But there's a split in the Cabinet over that: they can't decide whether to say 'WE LOVE THE GERMAN PEOPLE, REALLY' or 'SERVE YOU FASCIST BASTARDS RIGHT.'"

One of the men said: "Her contact list's missing, sir, and there's no trace of her special expense money. Everything else seems to be here." Another said: "I can't find any fingerprints, but I've got one of the bullets out of the door." The third, a big thick-necked man in a smart suit, spoke sharply: "Give me the bullet. Search the place more thoroughly, and go on searching until you find something useful. Don't make any noise. I'll report to Headquarters." He turned towards the phone, but the first man interrupted him with deferential urgency. "Don't touch the phone, sir, it may be tapped. There's a box fifty yards down the street." The big man nodded approvingly. "Good. Now get on with it." He slipped out of the front door as silently as a cat.

The talk had turned to politics and Moustache was becoming aggressive.

"Reds? Don't like Reds. Got one in the Mess—rotten sort of fellow, won't drink, always reading books. Tries to suck up to the troops, but they don't like him. Oh, no! They like 'n officer they reshpect—natural leader—right sort. This Red's like 'em all—can't keep his mind off money; always talking about wages and the cosht of living, thinks of nothing else."

He belched, exhausted by his oration. Desmond agreed. "I know. The working class are simply terrible. If they had a bath they'd keep coals in it if they had any coals. What did they do when they had money after the last war? Why, they bought grand pianos, lit fires underneath them and had baths in them."

Moustache pushed his face into Desmond's and breathed alcohol at him.

"You're a Red. *I* know. I smell 'em anywhere."

"They could smell you anywhere as well, I should think."

"You're insulting me, eh? You wan' a fight?"

He tried to draw himself up and nearly fell over. His voice was thick and angry, and the proprietor nodded to his second barman, a huge youth like a debauched plough- boy, who edged towards their corner. Desmond felt it was time to leave.

"Don' like Reds," repeated Moustache. "Don' like *you*." He hiccoughed loudly.

Desmond felt Dark pulling gently at his arm. He bent over to her.

"You give him a poke," she said unexpectedly, "he can't hold his likker, that's what's the matter with him. What he wants is a good poke."

Desmond had a better idea. He caught the man by the shoulder and pushed him round.

"Look, there's a friend of yours over there. I think he wants to buy you a drink."

Moustache swivelled glassily and peered through the confusion, while Desmond seized the girls by the arm and dragged them outside.

"Where's Jimmie? We've lost Jimmie!" shrieked Fair-Hair.

"Never mind Jimmie; let's go somewhere else. Taxi!" "Oh, yes, Tisky, let's! I'll fetch Jimmie!"

The taxi drew up. Hastily pushing them in, he told the driver to go somewhere nice and noisy.

"Poor Jimmie! He'll be hurt," said Fair-Hair. "Absence makes the heart grow fonder," said Desmond. "You should have given him a good poke," said Dark, "he doesn't think creatively."

The taxi-man's idea of somewhere nice and noisy was a cellar near Leicester Square dressed up as a Munich Beer Hall. In peace time it had prided itself on its German atmosphere, and served rissoles and two veg. under the title of *Konigsburger Klops mit Brat Kart, und Wirsingkohl.* This change of name, though it made the dish smell no sweeter, succeeded in quintupling the price. Since the war, however, there was a great pretence that the decor was Austro-Czech; and the Tyrolean orchestra offered the *Sambre et Meuse* and the *Marseillaise* as their contribution to the continental gaiety. The menu had reformed itself a little too far, and consisted now of such delicacies as *Central European Sausage with Sour Cabbage à la Danubienne.* The patrons of the place consisted largely of very young Air Force officers, all of whom seemed to be acquainted with each other.

Fair-Hair had forgotten Jimmie, and displayed a great capacity for drinking lager and flirting with groups of young men at a range of fifty feet. Her friend wanted to discuss the Eternities.

"You know," she declared earnestly, "I have a great gift for getting *inside* people."

"So have I. We must get inside each other sometime." She leant forward. "I get inside my friend, she has a lovely spirit really; she knows life is giving not taking; she gives and gives and gives."

"I thought that as soon as I saw her."

"Ah, you're intuitive! You've got a seer's eyes. What was your first impression of me?"

He gazed at her thoughtfully. "You're very sensitive and artistic: you had an unhappy childhood because you felt more keenly than others; you have an extremely strong character but you refrain from exercising it for fear you may hurt other people; you have one great weakness— you sometimes let your generous impulses betray your real purpose in life. I don't think I saw anything else."

She stared back at him.

"Why, Mr. Tisket, that's wonderful! I never met anyone who understood me so well!"

He blew his nose modestly.

"I studied astrology under Duleepsinghi. I expect that accounts for it."

He settled back in a pleasant coma and listened to the long and doubtless very interesting story of Dark's life.

At midnight the Tyroleans packed up their instruments, and waiters circled round the tables skilfully snatching undefended steins. By now Desmond loved himself and the world in general and welcomed Fair-Hair's suggestion that they go some place else. In the street, a last sliver of caution pricked him, and he saw the inadvisability of going to a bottle-party with several hundred one pound notes in his pockets. Where could he hide them? With a smile of pleasure at his own cleverness, he told the taxi to go to Leicester Square post office, and asked the girls to wait while he sent an important letter. Inside, he asked for their largest envelope and shut himself up in a phone box to count his money. He had nearly three hundred pounds, and put two hundred and fifty in the envelope. In one of his pockets he found Anna's diary, and glanced quickly through it. The pages, so thin that they scarcely turned without tearing, were covered with figures, apparently some sort of cipher. As he held the book, memories of how he had obtained it came filtering back through his artificial happiness. He shook himself and thrust it into the envelope. Where should he send it? Not to his own address, for if the police *did* happen to suspect him, they might somehow intercept his correspondence—he could even, his imagination heightened by drink, see the letter arriving while a detective questioned him, and feel his hand trembling as he slipped it into his pocket under the cold eye of suspicion. Better, he thought, send it *poste restante* to a false name, and in careful block capitals he addressed it to Walter Tisket, Esq., *Poste Restante,* Central Post Office—where? He remembered a village where he stayed as a child and would like to see again—Missenden, Bucks.

Easier in mind he went back to the taxi.

"Go to the best night club where one needn't dress," he said to the driver. They went.

The Snake and Ladder was the same as any other prosperous bottle party. John Bull, the business man, was buying champagne for a platinum blonde, so docile that she would obediently follow any man anywhere at any time, unless another man had her by the arm. Neural Gender, the poet, was recreating Athens with the help of five handsome young men and a paper cap. A cadet was sitting by himself and pretending to be blasé in a manner that revealed only too clearly that his past was in the future; and a good many other people were attempting to forget that any future they had was a long way in the past. Desmond wished he had gone somewhere else, and bought drinks for everyone within reach. Fair-Hair became .conversational.

"My," she said, "you are throwing your money about! " "Well, it's rather a special occasion. I'm celebrating in honour of a very dear friend who made me her executioner." "You mean executor," interjected Dark.

"Oh, yes, of course. Anyway, she left me money for a funeral feast in her memory; before she fell asleep she said she couldn't rest quietly unless she was waked. Dear woman! She always loved her paradox."

He sighed deeply several times, and noticed that a waiter was looking at him queerly. He must be getting drunk; better have another drink. The band thumped, a woman sang, a girl strip teased, a man told dirty stories. Presumably it was worth the money; at any rate, a great many people seemed willing to pay for it. Suddenly a loud clear voice spoke almost in his ear.

"Hullo, Anna, wherever have you been? I thought you were dead."

He spun round and saw two strangers talking at the next table. He laughed shakily at himself, but all his contentment had gone; he felt fuddled and ill, and breathed quickly as though he had asthma. He turned to Dark.

"I'm terribly sorry, but I must go at once. Here's money for the bill, it'll cover it easily. Buy yourself and your friend a present with the change. I hope you'll forgive me, but I don't feel very well."

He thrust a handful of notes at her and hurried out into the street. The full moon was half way across the sky, and the flat faces of the houses were like the backcloth to a cubist ballet. In the distance a clock struck the half-hour, and a train shunted over the river. He knew that he was caught in a net from which he could never escape.

The man who was sifting the ash-can in the kitchen stood up with a crumpled paper in his hand. "Here's something," he said, "a telegram, making an appointment for this evening." The big man snatched it from him. "Excellent. Finish your search as quickly as possible and destroy all the papers that I don't take with me. Leave quietly one at a time, and don't communicate with anyone until I permit you to do so. Stay at home during the usual hours and wait for my instructions. Good-night." He left. An hour later the flat was dark and silent. The fire had gone out, and it was difficult to believe that anything had ever been alive there.

Back at home, Desmond walked up and down before his bookshelves trying to calculate how much time and money reading had cost him. Happy the man, he thought, without mental or physical passions, ignoring with equal scorn the bookshop, the brothel and the travel agency. A pity one couldn't sell oneself to the devil nowadays; the decline of piety had knocked the bottom out of the market, and reduced the wicked to an unwanted proletariat, with nothing to sell but their already conquered souls. Faustus had got twenty-four years' power and glory for throwing over law, medicine, logic and philosophy; today every capital was crowded with scholars who were willing to abandon all four and a good many more for a guinea a thousand and an occasional lecture tour. There was over-production of vice as of everything else.

He stopped, swaying a little, and peered mistily at his books. "Ah, Plato! Used to read him once. Let's see how he's bearing up."

He took down a volume and opened it at random:

"Then taking it the other way about, if one tries to express the extent of the interval between the king and the tyrant in respect of true pleasure, he will find at completion of the multiplication that he lives 729 times as happily, and that the tyrant's life is more painful by the same distance."

Lucky George!—729 times more pleasure than a dictator. Poor Joe and Adolf! He began to read further, but the print melted into a jumble every few lines. Besides, there was something on his mind. What was it? With a little thought he remembered, and fumbled for another volume. Wonder what he thinks of murder?

"If a man gets into such an uncontrollable rage with his parents as actually to dare to kill a parent in the madness of his rage, then he that has done such a thing is liable to a number of laws: for outrage he will be liable to most heavy penalties, and likewise for impiety and temple-robbing since he has robbed his parent of his life. ..."

What a lot of nonsense! Why not charge him with arson for sending his parent to hell-fire, or with obstruction for stopping the motion of his parent's heart, or fraudulent conversion for converting his parent into a corpse?

". . .so that if to die a hundred deaths were possible for any one man, that a parricide or a matricide who did the deed in rage should undergo a hundred deaths would be a fate most just.

If he did it in cold blood he would presumably deserve about two hundred deaths—or perhaps only forty; you could never tell with Plato. When medical science discovered how to resuscitate people after some unpleasant death like suffocation, one might really sentence the criminal to a hundred deaths, reviving him after every execution but the last. There'd be a regular tariff, ranging from one death for *crimes passionels* to five hundred for premeditated robbery, sodomy and parricide upon a superior officer while in face of the enemy, the sentence to be doubled in case of an unsuccessful appeal.

"If a slave kill a free man in self-defence, he shall be liable to the same laws as he that kills a father."

Desmond became very angry. "Bloody old Plato! To think I wasted years respecting an unjust old bastard like that!" He began to tear out the pages one by one, reading a sentence from each, making a derisive noise and scattering them round the room. Then nausea swam up to his brain like bubbles in a quicksand, and he stumbled into the bathroom to be thoroughly sick. Directly the vomiting ceased he flung himself down on his bed, to get to sleep before sickness began again.

When he awoke it was morning and he felt as stiff and tired as an unsuccessful mountaineer. His nose and throat seemed stuffed, and his collar was choking him. He got up, still a little unsteady, and went into the sitting-room, to see rugs rucked up, an ink-bottle knocked over, and the leaves of his beautiful Plato scattered about the floor. He was too tired to try and think why he had done it, and did not remember Anna until he had turned on his bath. The memory meant very little to him: it was remote and already fading, as though it belonged to a distant period of history.

The day at the office was thoroughly unpleasant. Desmond, sick and heavy-headed, could scarcely keep awake, and his secretary had a cold that, since she was ashamed to blow her nose with the unladylike vigour its congestion demanded, kept her at a continual sniff. Every few minutes a crystal drop gathered on the rim of a nostril, and each time Desmond watched it with the depressed concentration of a pin table addict, betting with himself on its probable growth and duration. Proofs came in, the telephone rang, and the ten-storied intellectual factory worked at full blast. He thought longingly of his trip to Missenden in the coming week-end, and half decided to have a short nervous breakdown and blossom for a few weeks in Ireland or the South of France. He jerked himself awake and went for a glass of water.

After lunch he felt better, and carefully scanned the morning papers for a paragraph about Anna. He found nothing; and although common sense told him that delay made no difference, he had an irrational feeling that the longer the body remained undiscovered the better his chances of escape, and became correspondingly encouraged. His recovery was timely, for at three o'clock Mr. Poole returned from his club in a thoroughly pernickety mood.

"Really, Thane, I simply won't have you being facetious on serious subjects! What did you mean by your ridiculous sub-title to Captain Thompson's article on the offensive strength of the German Army?"

He rummaged through a pile of proofs and fished one triumphantly out. "There you are! 'Don't Hang Out Your Wishing On The Maginot Line!' What's that supposed to mean? I've had a note about it from Mr. Pink this morning and he said exactly the same as I: 'What Does This Mean?'"

"I only thought" began Desmond, but found he was too tired to argue. "All right," he said wearily, "I'll change it. How about, 'Hitler's Military Machine: the Real Facts'?"

Mr. Poole approved. "That's better, that's a good title. I'll make you into a journalist yet, if you'll forget all this highbrow stuff. I remember I was just like you when I was a young man; I was always trying to be clever, I wasn't *sound*. Then one day I decided I'd got to choose between a rackety bohemian life and the nine o'clock train each morning and a constructive job of work. I've never regretted my decision. You've got the right stuff in you. Thane; I know you're sound at heart."

"Sound without fury signifying nothing," thought Desmond. Mr. Poole rambled on.

"You young men are all the same; always trying to be clever. Now take those reviews you used to write, very bright stuff no doubt, but bitter, unbalanced. When I was editor of *The Montreal Chronicle* I used to say to my reviewers: 'If a book's bad, don't review it. If you find you can't enjoy the books I send you, don't do a notice at all. Remember that silence is the strongest form of contempt.' I used to tell them that the reviewer is the link between author and reader, and the less of his own prejudices he shows, the better."

"You mean that the weakest link is the.one that doesn't give the author and the publisher a break?" remarked Desmond.

"Thane, Thane, what are we going to do with you! Always cynical, never serious! I remember my old friend Max—Lord Beaverbrook—once said to me ..." He was off. Those who, like a Tibetan saint or a bad soldier, could sleep on their feet, need never be bored in Mr. Poole's company, once he was in top gear and well away.

Desmond leant against a bookcase and let Mr. Poole lecture on his own greatness. To hear him talking of the Humanities was as odd and embarrassing as to watch some thin-wristed astigmatic don demonstrate to his colleagues the Norse technique of swinging an axe, or listen to a patently dying consumptive discuss next year's political problems. Desmond felt that Mr. Poole's incapacities were so obvious that he himself must be aware of them; and that comment on anything he said would therefore appear as patronising personal insult. He had sometimes felt the same doubts when flattering an unattractive woman, and blushed to imagine his shame should she calmly rebuke him for a hypocritical liar. Actually, of course, though people may be conscious of defects in their own best qualities, they are seldom actively awake to those they wholly lack; and had someone gravely told Desmond that he had the eyes of a mystic or the calves of a cross-country runner he would probably have believed them and almost certainly have liked them the better for it.

At four, a boy opened the door and dumped in the evening papers. By twisting his neck a little Desmond could read the headlines: HEINKEL DOWN OFF SHETLANDS; MAYFAIR MAN IN COURT; DECREE NISI FOR BARONET; WOMAN DEAD IN FLAT. He stiffened and bent forward:

WOMAN DEAD IN FLAT

The body of a woman believed to be named Anna Raven was discovered early this morning in a Bedford Square flat. Death was apparently due to strangulation. The police have taken possession of a number of clues, and wish to interview a man in connection with the crime.

He felt himself going white and put his hand on the desk. They always said something of the sort; they couldn't have traced anything to him. But it was no use; the smudgy newsprint had brought the murder home to him—it had become "official" and he knew it had really happened. He was afraid he was going to faint. Mr. Poole suddenly noticed him.

"Is anything the matter, Thane? You're as pale as a ghost?"

"It's all right, thanks; I just feel a bit faint. I think I'll get some water if you don't mind; I'm all right really."

"Sit down here and I'll send Miss Prestwood for it. Put your head down—no, further down than that—and you'll soon feel better."

Mr. Poole fussed round, his natural kindliness struggling with his duty as an employer. Kindliness won.

"There, drink that. You'd better go home and lie down; we can manage without you for the rest of the day, and it would never do if you got yourself knocked up with dispatch-day coming. I'll ask Miss Prestwood to get you a taxi."

Desmond protested weakly, but, to his own fear and disgust, really did feel rather ill, and was glad to be led out and packed into a cab. In a few minutes, however, he felt better, and by the time he reached home was almost his normal self. His flat, like Anna's, was one of several in a converted house, and as he went upstairs he thought he heard his front door shut. He hurried up the last flight and found a large, strongly-built man with his hand on the knocker.

"Did you want to see me?"

The man turned slowly. His face was smooth as though he

shaved three times a day; his eyes were greenish and set wide apart. When he spoke his voice was husky.

"Does Mr. George Williamson live here?"

"No, I'm afraid he doesn't."

"I'm sorry; I must have come to the wrong address."

The man raised his black hat and went downstairs without showing any disappointment. Desmond shrugged his shoulders and let himself in.

Mrs. Fletcher, the char, had done her work very thoroughly that day, for Desmond noticed that everything, even his books, had been a little disturbed. He was relieved to remember that Anna's diary was safely hidden; the next thing was to get rid of the gun. He went to the suit he had worn the previous night and felt in the coat pockets. Yes, it was still safe.

When it was dark he took the pistol, walked rapidly down to Waterloo Bridge, and dropped it over the parapet. That, God willing, was that.

CHAPTER IV

MINUTES OF AN EXTRAORDINARY MEETING
OF THE CENTRAL COMMITTEE FOR WESTERN
EUROPE

Present: A (in the Chair), B, C (representing the Eastern Section), D, E, F, G (Secretary).
Held at: London Headquarters.
Date: 10.30   p.m.   17th inst.
It was agreed that the proceedings be held in English. B interpreted for D; E interpreted for F.
At the suggestion of the Chairman the Minutes of the previous meeting were taken as read.

The Chairman: I have summoned this Extraordinary Meeting at such short notice because of an occurrence that may have jeopardised the future of our whole organisation. I will be brief with you. Anna Raven, our principal liaison agent in this country, has been murdered by unknown persons and her Contact List stolen.

B: Oh my God, this is the Gestapo's work! What shall we do?

E: Gestapo? More likely the British Secret Service. You Germans think of nothing but your Gestapo.

B : You would not talk so lightly if you knew them as I do! I have seen them take people away; I myself have been present at the questionings. They will find my name and take me! I must go at once.

C: Stop him or he'll ruin us all!

An animated discussion then took place which was subsequently, on the instructions of the Chairman, struck from the minutes. The Chairman called for order.

The Chairman: Gentlemen, gentlemen, please compose yourselves; the situation is not so grave as you imagine. Mr. Foster, who collaborated with Raven in her work, has been investigating the matter and is waiting outside to present his report. I suggest we hear him before any further discussion.

Several Voices: Agreed.

B: Call him in, if he is still alive. I expect he has been murdered too.

Mr. Foster was then called, and made the following statement.

Mr. Foster: On Monday night Raven was to call on me at nine o'clock to make final arrangements for the transfer of her duties to me before leaving to take up her other post. At 9.45 she had not arrived, so I telephoned to her flat. Receiving no reply, I became anxious; and went in person with two assistants to see if anything were the matter. I entered the street door with my duplicate key, and encountered no one on the stairs. I found the flat door open; the lock had been shot away with two bullets. On the floor of the sitting-room I found Raven's body; she had been strangled with her own scarf after, apparently, a brief struggle. She had been dead only for a short time. The flat had been searched and was in disorder; her Contact List and a sum of money had been taken, but nothing else seemed to have been removed. I took possession of certain clues and left in the early hours of the morning. *The Chairman :* Has anyone any questions?

C: Of what exactly does the Contact List consist?

Mr. Foster: In this case it contains a short statement of our aims, particulars of our British contacts, detailed instructions for getting into touch with certain of our principal representatives in other countries, and certain notes on the members of this Committee.

B : God in Heaven, we are lost!

Mr. Foster: The book is written in a code which, I have reason to believe, the persons who stole it are as yet unable to decipher.

D: How do you know that ?

The Chairman: Don't answer that question. I am sorry, gentlemen, but for the moment I think it is in our best interests to enter as little as possible into details of this nature. At such a time caution is necessary even amongst . . .

B: What are you insinuating? How dare you accuse us in such fashion!

The Chairman: Herr B. Nothing I said was directed against any particular person present; I meant merely that there are a number of suspicious features in this business, and that until it is cleared up it seems safest to trust no one more than is absolutely necessary. I think, however, that it is as well for you that you are among friends who understand the reasons for your discomposure.

B : I am sorry. Forgive me. I don't know what I'm saying. It is hard to work for two masters.

E: Mr. Foster. Did you find any clue to the perpetrators of this murder?

Mr. Foster: In the kitchen ash-can I found a telegram dated that afternoon, in which a person signing himself D.T. demanded an interview at seven-thirty the same evening. Upon investigation, I discovered that it had been telephoned from the offices of International Features, an important Press Agency. I was able to trace only two members of their staff with the initials on the wire, and made enquiries about each of them. About the first I found nothing of interest: in the apartments of the second I found an automatic pistol which fitted the bullets I had extracted from the door of Raven's flat. I at once made all possible enquiries about this man, of which I have drawn up a short summary.

The Chairman : Please read it.

Mr. Foster: "Desmond Thane; aged about thirty; pale complexion; dark hair; about six feet in height. Employed by International Features in an editorial position. Married, but separated from his wife. No known interests outside his work, but is believed to speak several languages. During recent months he appears to have been away from home a good deal, but is very reticent regarding his movements, and his colleagues know little about him."—You must bear in mind, gentlemen, that I have had no time for close researches, and have had to observe the utmost discretion in questioning his known acquaintances.—"A careful search of his flat revealed nothing of importance, besides the pistol already mentioned. He has extravagant tastes in clothes and books and, from the evidence of a book of matches, appears to frequent the *Snake and Ladder,* an expensive night club. His papers consist largely of unpaid bills, and I should imagine that he lives above his income. I have been unable to connect him with any political organisation."

C: You didn't find the Contact List?

Mr. Foster: No, I did not.

G: What is your personal opinion of Thane?

Mr. Foster: I would not like to commit myself. I have observed before, however, that when a man is quickwitted, secretive, and uninterested in his work he usually has some other occupation that requires the first two qualities. Thane seems the sort of person I myself sometimes employ, and for that reason may be dangerous.

The Chairman: Does anyone wish to question Mr. Foster further? If not, I suggest we permit him to leave, as he flies to Paris in the morning, and has certain preparations to make.

E: One more question. How closely were you associated with Raven?

Mr. Foster: Very closely. We were collaborators.

E: Was your relationship purely a professional one?

Mr. Foster: Yes.

E: Did she ever refer to Thane or to anyone who could be connected or identified with him?

Mr. Foster: No. She always said she had no friends. I was her most intimate associate.

Mr. Foster then left. The discussion continued.

C: How reliable is Foster?

The Chairman: Most reliable. He is our principal British executive, and has always brilliantly accomplished the tasks allotted to him. His loyalty is beyond question.

E: Without questioning his loyalty, might he not have been implicated from personal motives? He is a determined and ruthless man; and I suspected, from the manner in which he spoke, that his connection with Raven was not wholly professional. Is it not possible that he killed her from, say, jealousy, took the Contact List to divert suspicion, and is attempting to plant the crime on Thane, who might even have been his sexual rival?

G : I think we may be sure that if anything of the kind is true, Foster will have done his work so thoroughly that we shall be unable to prove anything against him. And I would remind you that he is a very valuable and dangerous man whose work is above reproach and with whom we as yet cannot afford to dispense. I suggest we shelve such suspicions, and decide what steps to take about Thane.

E: I have thought for some months that we have been becoming too dependent upon this man. With his knowledge and abilities he might well become highly dangerous, and I think it is time that he was checked. I suggest, to begin with, that the investigation of this important affair be not left entirely in his hands.

G: I suggest that, while leaving the charge wholly in Foster's hands we send some man ostensibly to assist him in a minor capacity, but actually to observe him.

The Chairman : He will resent it, I am afraid.

G: Not if it is done carefully. I have in mind an excellent man for the job, an Irishman calling himself O'Brien. He is unknown to Foster, thoroughly reliable and incorruptible, and too stupid for Foster to take him seriously and hence be offended.

E: If he is stupid, what use is he?

G: A stupid watcher is often the best, as he is unable to do anything but report what he sees. He is also more trustworthy than a clever man.

The Chairman : Very well, I will send this person to assist Foster in his investigations. But now let us return to the Raven case. What is the view of the meeting?

B: The precise details of this affair seem unimportant; we know too much already. One of our most important agents has been killed, and the names of some of us are in the hands of our enemies. Unless we escape immediately, I shall end in Dachau, you in a salt mine, you with a bullet in the back of your head, you in a tropical swamp, and you, Mr. Chairman, in a comfortable castle awaiting a nice, fair trial, and a nice new rope for your neck—unless they break your backbone with a silken cord out of courtesy to your rank.

D: B's right; we're finished whoever has the list. We'd best scatter as quickly as possible, and waste no more time talking about it.

The Chairman : Gentlemen! To exaggerate one's weakness is as dangerous as to overrate one's strength, and to imagine ruin is the surest way to bring it about. I beg you to let me give an unimpassioned statement of the position.

First, a reminder. At the head of your agendas stand the letters I.O. which signify, as you know, International Opposition. We represent something new in history; the close international alliance of all those who, whatever their politics and intended policies, are at present out of power—we are, if you like, a Federal Union of the dispossessed. Between us we represent all the great ideological minorities of Europe, from C who would restore old Bolshevism to Russia and B who represents genuine National Socialism; to F who follows another Duce and I myself who hope to see Great Britain a benevolent autocracy instead of an unbenevolent oligarchy. We are, in short, the alternative government of the greater part of the world; a temporary united front of those temporarily in adversity. Today, we are on the edge of success, and perceptibly nearing the simultaneous coups in all the capitals that shall give us power—and revenge—in our separate countries. Then, we shall become enemies; now, we are partners who must stand or fall together, and in our partnership there is far greater strength than some of you seem to believe.

We have the advantage that whereas we are allies our opponents have become enemies. In peace, it is true, they often worked together—G will remember how Radek and Bukharin were betrayed to Stalin by the Gestapo because Krupp feared a revived Third International; while B will not have forgotten how the French Intelligence betrayed Roehm and Ernst to Hitler in the belief that State Capitalism in Germany would prove more amenable than National Socialism. Today, on the contrary, the powers are at war, and the links between their Intelligences are largely broken. Their ruling castes are fighting, their secret agents are spying on each other, and if one government discovers our intrigues against another, it is more likely to help than to betray us. We are the sole effective International.

Now let us consider the Raven case. She has worked on our behalf against both the British and the German Governments, and either of their Intelligence services may have removed her. They would not, however, have worked together or exchanged information, so at the very worst we are only half betrayed and thus but half destroyed. This is the worst; actually, I am sure, matters are not so grave if we consider calmly and do nothing precipitate. I may repeat that the list is in a code untranslatable without its key, of which our enemies, whoever they be, are not yet in possession. Now B, you belong to the Gestapo. Do you think they had any hand in this?

B: I cannot say. I don't know. For five years I have been in their service, and still I don't know all they do, even in my own department. They may suspect me and be keeping things from me; they may be planning to take me away. I know they are!

The Chairman: Please calm yourself and answer carefully. Do you suppose they knew of Raven's activities?

B: I don't know. I don't think so. Certainly she was not on the general list, but that's not final. She may have been down in one of the special sections.

The Chairman : Does what you have heard of this incident fit in with their usual methods?

B: No—No. They would not have strangled—they would have shot, clubbed or abducted her. They might have employed this Thane; they often use his sort for special work in England outside of normal espionage.

The Chairman: Mr. G. Do you think British Intelligence might be concerned?

G : It doesn't smell much like the Secret Service, although Thane sounds the kind of man they engage occasionally for unimportant business. But in any case why should they kill Raven? They're working in their own country; they could easily have arrested her had they wished. Might not the murder have been a casual or purely personal crime?

F: Surely not. Does a thief shoot open doors in an inhabited house? Would an ordinary criminal have taken a coded notebook and left silver ornaments and valuable jewellery behind. What other motive is there? A *crime passionel*? Would a man who shot open a door and rushed in to strangle his lover stay to search her desk, ignore her letters, and take the one notebook he would be unable to read? Was the telegram that of a lover? Besides, what evidence is there that Raven had associates of this kind, or that she had any connection with Thane?

G: The telegram presupposes an acquaintanceship.

F: True, but not necessarily a private and personal one. We can assume that Thane took the Contact List, whatever his motives in so doing; and until it is recovered we shall have no rest or safety. For my part, I have no use for coincidences, and everything we have heard convinces me that this murder is the work of one of our enemies. It is essential, in any event, that we immediately take measures on this assumption.

B: I propose Thane be killed at once, before he can do any harm.

C: I strongly oppose that. He is our only link with the Contact List which, code or no, must be recovered or destroyed. It is of the utmost urgency, too, that we discover who instigated this killing, and take appropriate steps to protect ourselves.

E: I suggest Thane be taken for questioning and disposed of later.

The Chairman: I agree with the last speaker. I propose that we leave the whole matter in the charge of Foster, who returns to London in a few days' time. We should, however, seize Thane at once and put him in safe keeping.

B: Must we wait on Foster? Can we not question this man ourselves? Put me in charge of the questioning and I will soon get the truth from him.

The Chairman: It is possible that the telegram was left in the flat on purpose, and that our enemies, unable to decode the list, are using Thane as a bait in the hopes of tracing us if we attempt to abduct him. If we leave his detention to minor agents for a few days we shall force our opponents to show their hands: even the British Intelligence would scarcely allow us to keep one of their number prisoner for long. Further, as Foster has taken over Raven's duties it seems best to leave things to him—and I might add that to put someone else in control at this stage would suggest a lack of confidence in him that he would certainly resent. I know, however, that we are all very grateful to Herr. B for offering us his expert services.

E: I agree. We cannot yet afford to offend Foster.

The Chairman: I take it, then, that we are all of one opinion? With your consent I personally will arrange all necessary steps for the immediate arrest of Thane.

G: And see that O'Brien receives his instructions.

C: Should not the code used in Raven's Contact List be cancelled?

The Chairman: That has already been done. Have I your approval, gentlemen?

B: I do not like it, but I suppose you are right.

B, C, D, E, F, and G assented to the'Chairman's proposal.
The Meeting was adjourned.

CHAPTER V

On Thursday morning, as he turned the corner of the street on his way to work, two men moved from behind a big black car and stopped in front of him. "You're Desmond Thane?"

"Yes, I am."

"We are police officers. You are under arrest for the murder of Anna Raven."

The world seemed to stop, and with the senseless clarity of a camera Desmond's brain recorded the cracks in the pavement and the house agent's sign on the other side of the road. The second man slipped round behind him and caught him unobtrusively but firmly by the arm.

"You'd better come quietly. You'd better not make trouble."

They pushed him unresisting into the car which moved swiftly off. After a few moments Desmond spoke.

"This is absurd. I don't know anyone called Raven." The men seated on either side of him said nothing. He continued more loudly.

"This is absolutely ridiculous; I'll get damages for this. I expect it's not your fault, but I protest most strongly. It's, it's absurd."

He noticed suddenly that the windows were frosted, and realised that, from the speed they were going, he was not being taken to the neighbouring police station.

"Where are you taking me? This is outrageous; I demand to see my lawyer."

No answer. He went on hysterically: "Where's your warrant? I insist on being formally charged. I wish to make a statement."

"Shut up," said the man on the left.

Desmond, used to courteous if not subservient treatment from officials, lost fear and temper simultaneously.

"What the hell do you mean? I demand to be taken to a station and properly charged. The police have no legal right to behave in this way!"

The man on the right turned sharply towards him. "We're not the police, so you can shut your mug. Anything more from you and I'll shut it for you."

He drew a little leather-covered blackjack from his pocket and gently tapped Desmond on the chin. The car must have got out of central London, for it seldom changed gear now and was travelling fast.

After his first shock, Desmond's chief feeling was one of relief, for, contrary to the cliche, the unknown is usually less alarming than the known; and a condemned murderer would probably feel unmixed pleasure were his prison to be invaded by tentacled Martians. He was afraid, but not as acutely as before; the stubborn and inescapable fact of arrest had become unpleasant but unpredictable fiction. He cautiously moved his head and studied his captors critically.

The man who had threatened him was the one who had made the arrest, and looked superficially like a policeman. Burly, hairy, what is sometimes known as "ripe," he seemed at first sight especially built for gross joviality, and would have made an ideal parent for a proletarian genius to react from. But there was, besides, something a little nasty and abnormal in him; he had the shifty brazenness of the race-course tough rather than the crude insolence of the happy bully. He clearly disliked his prisoner at sight, and Desmond hoped that he would not be left alone with him.

The other man belonged to a different type. Young, Jewish, smart in pale blue shirt and yellow silk tie, he belonged to Wardour Street or the wholesale dress depots of the East End. He was obviously vain, and even now carefully crossed his legs and pulled up his knife-creased trousers to reveal an expensive glossy sock. But his face was clever, and curiously austere. One could imagine him exploiting his employees and joking obscenely with his secretary all day, and at night locking himself in his room furtively to study. After an interval Desmond tried to question him, this time politely and almost conversationally.

"Where are you taking me? Are you sure you haven't made some mistake?"

The Jew smiled at him.

"Please be quiet. You're going to talk later. It'll be better for you if you keep quite quiet now."

He sounded friendly, but Desmond knew it was only a habit of speech and that beneath his apparent good-nature he was probably as ruthless as his gross companion. You could never trust courtesy; there were no doubt pleases and after you, sirs, on the way to the scaffold. He kept quiet.

They drove for what seemed an hour and a half, then slowed and turned into a short gravel drive. As they stopped Desmond heard a train whistle and the sound of shunting: apparently they were near a station or siding. The driver drew back the glass panel behind and turned to the Jew. He had a white, chubby face and spoke with nervous servility.

"Shall I take the car back to London, chief?"

The Jew considered for a moment.

"No. You'll stay here with me. Jackson can take her back."

He got from the car and beckoned Desmond to follow him. Directly he stepped out, the fat man pushed him into the house, before he could see more than a Victorian porch and a few trees. A minute later he heard the car start up and drive away.

"Come on," said the Jew.

Desmond glanced round and saw that he stood in what might have been the hall of a country doctor. A small polished table littered with circulars, an old fashioned hatrack, a good, slightly shabby carpet, and a framed certificate of some kind matched ill with the slick figure ahead of him, and the podgy little commercial traveller of a man sidling behind. He had a sudden intuition that apart from these two the house was empty, and felt that now, if ever, was his chance to escape. The Jew was slim and small-handed; the flabby plumpness of the other was still less formidable. They might be armed, but he had seen no sign of it, and was sure that he was physically stronger than either of them. A punch on the jaw for one, a kick in the stomach for the other, a dash through the front door to the adjacent railway, and he was free. He had often seen it happen in films.

He tensed himself, and as they reached the first landing hit desperately at the side of the Jew's head. The man ducked swiftly like a professional boxer and rode the blow over his shoulder. As Desmond struck again he knocked up the punch with his left hand and brought up his right with a jerk. Desmond's jaw seemed to explode and he found himself sprawling on the floor. As he tried to rise the fat man caught him from behind by the collar and held a thin-bladed knife an inch in front of his throat so that he dare not move. The Jew dusted his hands and grinned at him. He noticed, too late, that his shoulders were broad without padding and that he had the easy balance of an athlete.

"Now don't get tough," he said, "or I'll have to fix you. He can get up now, Fat; I think he'll be a good boy."

Completely cowed, Desmond got to his feet and let himself be led to a small room, with only a cheap bed and a chair for furniture. There was a small black-painted window high up in the wall, and a bulb set in the ceiling gave a harsh and unpleasant light. The Jew waved him forward like an old-fashioned inn-keeper showing his guest the best room, and leant against the doorway.

"If you don't want trouble you won't get it; if you do, you'll have plenty. Don't make a, noise, because I shall hear you first." He glanced up at the window. "You needn't worry about the window either—it's barred. And don't tamper with the black-out to-night, for if the police complain to me I'm afraid I shall have to complain to you." His smile became still broader and the fat man behind him tittered. "And I think," he continued, "we had better see what you have in your pockets. Search him."

Fat came forward and ran his hands expertly over Desmond, taking pen, wallet, cheque-book, handkerchief and a few letters, which he laid in a neat pile on the bed.

"That's the lot, chief."

"You can let him keep the handkerchief. Put the rest in Mr.

Foster's desk: he'll want to see them when he comes."

They went out. In the doorway the Jew paused.

"You'll find a pot under the bed, Mr. Thane, which my friend will empty for you now and then. You'll enjoy that, Fat, won't you?"

Fat leered and giggled like a dirty-minded boy of fourteen.

"Anything you say, chief."

The door shut behind them and the key turned in the lock. As far as his aching head permitted, Desmond tried to make out what exactly had happened to him.

These people were plainly nothing to do with the police; their behaviour was rather too unorthodox even for the War Reserve. Anna was a foreigner, so might they not be Connected with Intelligence, or even be enemy spies? Or a criminal gang of some kind?—though it was difficult to guess what was their line of crime. But in any case what could they want with him: what could anyone save Scotland Yard have to do with him? They might possibly be friends of Anna's seeking a Latin vengeance, but in that case would there be so many in it? He had already seen three, and there must be at least another—the important Mr. Foster who apparently had a right to the contents of his pockets. And how had they found him at all? Had Anna told them about him, had they found his telegram or some other clue in her flat, or was it all an incredible coincidence of the sort that occurs too often for logic, like a roulette number turning up ten times running? He was no longer frightened; the shock and surprise had worked on his normal feelings like cocaine on a nerve, and he was prepared to accept anything. With a sigh of resignation he lay down on the bed, and in a few minutes fell asleep.

When he awoke the room and its glaring light were exactly the same, but he sensed that it was late afternoon.

He lay on the bed staring at the ceiling and not thinking at all; he was in the grip of forces beyond his knowledge or control, and felt almost happy because, for the first time since early childhood, the initiative was wholly out of his hands. At about six the fat man slid in with a glass of water and a plate of crudely cut sandwiches; four or five hours later the light, which had no switch inside the room, snapped suddenly out. Desmond did not even blink, but lay still and felt reality drifting away from him.

So began a queer half-life that continued for days until Desmond lost all count of time. The light burnt for stretches of what must have been twelve or sixteen hours; then went out, presumably for the night. Twice a day one of the men came in with unambitious but adequate cold food, and sometimes he could hear them moving about in the next room or on the floor above. Once the phone rang—that was an event and set his heart beating; and once or twice he heard a wireless playing dance numbers. All the time, on and off, the trains shunted and whistled, and every hour or so a long rattling chain of trucks rumbled past to an unknown but enviable destination. It was as if he was buried, or in the deepest , cell of an asylum for the incurably insane, and once, waking in the thick darkness, he began to believe he was dead and had to bite his hand till it bled to stop himself screaming. The next day when the Jew brought his food he gripped his arm and told him that he must have a candle or he would go mad. The man had looked alarmed and had twisted quickly out, but returned a few minutes later with a little electric torch.

Desmond tried to make friends with his guards. The fat man would never talk except to his colleague, and seemed as shy of Desmond as a small boy of an unfamiliar adult. The Jew, being naturally voluble and fond of company, was easier to approach; and soon fell into the habit of staying for a few minutes' chat when it was his turn to bring in the food. At first Desmond was careful to keep to general subjects, for while the other was quite prepared to discuss films or the war, he left abruptly at the first appearance of personalities. On the third or fourth day, however, Desmond stepped between him and the door, and begged him to say what was going to happen to him. The man was evasive and nervous, but at last sat down on the chair and talked rapidly.

"I can't tell you anything, and I'm not going to, but I'll give you a good tip. There's a man coming to see you in a day or two and he'll ask you questions. If you want to keep whole, tell him the truth; and for God's sake don't let on I've talked to you."

He seemed to think he had said too much and made to leave, but Desmond caught him by the sleeve.

"Don't go; I swear I won't say you spoke to me. Can't you just tell me who you are? Are you German spies or what?"

"Nazi spies? What the hell do you take me for? Do you think I'd work for those bastards after all they've done?" "Well, who *are* you then?"

"I can't tell you."

"Who's this man who's going to question me? What does he want?"

"He calls himself Foster. I'm not talking about him." "Well, for God's sake tell me what's it all about?"

"I can't tell you and it's no use asking me. But you may as well know this: It's a bloody big thing—about the biggest there is—and if you cross them, God help you. I don't know who you are or what you're up to, but you probably think your bosses can protect you. If you do, forget it; we're the biggest thing yet, I tell you, and you won't have a chance."

"I haven't got any bosses. I don't know what you're talking about."

The Jew smiled incredulously.

"Have it your own way now, but I tell you that won't go down with Foster; he'll expect more than that, and he'll get it. I don't like his methods, but they work all right."

"But won't you at least tell me   "

The Jew had had enough and opened the door. Desmond stopped him.

"Look, you've got my cheque book and I've a good deal in the bank. How much do you want to let me out of here?"

The man shook his head.

"Not enough money in the budget."

"How much just to tell me what's it all about? I'll give you a bearer cheque—if you like I'll give you a note to a friend who'll pay cash."

The Jew shook him off and spoke with unmistakable sincerity.

"How much would you ask for a knife stuck in your guts?"

He shut the door. It was quite some time before Desmond felt like eating his sandwiches.

The next day there were sounds of activity in the house. The telephone rang repeatedly, there were noises as if furniture was being shifted somewhere at the end of the passage, and a car was driven up to the front door. The fat man, who seemed barely to be suppressing some urgent excitement, kept sticking his head in at the door, and broke his silence, to ask Desmond if he would care for an apple or a glass of claret. Desmond accepted both, and persuaded the man to leave the bottle, with the result that he became a trifle tipsy and was almost anxious to meet his mysterious inquisitor. He was still light-headed an hour later when the Jew led him down the passage and pushed him into a room at the far end.

"Here he is, Mr. Foster."

CHAPTER VI

He found himself in a large, brightly-lighted room, with a long mahogany table running down the centre and a Victorian chandelier blazing in the ceiling. At either end stood heavy antique chairs, and in that facing him sat the green-eyed man he had met, several centuries ago, knocking at the door of his flat. Behind him was the fat man like an unhealthy attendant seraph; in the corner, a wireless played dance music very softly. The room might have been staged by an Academy problem painter of an old-fashioned kind, and Desmond, standing foolishly in the doorway, felt like a nervous applicant for an unobtainable position. The man in the chair stared at him silently, like a sleek, bored cat examining a stranger, until Desmond felt clumsy, gauche and ill-bred; and, as often when he was nervous, became loud voiced and insolent.

"So you're Foster, are you?" he said, putting his hands in his pockets, "fancy meeting you here! Sure you haven't mistaken the address again?"

Foster's placid stare remained unchanged.

"Please sit down. Answer my questions fully and truthfully. Don't try to waste time, for I shan't be very patient with you."

His husky voice had an ominous quality of decision, and quite deflated Desmond's precarious aggressiveness. He sat down in the chair facing his questioner and the Jew stood behind him. It was a conference between princes, or a scene from one of those nineteenth century novels in which husband and wife, with footmen standing behind them, dine at each other every night down a furlong of table and never exchange a word for twenty years. Foster straightened the papers lying in front of him, took out a fountain pen, and leant a little forward.

"Who ordered you to kill Anna Raven?"

(Don't admit anything. If you confess you'll probably be hanged in the end; even this thick-necked beast can't do worse than that.)

"I don't know what you're talking about; I've never heard of the woman! I demand an explanation of your fantastic behaviour! What the hell do you—"

The other interrupted.

"Have you seen this telegram before?"

(So she didn't destroy it after all! I expect it was lying in full view the whole time.)

"No I haven't! This is all absolute nonsense! If you have any charge, go to the police!"

"This telegram is initialed by you and sent from your place of work. The bullets that shot open the door of Raven's flat were fired from a gun in your possession. It's no use lying to me, Thane, and it'll be the worse for you if you attempt it. Who ordered you to kill Raven?"

(I won't confess. The police can't prove anything now these people have the evidence.)

"I didn't kill this—this Raven of yours! It's impossible to talk to you if you persist in such an absurd idea! I'll answer nothing more until I see my lawyer."

"Why did you kill Raven?"

Silence.

"Why did you kill Raven?"

Silence.

"For the last time, why did you kill Raven?"

Silence. Foster flicked his fingers, and the Jew stepped round and slapped Desmond violently across the face. He leapt to his feet in fury and saw a gun appear in Foster's hand. The round, black hole of the muzzle, as threatening as the spot of a fatal disease, deflated his anger, and he sank back into his chair, for the first time thoroughly frightened. His mind remained calm, but his body could already feel the thud of the bullet breaking bone and muscle; and he reacted to this new world of threats and death as promptly and rightly as a fledgling sparrow does to a prowling cat. These people, he thought, with a fading flicker of his usual cheerfulness, had done what eight years of Christian education had failed to do: shown him the propriety of turning the other cheek.

Quite unperturbed, Foster continued.

"Why did you kill Raven?"

Silence. The Jew struck him.

"Why did you kill Raven?"

Silence. The Jew struck him so hard that his head rang. He folded his arms and said nothing. Foster looked at the Jew.

"If he doesn't answer this time, hit him under the jaw and knock out a few of his teeth. Now, Thane. Why did you kill Raven?"

The Jew stepped back and measured his distance. Desmond gave way.

"I didn't kill her, but I admit I was in her flat the evening she died."

"That's better. Now tell me the story in detail."

His tone was not encouraging, but Desmond went fluently ahead, and by the end of his third sentence began to believe himself.

"I know it sounds improbable, but it's true. I met Anna quite by chance when she picked me up in a café. We had an affaire; and I soon got very jealous because I suspected she had other men. I'm afraid I must have become rather impossible; and last Monday after she had missed a lunch appointment I sent her a silly wire—the one you must have found—saying I'd got to see her and would call that evening—I thought, you see, that she'd decided to leave me for good and that the wire might make her change her mind and see me once more. When I arrived I got no answer, but thought I heard laughter and a man's voice inside the flat. I completely lost my head, and shot open the lock—if I'd caught her and her lover I admit I might have killed them—and was horrified to find her body lying on the floor. I was very frightened and left at once; for all I know the murderer was hiding in the next room. I suppose I should have gone to the police, but I was afraid they might suspect me. I may as well confess, too, that I'm suing my wife for a divorce and couldn't afford to come into court and admit I'd been sleeping with Anna. I've behaved stupidly throughout, but there it is. That's all I know about it."

It was a good story and Desmond felt pleased with himself. Foster stood up and came round the room; his voice was calm but one of his eyes was twitching slightly.

"You say that your only connection with Raven was a sexual one, and then when you arrived on Monday she was already dead?"

Desmond decided to embroider a little.

"Yes, that's all. I'd caught her with a man once before and threatened to kill her if it happened again. I won't swear," he continued with endearing frankness, "that I didn't intend to kill her myself that evening. Luckily for me, however, the job had been done already."

Foster's twitch became more pronounced.

"And who do you think killed her?"

"Oh, some man or other. I expect she was always picking people up—it was bound to end in trouble some day." "That's a lie!" said Foster, and his face contorted. With a shocking jolt Desmond realised he had made the worst and probably the last mistake of his life, and that whatever he said now would probably be useless to save him. He knew, beyond the possibility of a doubt, that Foster, too, had been in love with Anna.

Foster straightened up, his face calm and his thick voice cold.

"This man is lying: we shall have to use stronger measures. Tie him to the chair."

The fat man took a coil of rope from a drawer and expertly bound Desmond's ankles to the chair legs, passing the ends of the rope round his waist and arms. As he worked he tittered to himself, and twice asked if he were pulling too tightly. The Jew strolled away and stood staring at a Turner reproduction on the far wall; Foster sorted his papers. Suddenly the bell on the front door rang and all three stiffened. Foster turned to the Jew.

"That must be this man Headquarters are foisting on us. Go and let him in."

A moment later the Jew returned with a heavy, fair- haired man who stood blinking in the light.

"I suppose you're from Headquarters?" Foster's voice was cold and hostile.

"Yes, sir. O'Brien's my name, and I'm glad to meet you gentlemen."

"Have you seen either of my colleagues before?"

"No, sir." He gazed at Desmond curiously. "So this is the Secret Service man we've been hearing tell of."

Foster interrupted sharply.

"You can keep your talk to yourself, O'Brien; you weren't sent here for that. Sit down and hold your tongue; I'll explain your duties to you later."

The friendliness went from the Irishman's face as if a light had been switched off, and his eyes narrowed as he plumped noisily down into a chair. Fat and the Jew drew away a little, and studied him warily, like second-term boys eyeing a formidable newcomer, before pointedly ignoring him.

Desmond's mind came awake again. So they thought he was in the Secret Service! Who were they, then? German spies? None of them seemed to fit the part; they were all British, and the Jew's denunciation of the Nazis had sounded sincere enough. Communists? Ridiculous. Some sort of International gang? Foster's voice broke in.

"Now we'll see if you'll talk; I've had enough of your lying. Where's the Contact List?"

'Contact List?' What the hell did he mean? He'd seen no list.

"I don't know what you're talking about."

"Right, now we know how we stand." He beckoned to Fat. "Get to work; go slowly at first."

The fat man rolled up Desmond's left sleeve and tied tightly round his forearm a thin knotted cord with an iron skewer thrust through one of the knots. It was like a crude tourniquet.

"What are you going to do? You can't torture me!" "Where's the Contact List?"

"I don't know. I've never seen any List!"

Fat's face set in a grin and he wriggled and shifted his soft body as though he had diarrhoea. Foster nodded to him, and he rapidly twisted the skewer three or four times, so that the knots dug into the flesh. Desmond gave a gasping grunt, and the Irishman ran forward and pushed Fat aside.

"Leave him be, ye little runt, or I'll break ye! You can't do this to a helpless man, Mr. Foster, it's not right!" Foster's face flushed.

"Get back to your chair, O'Brien, and control yourself. Worse things have happened to people who interfered." The Irishman shuffled doubtfully, then slouched unwillingly back to his corner, and sat muttering to himself. The fat man came forward and twisted the cord again. "Where's the Contact List?"

Pain swept through Desmond like a tide.

"I don't know what you mean! "

Fat twisted again. He was humming to himself. "Where's the Contact List?"

Desmond gave a scream. "I don't know what you're talking about! Let me alone! I admit I killed Anna! I took some money, but I saw no list! "

"I know you killed Raven, but I'm not interested in that at the moment. Where's the Contact List?"

Fat dribbled a little and twisted again; the Jew turned his back and examined a bookcase; the wireless played softly on. Desmond could feel the blood trickling down his wrist, and from each knot pain spurted up his arm into his shoulder and through his whole body. He could see nothing but a bronze haze with fluttering lists swirling whitely through it. Foster's voice beat on like a drum. "Where's the List?"

Fat twisted viciously, and with a scream Desmond fainted. He came to himself to find the cord relaxed and the fat man throwing water on his face. Through the mists of returning consciousness he heard Foster's unchanging voice.

"Where's the List?"

"I don't know," he mumbled. "I don't know, I don't know, I don't know."

"His arm's bleeding rather badly, Mr. Foster," bleated Fat, "shall I put some iodine on it?"

Without waiting for an answer he took a bottle from his pocket, pulled the largest wound open with his fingers and poured on the antiseptic. Desmond fainted a second time and again they revived him, questioned him, and twisted the cord until he fainted once more. He lost all measure of time and fell through a cavernous eternity filled with a vast snowfall of all the lists he had ever seen; and went on muttering "I don't know, I don't know, I don't know," until he forgot the meaning of the words. At last consciousness fully returned and he realised they had left him alone while Foster answered the telephone.

"Yes . . . yes, I'm questioning him now. . . . No, not yet, but I think he soon will . . . yes . . . now? I'm busy with Thane, sir, and I think. . . . Yes, very good; I quite understand. I'll get it through at once and phone you back. Good-bye."

He hung up the receiver and came over to Desmond. "I'm going to give you an hour or two to think things over. If you don't talk then I shan't waste any more time on mild methods, but break your fingers, and burn your feet and crush your testicles." He spoke each threat with the slow, vicious sincerity of a man swearing a vindictive oath. Taking a little leather book from his pocket, he tapped his knuckles with it. "Unless you tell me what you've done with the duplicate of this list I'll cut and burn you piece by piece. Now take him away."

As the Jew helped him down the passage Desmond realised numbly that the "Contact List" was the same as Anna's diary, and that his visual imagining of it as a sheet of paper had made him temporarily into a hero. He swayed down on to the bed and laughed weakly. The Jew gazed at him with admiration.

"I like your guts," he said, "but for God's sake come clean when he sends for you again. The man's a devil, and what he and that little fat bastard'll do to you if you don't talk'll be enough to turn my stomach."

He shut the door, but peered in again a moment later.

"Here," he said, "have a drink. You'll need it." He flung a flask of whiskey on the bed and backed out. This time the key turned.

Desmond lay back on the bed and his mind ran on like an uncontrollable engine. "I'm Desmond Thane, and I work in an office in twentieth-century London, and I've been abducted, imprisoned and tortured, and unless I tell them something I don't know they're going . . . " Then he remembered that he *did* know; that he had only to tell Foster about the registered letter to be left in peace. He staggered up and rattled frantically at the door-handle.

"Here!" he shouted, "fetch Foster! I'll give you the list, I'll give you ..."

Abruptly he came to his senses. What would happen when he gave them the book? They could scarcely let him go after what they had done: they would have to kill him. But if he refused to give in they would certainly torture him until he did. He sat down on the bed and went carefully over everything he knew about his captors.

"They think I'm in the Secret Service, so they can't be ordinary criminals—besides, Anna was apparently one of them, and its impossible to imagine her as a crook— but must be political; perhaps they're an English fifth column, although the Jew's certainly not pro-Nazi. . . . This Contact List must be very important for them to take all this trouble, especially if, as it appears, they believe I'm a Government agent: it might be worth a lot of money to me if only I could get away from here. I mustn't let them know where the diary is, for as long as I've got it I've something to bargain with and they obviously can't kill me. In a queer way I'm in a strong position, and since they've got the telegram, the police can't connect me with Anna's murder. If I can get away from them, I'm safe!"

An unreasonable exultation seized him, until a stab of pain

brought him back to reality. He gently pulled off his coat and found his shirt-sleeve damp with blood. His arm was pocked with four deep indentations, pinkly ragged round the edges and welling deeply in the centre. He whistled involuntarily with pity and disgust, and tore off the tail of his shirt to make a rough bandage. When he had done he felt sick, and paced up and down the room until the nausea passed. Outside, a train whistled.

"I don't know who these people are, but they belong to the wrong period of history. Guns, knives, knotted ropes and all the anachronistic machinery of tyranny don't belong to the twentieth century, in spite of Hitler and Stalin. They aren't really efficient any more in this sort of society, and in spite of their atrocities these people couldn't get what they wanted from me because they've no sense of reality. Anyone with the slightest grasp of common sense psychology would have seen at once that I'm not the sort of person who holds out under torture, and have realised that there must have been some kind of mistake. They're so far detached from the real world of ordinary English people that they couldn't see I was speaking the truth, and credited me with the valiant obstinacy of a medieval heretic!"

In spite of his superior contempt for unreasonable behaviour he felt illogically flattered at their painful misjudgment of him.

"Yet they're not fools: that man Foster's certainly got brains, and the Jew looks quick-witted in his own way. They must be a little mad, like all clever men who deliberately try to live outside the society of their time —anyone of Foster's intelligence who goes in for a job that depends on guns and instruments of torture must be emotionally arrested or perverted in some way or he wouldn't waste his time fulfilling a schoolboy's daydreams. In a world of penny papers and elementary education he's hopelessly out of date, and however able and ruthless he may be, is bound to be destroyed. He and his gang are like tigers loose in Piccadilly: terrifyingly formidable for a moment and within a short radius, but inevitably doomed because they're out of place. I know he isn't infallible even in his own metier, for he's already made two ludicrous mistakes about me, and will probably make others. In his world, probably, everyone is the same as himself, and all live in a stupid alternation of persecuting and persecution mania. Well, I'm not one of their kind, though they obviously think so; and so long as they don't know how dull and sensible I really am, I've got a winning advantage over them. They're gullible because they can't get away from their preconceived notions about things. They might not believe the truth if I told it, but they'd probably swallow anything, however ridiculous, that squared with their own ideas. I once argued that a modern man could have talked himself unscathed out of the Spanish Inquisition. Here's my chance to prove it."

Though his mind was cool his body was terrified, and as he felt the pain of the past torture and imagined the horrors of the next he trembled uncontrollably. He could already feel flesh tearing and bones breaking, and the final slow sickening thrust of a knife in the stomach, and it took several minutes of deep breathing, and concentration on algebra, politics and past lusts before he became calm. He noticed the Jew's whiskey and unstoppered it to drink, but had a better idea; and after swallowing a gulp and dabbing a little round his mouth like eau de cologne, emptied the rest in the chamber-pot under the bed and dropped the empty flask in the middle of the floor. So they thought he was in the Secret Service, did they? Time passed.

Minutes or hours later the Jew opened the door.

"Come on, Foster wants you."

Desmond stood up and reeled against the wall.

"Okay, okay, I'll come and see your Fuhrer!"

He gave a grotesque salute. The other looked at him, then picked up the empty flask from the floor. Desmond, feeling thoroughly foolish, talked thickly and rapidly.

"Bloody good whiskey, old man, bloody good! Haven't left you much I'm afraid; ask Foster to buy you some more. Well, what are we waiting for?"

Pushing past the man, he strode down the passage with careful steadiness and walked into the big room. Foster was still seated at the head of the table with Fat standing by his side; the Irishman leant glumly in a corner.

"Hallo, Foster," he said loudly, "I've been thinking things over and I'm going to come through. I'll make you an offer."

He sat heavily down and the Jew moved behind him.

He could sense that the man was making signals, though Foster gave no trace of acknowledgement.

"Good. Make your statement."

Desmond took breath, clenched his toes, and began.

"I did kill Anna Raven, although it was all a mistake. I do know where the Contact List is, though I haven't got it myself. I am a member of the British Intelligence Service." The Jew made a sucking noise.

"Go on," said Foster quietly, "tell the whole story from the beginning."

Desmond, wishing he really had drunk the whiskey, spoke rapidly. Fear made his voice high and stumbling, reproducing the effects of alcohol better than he could have done of his own will.

"I've been in British Intelligence for years. I'm not exactly a regular member of the service—I do special jobs for them, and they call me in whenever they want an intelligent man, or something a bit different from their ex-officers and civil servants. Of course they're pretty mean about money, but I don't mind that, as it's something of an honour to work for them."

There was dead silence in the room. He hurried on. "Well, they told me to watch this Raven and make her acquaintance—they thought she was up to something, but didn't want to arrest her as she had an American passport. You know what Americans are," he interposed confidentially, "still think they're living in the nineteenth century—quite capable of sending their fleet to bombard Bristol if we'd done anything to Anna. Doesn't do at all to treat Americans as badly as you do your own citizens." He began to laugh. "Go on," said Foster.

"Anyway, it was my job to watch the woman and try and find

something about her. After a bit I got to know her—picked her up in the Caféε Royal—I'm good at that sort of thing, you know; wish it was a whole time profession."

He grinned conceitedly. Foster nodded slightly.

"Well, I got quite intimate with her, though not as much so as I'd have liked—she must have been frigid, or something." (He watched Foster to see how he took this little apology, but the man's broad face remained expressionless.) "But I hadn't got anything worth while—I'm paid by results, you see, apart from expenses, and damned close they are about those—when I heard she was going away. I sent the wire you found, and called round to make a last effort to pump her. She went into her bedroom to change and I looked through her desk; it was the first chance I'd had. I'd just found a coded notebook—your Contact List, I believe—when she came in and stuck a gun at me. There was a struggle and I accidentally killed her. I was pretty scared, for I'd exceeded my instructions and knew that my chief probably wouldn't protect me, and stupidly shut myself out without taking the diary. I shot open the door, took it, left, and here I am."

It sounded very thin, especially the parts that were more or less true. Foster drummed on the table; Desmond could see him analysing the story, and felt it might have been better to have told the truth. But they wouldn't have believed that either, and certainly wouldn't have spared him once they recovered the list. Foster looked up.

"What did you do with the Contact List?"

"I gave it to my chief at the Home Office saying I'd found it in Raven's flat and stole it because I couldn't decode it on the spot. I didn't tell him about killing her; they'll have to fix that on me for themselves. I don't think they'd dare bring me in court on a murder charge, as if they did I'd swear it was done on their instructions. Even in war-time they couldn't stop it from being a very dirty scandal, so I think they'll leave well alone."

This was plainly the way in which Foster's own mind worked, and Desmond could see him hesitating on the edge of conviction. He hurried on to his only chance of escape.

"Look, I'll make you an offer. I'm in this business purely for money and excitement; I don't care whether I work for the German Government or my own. If you'll pay me reasonably I'll come in with you, and although I'm a bit tight at the moment I can tell you I'm pretty good at my job. Why," he went on, "I might even find some way of getting back your Contact List."

As soon as he spoke he saw he had made a mistake. After the free-lance mercenary portrait he had drawn of himself, Foster would immediately assume from his last sentence either that he still had the List and was playing for a high price, or that if he was sufficiently trusted by British Intelligence to be able to recover material he had sent them, he might even now be acting in their interests and laying some elaborate trap. He had forgotten that to the Fosters of the world nothing is ever simple, but that in every subtilty they find another, like a nest of Chinese boxes. His fears were justified. Foster's whole attitude stiffened and he began a staccato interrogation.

"Why didn't you talk sooner?"

"Because I can stand pain well enough, but don't fancy mutilation. I gave in as soon as I was sure you really meant business."

"Who is your superior in Intelligence?"

"I don't know. I address my reports to him as A.5." (He *can't* believe that!)

"Where do you send these reports?"

"I give them to him personally. We meet for lunch at stated times."

"What does he look like?"

"Like an Indian Civil Servant, more than anything. It's no use asking me about him; none of us in the lower ranks know a thing."

Foster flicked his fingers and snapped out,

"Us? Who are 'us'?"

Desmond felt his heart beating and saw the pit opening in front of him.

"Why," he stammered, "just some of my colleagues, no one of any interest."

Foster smiled at him.

"That's not quite good enough, Mr. Thane. I want the names of these colleagues of yours."

"I don't know their names! I..."

"No, Mr. Thane, that won't do! Unless you identify some of these mysterious persons.... He clasped his hands and his smile became still broader. With a sick fear Desmond noticed that Fat, who obviously knew all the signs, had started to sidle round the room towards his chair.

"I daren't speak!" he cried desperately, "they'll kill me if I do!"

Foster's smile snapped off.

"I'll kill you if you don't."

Desmond knew he meant it, and flung his mind wildly round for a name. Mr. Poole? Absurd. Any of his friends? Equally ridiculous. He glanced despairingly round the room and suddenly with a mad memory of that stable of detective stories, the Most Improbable Person, pointed melodramatically at O'Brien.

"That's one of them, the man you call O'Brien! His real name is Stanhope and he's an officer of Military Intelligence! "

The Jew gasped, Foster's mouth dropped, and the Irishman roared like an epileptic bull.

"You bloody lanky lying sod, you!" he bellowed. "I'll have the guts from you!" and flung himself at Desmond so that both went crashing to the floor, O'Brien's thumbs dug into his victim's throat. The man's wrists were as hard as iron, and Desmond barely heard Foster's voice through the drumming of his ears.

"Let go, O'Brien, or I'll shoot."

The Irishman's hands relaxed and he stood up.

"I'm sorry, sir, I've the divil of a temper, and that long bastard ..."

His voice petered out as the others stood looking at him. Foster did not put back his gun.

"I think we had better talk," he said. He nodded to Fat. "Take

Thane away and come back here."

At the door Desmond turned.

"I'm sorry, Stanhope, I deserved it. Thanks for trying to stop them torturing me. I wish I had your guts."

He walked nobly out after the fat man who paused half-way down the passage to turn down a switch, presumably that of the light in Desmond's room. The door shut and he was left alone.

When his elation faded he knew he had made a fatal blunder. By attacking him, the Irishman had played into his hands, but it could not be long before Foster got in touch with his mysterious Headquarters and checked the man's credentials. Even should O'Brien remain for some time under suspicion it would do Desmond no final good; the most he could hope was a few hours' or days' further imprisonment. Worse, when Foster found he was lying, nothing he said would be believed; and after forcing him to disclose the whereabouts of the List he would certainly kill him. The accusing of O'Brien had been, like so many of his inspirations, more brilliant in the conceiving than in effect.

Now that there was nothing to be lost he determined to make a fight for it, and smashed the little window with his shoe. It was barred on the outside as the Jew had said, but the light should soon attract attention, and it was better to be hanged in due legal form than tortured and obscurely murdered. Standing on a chair by the broken pane he began to call softly for help.

Footsteps sounded in the passage. Hastily pulling back the chair he crouched down at the doorway as if trying to listen through the keyhole, falling clumsily into the passage when Fat opened the door.

"Listening?" said the man. "You won't hear much. Get up and come along; Mr. Foster wants you."

As Desmond had hoped, he turned away without looking into the room and seeing the broken window. Passing the switch he flicked it off, and Desmond, reaching behind his back, turned it on again. There was nothing else he could do.

The Irishman, Desmond was glad to notice, had apparently

not yet been able to clear himself, and was standing at the end of the table uneasily clenching and unclenching his hands like a prisoner in the dock. As soon as he entered the room Foster began without preamble.

"When did you first meet this man?"

Desmond decided to play for time.

"I shan't answer your questions unless you promise me full secrecy and protection."

O'Brien snarled something unintelligible and the Jew gestured him to silence. Foster spoke sharply.

"If you are speaking the truth we shall take care of you. When did you first meet him?"

"What will you give me for this? I'm worth good money, you know, and I won't help you for nothing. How about retaining me for a couple of hundred, and paying me on a piece-work basis?"

"Hear the grasping insolence of the bugger!" shouted the Irishman, "let me deal with the black liar, Mr. Foster!"

"Shut your mouth!" said the Jew nastily. He nodded to the fat man, who put his hand to his hip pocket, and the Irishman muttered and fell silent. Foster spoke very patiently.

"Mr. Thane. I don't think you fully realise your position. Answer my questions plainly and promptly or I shall make you do so. Do you understand me?"

Desmond understood. "Well," he began hopelessly, "it was like this ..."

There was a peremptory and unmistakable knocking at the front door.

"Good work, Stanhope! " cried Desmond. "The police! " The Jew turned on him with a gun in his hand and he stopped abruptly. The fat man's pastiness faded to grey and he put his hand to his mouth. Foster smiled slowly.

"I'll deal with this. Turn up the wireless and see that our guests keep still. If you hear shooting get out by the back way." He glanced at Desmond and the Irishman. "You needn't take these two with you."

The knocking began again, and he slipped out of the door. They could hear him going slowly downstairs: Desmond noticed that his steps had perfectly assumed the gouty dignity of a country gentleman. The wireless sang loudly.

"All the lads love Susie,

The democratic floozie,

Who sees the boys on leave get equal rights," crooned a nasal voice inappropriately. O'Brien suddenly realised the purport of Foster's last remark, and, desperately eager to show his loyalty, made for the door.

"I'll go and help Mr. Foster," he said violently. "I'll fix those blue bastards for him!"

The Jew stepped in front of him.

"Oh no you don't! You're staying here."

The Irishman shifted from foot to foot like an angry ape. "An' who's goin' to stop me? You, ye dirty little Yid?" Fat moved to his side without a word and a thin knife appeared in his hand. The three stood posed like waxworks, oblivious of everything but each other's eyes and Foster's footsteps stumping along the hall. The wireless drew breath.

"She's for freedom and fraternity,

But keeps clear of maternity,

And gives her squires most satisfactory nights."

Downstairs Foster fumbled with the catch, and Desmond knew this was his last chance. Desperately he charged at the Jew, sent him spinning across the room, and flung himself through the door. With a snarl O'Brien leapt after him.

"Stop him!" cried the Jew; and the fat man, faithful to what he thought were his master's orders, drove his knife up to the hilt in the small of the Irishman's back.

CHAPTER VII

Outside the room Desmond paused for less than a second, and in the same suspended instant saw ahead of him the passage that led blankly to his cell, and heard behind him the triple thump as O'Brien's knees, hands and face struck the floor like three tumbling sacks. The stairs on the left were his only hope, and leaping down them he ran at the front door where Foster stood with a policeman. They turned towards him and involuntarily he paused. Foster smiled with perfect self-possession, and Desmond noticed that now he wore pince-nez and bore a stoop that made him look many years older.

"Well, Desmond, precipitate as usual! This officer tells me that you failed to black out your room properly and that he'll have to apply for a summons. You really must be less careless—you remember the trouble your foolishness over the telegram cost you?"

He spoke with the testy good-humour of a crotchety, middle-aged man, but his right hand was grasping something in his pocket and his eye twitched at the corner. He continued gently.

"Please go upstairs, and switch off the light, and I'll try and persuade the officer to forgive you as a first offender."

Desmond glanced behind him. At the head of the stairs stood the Jew with his hand thrust Napoleonically into his coat, and at his back the fat man lurked in the shadows. Desmond knew that if he denounced Foster he would probably be shot at once and certainly hanged afterwards should he escape; while if he tamely let the policeman go he would get no second chance.

"To hell with the police and the black-out," he shouted. "I turned on my light once and I'll do it again. If you serve me a summons, you silly bumpkin, I'll stick it where it belongs. This is a free country and you can bloody well mind your manners."

The policeman's face reddened and he reacted just as Desmond had hoped.

"You'd better not talk like that, sir. I'm here to do my duty, and unless you mind your language I'll have to take you in charge for insulting behaviour."

"Go and bugger your helmet, you stupid bluebottle! You dare arrest me and see what happens!"

The policeman stepped forward, but Foster intervened. "Desmond, you're drunk again! Get back to your room at once. Officer, you must excuse my young friend—he's had a severe accident and is not quite himself." He drew the constable aside and talked in a rapid undertone. Desmond caught the words "air force . . . most gallant exploit . . . discharged as unfit . . . effects of shock . . . looking after him..."

The constable nodded sympathetically.

"I quite understand, Mr. Foster. All the neighbourhood knows what you've done for A.R.P., so I won't press the matter if you'll put it right now and see it doesn't happen again. And now I must get on my rounds, so I wish you good-night."

He threw a commiserating glance at Desmond, who realised suddenly how haggard and ill he must look, and stepped out into the porch.

"You can't do this!" cried Desmond wildly, "you've got to arrest me! "

The man looked embarrassed, and Foster called up the stairs.

"Come down here, Cartwright, and help your master up to bed. I'm afraid he's a little over-excited."

The fat man hurried down and Desmond pushed Foster violently aside.

"I need a breath of fresh air," he cried, and ran out round the corner of the house.

To his surprise there was no noise of pursuit, and as soon as he was clear of the gravel and on the soundless grass he stopped to take his bearings. The night was moonlit though cloudy, and save where the shadow of the house, or of the trees round it, threw slabs of blackness, he could distinguish the shapes of bushes and the frontiers of the drive. In the silence he heard the voices of Foster and the policeman clearly but indistinguishably;

then footsteps moved away and a gate clanged heavily. A moment later Foster called something sharply and the Jew answered him. Then, as if a glass door had shut on him, absolute and terrifying silence. He hesitated no longer, but, avoiding the open spaces and keeping in the deepest shadows, crept as quietly as he could towards a tall hedge that seemed to bound the garden. As the moon shone through a gap in the clouds, he saw Fat standing by the gate fifty yards to his left, peering this way and that like an anxious tortoise; and beyond him a white road curling round into a village. Right away on the other side he heard the pad of slow footsteps.

His best course, he decided, was to push through the hedge and make a dash for the houses; they would hear him at once, but he should have fifty yards start. He put out his hands and tried cautiously to part the tough fibres of the hedge which seemed to be a mingling of evergreen and thorn. Then as the moon came out again, something glistened among the leaves and he saw that intertwined with the branches was an impenetrable thicket of barbed wire. It was not the thin strand that forbids trespassers, but the thick, knife-sharp clumps and tangles that resist armies and have revolutionised war as much as tanks or poison gas. Desperately he doubled sideways, searching for a gap, but found none. The hedge was nearly six feet high and at least three broad, impossible to be clambered except with terrible mangling; and faced with a welter of small bushes that left no room for a hopeless leap. He was caught, and realised now why Foster had not bothered to pursue him. With a man at the gate and others systematically beating the garden the place was as strong as a prison and left an unarmed fugitive without the smallest hope of escape.

He ran back the way he had come, and heard a whistle to the side and a hurry of footsteps. Making no attempt at silence now, he plunged through what felt like a rockery, snatched up a piece of stone for a weapon, and rushed towards the gate and the fat man with his knife. At the turn of the drive the moon shone through again, and he saw that Fat had been joined by Foster. Hopelessly he hurled his rock at the pair on the absurd chance of halving his enemies, but it missed by twenty feet and crashed into the bushes behind them.

Foster spun round at the noise.

"Over there! " he cried, and the Jew spurted out of the blackness and dashed towards the sound. While all three pointed like homicidal setters in the wrong direction, Desmond ran back towards the house. As he passed the porch a voice called:

"There he is, you fools, after him! "

There was but one thing to do. He swerved into the house and slammed and bolted the door.

Inside, he ran across the hall, pushed into a room at the end and flung up the window—to find it opened on to the fatal garden from which he had fled. But on the right the building jutted out past the hedge, and overlooked a dark freedom below. Roughly calculating its position from inside the house, he turned back to the hall and hurried upstairs. As he reached the landing he heard a window below smash and someone jump heavily into a ground-floor room. According to his reckoning he must turn left and then left again to reach the projecting wing. Yes—here it was, a bathroom. Pushing open the window, he peered blindly down, but the shadow of the house made a pool beneath him. With the footsteps of Foster's familiars already pounding down the passage, there was nothing for it but to climb on to the window-sill, lower himself to the full extent of his long arms, and let go.

He landed sideways on a gravel bank and rolled over on to a metal bar—a railway line. All round him he could see the hooded outlines of trucks, huddled together as if for company, and in the distance the green light of a signal. He staggered to his feet and stumbled clumsily towards it.

"You two take the left and right; I'll follow here myself," barked Foster's voice above him, followed a moment later by the thud of a heavy man jumping. Desmond crouched behind a wagon holding his breath and listening for the scuffling as Foster got to his feet. The man kept absolutely still for half a minute—a minute—two minutes, without Desmond daring to stir. Then he called out.

"Thane. Listen to me, Thane. I know you're hiding amongst those trucks. You can't get away, you know, why don't you give up? If your story's true, we'll forget this business. Come out and talk it over."

No answer. In the stillness Desmond could hear Foster moving stealthily down the bank. When he reached level ground he spoke again, in a soft, husky coo, like an amorous woman.

"Come on, Thane, give yourself up. The others are working round on each side of you; you'll never get away. If you make a noise or try to resist we'll have to shoot you—you do see that, don't you? Come on, Thane, give yourself up."

The moon was out now and the track was caught in its bright, sterile light. Desmond could see Foster's shadow across the sleepers; the man was out of sight behind a buttress of sandbags projecting from the wall of the house. Desmond, himself completely hidden in blackness as long as he kept still, began to weaken. Foster was quite right; he couldn't get away. On the near side of the line the house and the barbed wire hedge stretched for a considerable distance with, presumably, Fat and the Jew working towards him from either end. On the other side of the tracks were a few straggling houses and open country, but the distance between was, with the sidings, at least sixty yards, and bare of any cover beneath the now cloudless moon. He would be overtaken or shot before he could traverse half of it. Foster tried again.

"Be sensible, Thane. I can come and get you whenever I want, but I might have to shoot, and I don't want to do that. You can't hold out long; it will pay you to be reasonable."

After all, why not give it up and get it over? Desmond began to raise himself to surrender; then, like a polar explorer falling asleep in the snow, forced himself back to sense. Surrender to Foster, give up this apparently valuable Contact List, and then be quietly murdered? He would sooner be killed. With a feeble twist of amusement he remembered that he probably would be.

"For the last time, Thane, give yourself up. If you don't come out in thirty seconds, we'll come and fetch you."

The man's voice was sharply insistent, and it suddenly occurred to Desmond that his capture had become a matter of urgency; that, unknown to him, there was an approaching time limit, and that if he could hold out for a little longer he might be safe. With sudden resolution he quietly picked up a lump of coal.

"All right. I give up. Where are you?"

As Foster stepped out, gun in hand, from behind the sandbags, Desmond stood up, threw the lump full into his face and darted back into the pools and reefs of darkness formed by the trucks. Foster's gun went off with the muffled plop of a silencer, then he ran out on to the open track and signalled rapidly with his hands like a tictac man. In a few moments Fat and the Jew joined him, and all three advanced in open order against the wagons.

Then began an intense and ridiculous battle. Desmond, with his back to the wall and blackness for his shield, dodged from truck to truck pelting his attackers with jagged chunks of coal; while they, in full view and without cover, tried simultaneously to close with him, to drive him into the open and to avoid his shower of missiles. Fat had little stomach for close-quarter violence in the dark, and after a lump had caught him on the leg, took care to venture as little amongst the trucks as his fear of Foster let him; while Foster himself—Desmond was glad to notice that his eye was closing and cheek bleeding freely—stood back out of effective range to meet any attempt at a break for the open. The most dangerous of the three was the Jew, who climbed and ducked across the wagons with a calm and remorseless certainty, cleverly sidestepping his quarry's increasingly wild bombardment until there was but a single barrier left between them. Quite near a train whistled. "Hurry up," called Foster, "get him quickly!"

"O.K.," answered the Jew, and sprang over the last coupling.

Desmond backed away.

"I've an iron bar," he shouted, "and I'll smash your skull in if you come a yard closer! "

The Jew laughed.

"The hell you will!" he said, and rushed at him.

Faced with the Jew's fists or Foster's bullets, Desmond did not hesitate, but ran out across the line against the unfamiliar danger, and saw a long goods train clanking round the bend towards him. Behind came the stifled clap of Foster's gun, and two bullets smacked against the ground almost between his feet, and a third clanged on a rail just ahead. "So he still doesn't want to kill me, he's shooting at my legs: he wants to bring me down and take me prisoner. He'd sooner let me get away than kill me without getting his list," flashed through his brain. Then he was across the line almost under the engine (was that a shout from the driver?) and the interminable line of wagons rumbled past, a moving wall behind him. Gasping, he dragged himself up a bank at the edge of the track and climbed through a wire railing into a narrow road. To the left were houses; on the right a hill and open country. He began to go to the left to find help, then realised that this was precisely what they would expect him to do, and that after the incident with the constable the local police would smile sympathetically at his story and take him back to Foster. He turned back and went at a trudging run up the hill and into the lunar heart of the empty and unknown countryside.

At the crest of the slope Desmond halted for breath. Before him, the road ran for miles like a trickle of water, its white continuity broken only by clumps of trees and an occasional low hill. On either side stretched acres of ploughed fields, and nowhere could be seen the least sign of human habitation. It was hard to remember that this was in the home counties some thirty miles from London: in the white floodlight of the moon it seemed as desolate as planetary space or the uplands of Alaska.

By the side of the road stood a notice board and with a little effort he made out its message.

NOTICE

Every driver who injures the roadway by descending the hill
with a locked wheel which has not a properly adjusted
skidpan will be prosecuted.

By order of the Herts. County Council.

Now, at any rate, he knew the county. But how far was the
nearest town and where did the road lead? His arm began to hurt
again, and felt as though it were bleeding. He sat down on the
bank waiting for the pain to cease and speculating upon the
nature of skidpans, when all at once he heard footsteps coming
steadily up the hill, and fear swam to his head like a fog. Stupidly
he listened, hoping they were the steps of a casual walker, until
they reached the bend below him; then instinct took charge and
he found himself running very fast, paced by the interminable
white line down the middle of the road. Cowardice proved a
better spur than team spirit had ever been, and he must have
covered nearly half a mile before his wind gave out and he
dropped panting to the shelter of a dry ditch. The road was in
the heart of the moonlight now, as exposed as a crack on a plate,
and only in the narrow shade of the hedge was there any hope
of concealment. Cautiously he peered behind and saw a dark
figure running evenly after him. The man went quite slowly,
glancing continually from side to side to see if his quarry lurked
in the shadow, but never slackened step and ran with the tireless
lope of the cross-country runner. As he came nearer, Desmond
saw that it was the Jew, and again forgetting concealment,
plunged to his feet and rushed wildly on. Glancing over his
shoulder he saw that his pursuer had lengthened stride but not
perceptibly increased his pace: he knew he would soon outrun
his victim, and meant to be fresh for the kill.

Almost at the end of his strength, Desmond dashed between
the black walls of a little copse, and saw as he emerged a cottage
by the side of the road. Behind, he heard the Jew slow to a walk
and guessed that he was going to search the wood. Stumbling

through the gate, he knocked as loudly as he dared on the cottage door. No answer. He knocked softly again, and this time thought he heard a murmur in an upper room, but still there was no reply. In a few minutes the Jew would be out of the coppice and find him in full view. Running round to the back of the house, he pushed violently at the first door he reached. It splintered, and gave on to a junk-strewn outhouse, and he saw, in the path of the moonlight, a double-barrelled shotgun leaning against the wall. He snatched it up and looked round for cartridges, but could find none. Back on the road he heard footsteps: the Jew had left the wood and was coming towards the cottage.

Desmond slipped round the further side of the house and ducked in among a group of fruit bushes. He could see the Jew now, moving slowly along the line of the trees with an automatic in his hand, stopping every few paces to glance round him and listen intently. As he came nearer, Desmond saw that his mouth was open and his eyes darting ceaselessly this way and that. An owl hooted surprisingly on a branch just above him, and he swung round tensely, pistol at the ready; then relaxed and gave an audible sigh of relief. Desmond suddenly realised that the man was frightened. Without physical fear; at home, no doubt, in the gangster quarters of great cities, the moonlit emptiness and odd nocturnal noises of the countryside had bitten at his nerves, and the last search through the whispering blackness of the coppice had brought him near to panic. It was probably the first time he had ever been alone in the country at night; and while he pursued Desmond down the empty road, he must have been imagining a dozen fearful fiends treading closely at his own heels.

At once Desmond forgot all his own terrors, and crept from bush to bush until he was scarcely twenty feet away from his adversary. The wind had risen, and the noise of his movements was lost in the rustling of the wood. In the Jew's world, he remembered, guns were always loaded and their bearers meant to shoot—Anna had assumed that the sight of her pistol would cow him; a mere threat to fire had restrained the homicidal

Irishman. He waited till the Jew had turned his back towards him, then called out softly from the bushes.

"Stand quite still and put up your hands. I've got a shotgun from the cottage, and if you move I'll blow your head off."

The man stood perfectly still but did not drop his gun, and with a spurt of uneasiness Desmond realised that he was on his own ground now, and once more self-possessed. It would have been better to have made a noise like a ghost, or hopped hastily from shadow to shadow, instead of calling him back to his safe and familiar environment.

"Come on," repeated Desmond, "drop your gun." Without moving the other said:

"You daren't shoot because of the noise. You might risk it if I came at you, but what if I stay put? "

"That's where you're wrong. In the country they shoot all night, at partridges and so on. If I fired a shot no one would bother in the least."

As he had expected, the Jew's rural knowledge was of the slightest, and Desmond could see that he believed him. He went on: "I don't want to kill you because you treated me decently when I was a prisoner. If that sod Foster was here I'd shoot, so to speak, like a shot."

As he spoke he knew, surprisingly, that he meant it; more—that had the gun been loaded he would probably have killed the Jew without compunction; and regretted his present hypocrisy more than his bloody intentions. Did it need so little, then, to make one a conscienceless murderer, or was it that only detached people like himself were prepared to be soldiers in the cause of their own enlightened self-interest? He checked his philosophic maunderings, and noticed with growing disquiet that the other still clutched his pistol, and was shifting his feet, ever so slightly, as if for a quick turn. He spoke in a tone he tried to make sharp and ominous.

"Keep your feet still and drop your gun or I'll give you both barrels. Perhaps you think I'm not armed—why not turn round and look? May I remind you of two things: firstly that your little pistol won't do much good—at this range the shot would cut you in two; and secondly, that if I haven't a gun you won't want yours to handle me. Well, what about it? I'll give you ten seconds."

For a horrible instant the Jew hesitated, then jerked his weapon thirty feet into the copse.

"All right," he said, "now go and get it. You can bluff me into dropping my gun, but by God I'll see you don't bluff me into giving it you."

He turned slowly round, his hands above his head, and broke into a broad grin.

"So you have got a gun! I was a mug to think anything else—you wouldn't have had the guts without it. Well, what do we do now? If you feel like tying me up there's some cord in my pocket."

"Oh no you don't! Stop where you are and face the other way."

Desmond spoke firmly, but he was far from confident. What *was* he going to do with his prisoner? To attempt to bind him was out of the question—he was acutely aware of what would probably happen if he got within striking distance—yet he could scarcely hold the man up indefinitely. The Jew was unarmed now, and less dangerous; the best thing was to let him go, and so gain at least a considerable start.

"Walk ahead of me," he said, "and go back along the road we came by."

They walked in silence. At the farther edge of the copse Desmond stopped.

"If you give me your word not to tell Foster you found me, I'll let you go. I might add that you'll look pretty stupid if you confess that your quarry captured you, and Foster's not the man to forgive mistakes; so it's in your own interests to keep your mouth shut. Do you promise?"

"O.K.," answered the man earnestly, "on my solemn word of honour. Do you think I'd tell that bastard Foster about this? Not likely!"

"Right. Go straight ahead down the middle of the road and don't stop or look round. I'll follow you some of the way, and at the least funny move I'll shoot. Now get on."

The Jew marched promptly off, and Desmond stood watching him. All at once he knew with omniscient clarity that of course he would tell Foster what had happened, and that in half an hour the whole trinity would be after him, probably in a car.

"Stop!" he cried.

The man stopped; and Desmond took four paces forward and swung the butt of the gun smash on to his glossy head. With a puffing sigh like a punctured tyre he pitched face downwards on the road, twitched a little once or twice, and lay still.

Desmond knelt beside him and began to dab with his handkerchief at the gaping wound in the back of the head. Then he snapped his fingers, caught hold of the Jew's wrists, and dragged him back to the dappled darkness of the edge of the wood.

"He can't be dead," he thought, "but he'll certainly keep quiet for a couple of hours, and not feel fit for much at the end of that." He decided to drop the man over the fence into the coppice, where he could not be seen by passers-by; and went quickly through his pockets, taking a wallet and some loose change. Then he picked him up in his arms (how light he was!) and heaved him over the hedge. There was a splash and a gurgle—then silence. The ditch was full of water, pretty deep from the sound of it; and as he peered over the brambles he could see nothing but the glister of widening ripples. His half murder had become complete.

He thought: "I don't think he'd have told Foster after all. I think he'd have kept his word."

He thought: "I wonder if I really meant to kill him all the time?"

He thought: "How stupid of me! I ought to have questioned him: I ought to have found out where I am."

He ceased thinking, and walked on through the coppice. His hair was wild, his clothes dishevelled, his face as pale as ice. Anyone who saw him might have thought he had dwelt iii the dark wood for a long time.

CHAPTER VIII

Opposite the cottage he came to himself, and found he was almost exhausted. He could go little farther without rest, and it was likely that when the Jew failed to return Foster and the fat man would come out to look for him. The sensible course was to leave the road and take to the fields, but he knew that after a few hundred yards through soggy ploughland he would probably collapse and fall asleep. With weary resolution he resolved to ask the cottagers for shelter, and leave the story he would tell them to the moment and his unfailing power of invention. He noticed that he was still hugging the shot-gun, and, wiping the stained butt on the grass, slipped round to the outhouse and leant it back where he had found it. Then, going up to the front door he began to knock as loudly as he was able.

After a few minutes the window above him opened and a scared feminine voice called down.

"Who's there? What do you want?"

"I've met with a slight accident. I wondered if you could give me a glass of water."

He heard a whispered confabulation punctuated by frightened giggles. Then a second woman spoke, this time in a tone of nervous arrogance.

"How dare you disturb us at this time of night. Who are you?"

"My name's Tisket and I'm quite harmless. I've had a trifling mishap, but the priest and the Levite have passed me by, so I wondered if you could oblige me with a glass of water."

The whispering began again, and he thought he could catch the words, "Tisket . . . got a friend called Levy. ..."

"I have no friend called Levy," he shouted, "I just want a glass of water!"

This provoked further stifled giggling, and he heard the second voice say, "He sounds like a gentleman."

"Yes, I'm definitely a gentleman," he interrupted. "I was at

Winchester and the House, I hunt, I belong to the Junior Carlton, I play squash, travel first class and have stayed at Brown's Hotel. If you'll please answer the door I'll give you both lunch at the Berkeley."

There was a pause. Then the first voice said:

"All right; wait a minute and I'll come down."

The door was opened by a tall young woman in a red dressing-gown, with another, holding a lamp and a poker, peering over her shoulder. As he stepped forward into the light they both gasped, and he realised that he must look battered and dishevelled.

"Why, your arm's bleeding!"

He glanced down and saw that his cuff and left wrist were flecked with blood.

"Yes, I've had a slight cut, but it's nothing serious," he said bravely; and resolved to ensure his night's harbourage by simulating a little faintness—just enough to excite pity and prove his incapacity for harm, but not so much as to cause serious alarm. "If you'll excuse me," he went on, "I'll sit down for a moment; I feel a trifle unwell." He clutched his brow and sank into the nearest chair; and to his surprise blackness tilted before his eyeballs and starshells burst in his head. For an instant he fainted in reality, then came to his senses to find his head between his knees and a cold sponge on the back of his neck. He straightened up.

"Thanks; I'm better now. If you'll tell me the way to the nearest town I'll be getting along."

"Nonsense," said the taller of the girls briskly, "you can't go like this. Let's have a look at your arm."

He took off his coat and rolled up the shirt sleeve. The blood had dried in streaks down the forearm and the wounds looked impressively nasty. The girl gave a little cluck, and turned to her companion.

"Annabel, go and fetch the lint and a sponge. I'll put on a kettle."

While she was sponging his arm he began to make his explanations.

"I had a very silly accident, really. I was in a train on the way to London and leant out of the window to look at the moon, when the door flew open and I fell on to the line. I must have been stunned, for I don't remember anything more until I woke up and found myself on a lonely road without a house in sight. My arm was hurting, so I bandaged it as best I could—a pretty rotten best as you saw. I had some iodine with me," he remembered suddenly with a shudder, "and poured that on as well. Then I walked on till I came to your cottage. I knocked at the door but you didn't hear me. ..."

"Yes we did," interjected one of the girls, "but we thought you were a tramp. Go on."

"So I went on walking, but soon felt a bit faint, and thought I'd better come back and try again. It does sound ridiculous, doesn't it?—when I tell it like this I scarcely believe it myself. But that's all there is to it: I'm only thankful the train wasn't travelling very fast."

"Good lord, how absolutely too priceless! " exclaimed the girl who was sponging his arm.

He was as offended as though he had really experienced the mishap he described.

"Well, I suppose it was priceless in a sense. Certainly no one would have paid a price to experience it. But tell me," he continued, "where precisely am I? I know I'm in Herts, but that's about all."

"We're about six miles from Bishop's Stortford, and a mile and a half from the Buntingford Line. You were travelling on that, I suppose?"

"Yes, yes, the Buntingford Line—that's right. As a matter of fact," he hurried on to sidetrack any detailed questioning about his imaginary journey, "I've been wandering haphazard about the country for weeks, collecting material for a book of poems. That's why I haven't shaved."

"Oh, are you a poet?" interrupted the girl called Annabel. "You may have met the man I'm engaged to —Bob Paget. He writes a good deal in *New Poetry* and *Cervix*—you know, the one they used to call *Axis* until the war made it sound unpatriotic. Stephen and Tom Eliot thinks very highly of Bob."

"Why yes," lied Desmond, "I think I did meet him once at a party. Let me see, isn't he the good-looking one with longish hair and a very intellectual face?"

This won Annabel, and she immediately adopted him as her friend. She was attractive, with her slim calves and the fair hair falling over her face; and he played with the idea of trying to compete with Bob. He had always believed that one could seduce warm-hearted women by persistently praising their men (a fortnight's lovably selfless admiration of the creature, then a gentle advance —"Oh no, you mustn't! You're Bob's friend!" "But, Annabel, I admire him so much because he likes you. I know he'd understand; he's often made love to women whom I . . . No, no, you mustn't tell him! It would spoil our friendship if he knew I betrayed his confidences, and I shouldn't like that to happen, as in spite of the things he's sometimes said about you I admire him more than any man I've met," etc. etc.), but had never yet put his theory to the test, since he invariably despised his sexual rivals too heartily to be able convincingly to praise them even for their own undoing. But a sudden twinge as the sponge scraped a raw rim of flesh brought him back to the present with a jolt and drove the amorousness from his head, which was, after all, the place where it had mainly resided.

Annabel sat beside him, leaving the first aid to her more efficient friend.

"What school of poetry do you belong to?"

"I'm a wandering scholar of all schools. Sometimes I attempt the

Love, like a bomb,
Shakes sober sense's sooty cities down
*And flames like spring on reason's whited tomb*style, but I'm often

more homely. Housman's influenced me a great deal; I'll recite you the opening stanzas of a sequence I wrote in imitation of him—The First Rung of the Ladder, I used to call it:

Oh, there lies a Lad under Ludlow Who'll never strike ball with bat. He wedded death with a gas-ring The day the Assizes sat.

And, naturally, I've done a fair amount of *fin de Zeitgeist* stuff:

The roc broods in the empty factory, making its nest from girders;

The upas sprouts in the Major's well-kept garden; The banks are covered with grass; the mad vicar Plays an astonishing voluntary on his ruined organ.

I'm very versatile."

The other girl sat back.

"There!" she said. "I think that arm'll be all right now—it wasn't as bad as it looked. But I can't imagine how you hurt yourself like that by falling from a train." "No," he agreed sincerely, "it's so extraordinary that I can scarcely credit it myself. But it's nearly two o'clock, and I mustn't keep you up any longer, so I'll get along to Bishop's Stortford—it was only ten miles you said, wasn't it? Thank you so much for your succour and kindness; you must have dinner with me next time you're in town—give me your address and I'll write to you as soon as I'm settled."

He got up and went nobly to the door, staggering a little at first, and supporting himself on the lintel. It worked.

"Oh no!" cried Annabel, "he can't walk to Bishop's Stortford, can he, Mary?" She turned to Desmond. "You must stop here to-night; there's a bed in the spare room." "Yes, do stay," said Mary, "you don't look up to walking six miles. Besides, you wouldn't find anywhere to sleep in Stortford at this time of night, even if you got there."

"That's very nice indeed of you; I should be very glad to. To tell you the truth, I do feel a trifle unsteady; and though it's really shameful of me to trespass on you like this, the prospect of another walk to-night does rather appal me."

"Good, then that's settled. The sheets were aired only yesterday, so they won't be damp."

They escorted him upstairs to a low-ceilinged, white- walled room and left him a candle. Securely alone, he examined the Jew's wallet and found thirty shillings and a typewritten card:

DEREK MARCH
Dealer in Rare and Second-hand Books
Hampstead Passage
Hampstead
*In answer to your enquiry, item 87 of my current catalogue
is no longer in stock*

The card was addressed to "A. Samuels, 1 Charing Cross Hotel." That was all. It was hard to imagine the Jew a customer of an antiquarian bookseller, and Desmond began to speculate sleepily on the sort of book which might be expected to interest him. Item 87 was probably a handbook of boxing or the sort of work listed as "Very curious. Sold only to bona-fide members of the medical profession." To-morrow, he resolved, he would go to Missenden and collect his registered letter—Mr. (Poole could well do without him for another day—and, on his way, he might visit Mr. March and satisfy himself as to his late victim's literary tastes. Common sense told him to leave ill alone, but curiosity and a growing aggressiveness argued that here was a chance to take the initiative and find out something about his mysterious enemies.

After a little internal conflict he decided, typically, at least to walk past the shop and look in the window, and immediately fell asleep.

The morning was bright and sunny, and Desmond felt inappropriately pleased with himself. His arm was comfortable, the chintz curtains flapped cheerfully in the breeze, the stubble on his chin had attained a handsome thickness, and he looked forward to collecting his registered letter with the carefree enthusiasm of a child waking up on its birthday. Always resilient where other people's troubles were concerned, the thought of the Jew's body in the ditch failed to disturb him in the least.

"He won't be found for a day or two," he thought, "they mayn't even smell him out till the summer." Irrepressibly elated at having proved fatal to one of his enemies, he turned down his thumbs and made insulting noises with his lips. He felt ready for anything.

At breakfast he told his hostesses more about himself. "I used to work on the *Daily Telegraph,* you know; I was sub-editor of the Births, Marriages and Deaths; but I soon became sick of that job and ended by getting myself fired. How did it happen? Well, it struck me that the Died on Active Service column was a good deal too dull, so one day I tried to touch it up by inserting entries like 'He Fell Asleep while on Patrol,' 'Passed Over to the Other Side,' or 'Found Peace while Leading an Air Raid.' At the end of the month I found peace myself."

Annabel looked up from a letter.

"You said you wrote poetry, didn't you? Bob's written and sent me his latest poem—would you like to read it?" "I should love to."

She handed him a typewritten sheet and his eyes automatically ran to the top of the page.

"...like Baudelaire. Your creative understanding and ardent integrity are as necessary as my Kant to me. Your passion buoys me spiritually as a warm sea laps the limbs of a bather ..."

This was too sacred for the early morning, and although he was sure Annabel meant him to read it, he fixed his eyes firmly on the last paragraph.

"I do think the present war has become an important spiritual experience for the creative writer, and I agree that it is the duty of the poet as a leader of the common consciousness, to interpret this popular feeling in intense and passionate form; and show by the resolution of his own emotional conflicts the way to a lasting peace based on justice and democratic rights. Spender and Macniece— and to a lesser degree, Dante, Shakespeare, Blake, Goethe and the poets of the Greek Anthology—all realise this vital truth, and poetically precipitate the political praxis of their periods. Here's the rough draft of a sonnet I've just written about my love. It's not at all in my usual style, but, as I think Stendhal said, *Te poete, comme l'amoureux, n'est pas le moins serieux parcequ'il fait des variations de son technique."*

POEM

Shall passion like an ostrich hide its head In sands of abstinence when armies move?
Did cannon balls displace the need for love When towering Tolstoi kept his turgid bed?
A butcher's-shop-hung-heart is hideous:
To call a helm a metal hat's absurd,
But both are nobler far than love deferred; Unlicensed lust is simply ludicrous.
Where Shelley wore the bays we pour bay rum, And yet our minds are not intoxicate.
As Marvel said, "Tomorrow never comes,"
And age or gun-fire make a final date.
The act may end before it really starts,
So let the actors-haste to play their parts.

"Will you be in town next week? We might go for a walk on Clapham Common and read Rimbaud together—he's like me in many ways. . . ."

"That's a fine poem," said Desmond, "from what I know of Bob it's just what I should have expected of him. It ought to be put in a casket and buried for the edification of all future ages. . . ."

He paused abruptly as, outside on the road, a car swerved round the corner and came to a stop. He ran to a window and saw a man get out and walk towards the cottage, while another, whose shape he could not distinguish, sat at the wheel with the engine running. He felt his stomach sink and his face pale; and, making an effort to keep his voice steady, turned urgently to the two women.

"I can't explain now, but if this man asks after me, say you haven't seen me. They aren't the police or anything like that, but it's desperately important, and for God's sake don't say I've been here, I'll tell you about it when he's gone."

As the girls gaped with astonishment, he slipped behind the door and stood with his back against it. There was a knock which Mary answered.

"Excuse me, madam, but have you seen anything of a tall young man, possibly with an injured arm, either late last night or this morning?"

Desmond did not recognise the voice, but it was clipped and a little unnatural as though the speaker were trying to disguise his accent. Mary hesitated a moment and glanced at her friend who still sat at the table in mouth-filled surprise. Then:

"No"—a pause—"No, I don't think I've seen anyone at all since yesterday afternoon."

"Thank you; I'm sorry to have bothered you."

The man turned and walked back towards the road. Mary stood looking after him and as he reached the gate called out:

"Who is this man you're looking for? Why do you want him?"

He paused and called back.

"I'm from West Herts. Mental Hospital: one of our patients escaped last night."

Annabel gave a little gulp and Mary drew in her breath for a shout. Desmond clapped his hand over her mouth and snatched up the bread knife.

"Keep quiet," he hissed, "or I'll cut your throat."

He kicked the door shut and stood in front of it until, an interminable moment later, the car drove off. He sighed with relief.

"That was a near thing! I'm sorry I had to behave so melodramatically, but it's quite simple. ..."

The girls were backing away from him and staring with horrified incredulity. It looked like the climax of the tenser sort of one-act play.

"Good heavens!" he said, "you don't really imagine ..."

They clearly did. They were standing together in a corner now, clutching each other rather pathetically, like the little princes in the tower.

"Look here . . . " he began, and moved towards them; but panic exploded in their eyes and he stopped.

"Look," he began again, sitting pacifically down on a hard chair. "You don't really believe I'm mad, do you? That man didn't come from a mental hospital; he's the agent of a gang that want to kidnap me..."

He petered into silence. Of course they wouldn't believe his story; he scarcely believed it himself. Even in normal circumstances it would have seemed incredible, and, after his arrival in the middle of the night, his absurd tale of falling from a train, and his febrile and unorthodox witticisms, he must appear the perfect specimen of an advanced mental case. This morning, with marmalade on the table and sunshine outside the window, he almost believed they were right and the memories of the previous week only the delusions of a maniac. There was not a sound in the room, and he and the girls stared at each other with an increasing awareness of their mutually unpleasant position. Hopelessly, Desmond tried again.

"I'm not mad, you know."

Mary drew breath and answered firmly, if a trifle loudly.

"No, of course you're not—I'm sure it's all some mistake. Let's go on with breakfast."

She had adopted the soothing tone of a hospital matron, and he knew that she had made up her mind beyond all conviction.

"No, thanks," he said, "I've had enough; I must be going. Where's the next village?"

Their eyes flickered with relief.

"Braughing's the nearest. If you take the path through the wood and across the fields it's not more than half- an-hour's walk."

"Good. I'll go that way. Perhaps you could point out the route?"

He opened the door and beckoned them out. As they passed him he caught them affectionately but firmly by the arms, and felt Mary's muscles tense and Annabel's go completely limp. He led them to the edge of the wood and halted.

"Now, where's this path?"

Mary pointed to the right.

"It starts at that gap in the hedge and goes round to the right. When you come out of the wood follow the line of the trees and you can't go wrong."

He released their arms.

"Right, I'll go then, and thank you for your charming hospitality. I'm not mad, you know, just unlucky, and one day I'll write to you and explain it all. Good-bye."

He went into the wood without looking back. As soon as he judged himself to be out of sight, he crept round and peered at the cottage through the trees. The girls were standing in the doorway chattering like appalled sparrows, apparently in argument. After a minute or two Mary said something decisive and walked firmly round the corner of the house, followed less eagerly by her friend. In a few moments they reappeared with bicycles and, after a last anxious glance at the wood, set off down the road. He noticed, in the daylight, that there was a turning to the left about a hundred yards beyond the cottage, and saw them wheel round it and pedal rapidly down the lane, their heads bobbing over the hedge like targets in a shooting gallery. As soon as they were gone he came out of the wood and hurried up the main road. There was a sign-post at the turning, and he saw, as he had expected, that it pointed to Braughing. He grinned to himself to think that when they breathlessly told the police their story of an approaching lunatic who not only failed to arrive but was found never to have escaped, they would learn at first hand what it felt like to be thought mad. He waved his hand after them and strode straight ahead— six miles to Bishop's Stortford.

He reached the town shortly after eleven, had a shave and took a ticket for the 11.40 to London. Waiting for the train, he amused himself by reading the L.N.E.R.'s regulations—from which he learned that any person driving an "Improper Engine" (presumably one in the shape of a sea-shell with gilded panels depicting unsuitable mythological scenes) was liable to a fine of £20, and that for the inclusive sum of £15 one could travel without a ticket, be drunk and insulting to the other passengers, expose one's person and pelt the plate-layers with fittings torn from the Company's carriages. Tired of this, he studied the map to determine exactly where he had been imprisoned. Suddenly it occurred to him that since Foster had been known by that name to the policeman, his address would probably be in the telephone book, and finding a call-box, he looked through the local directory. There were only eight Fosters, of whom five were tradesmen and one a woman. Of the remaining two, one lived in Bishop's Stortford itself and the other was *A. C. K. Foster, Hill House, Standon.* Impulsively he picked up the receiver and called the number. Almost to his horror, it was Foster's voice that answered.

"This is Foster speaking. Who is that?"

"I'm Thane. How are you?"

There was a moment's silence, then Foster spoke without any trace of emotion.

"Good morning. What can I do for you?"

"I thought you might be looking for your Jewish friend. He's stopping at present in the first wood on the main road to Bishop's Stortford. I don't think he'll be back."

"Is that what you rang up to tell me?"

"Yes. I thought you might like to take him home before he bothers the neighbours. He may get disagreeable in a few days, and that would inconvenience both of us."

"Thank you. I'll see about it."

There was a whispered scuffling at the other end of the line as if several people were moving about, and the faint tinkle of a bell. With a horrid certainty Desmond knew that Foster had another telephone, and that someone was even then calling the exchange to trace the number from which he spoke. Cursing the stupid bravado that had made him 'phone, he thought quickly.

"I expect you'd like to know where I'm 'phoning from. I'm at Bishop's Stortford station and my train leaves in five minutes, so you can't get here in time to see me off."

(They'll find that I'm speaking the truth and try and intercept me at Broxbourne Junction or meet me at London.)

"Why do you tell me this?"

"Because I want to do a deal with you. I can get back the Contact List in two days, and I'm prepared to sell it you."

(And why not, after all? I ought to have thought of it before.)

"How much do you want?"

Desmond glanced at the number on the dial—Bishop's Stortford 1572. "Fifteen hundred pounds."

Foster answered without the briefest hesitation. "I accept; payment on delivery. 'Phone me here and make an appointment directly you've obtained it." "Good-bye. I must catch my train."

He ran off as the London express panted into the station. They could certainly meet the train, and perhaps send someone to Bishop's Stortford on the chance of catching him before he left—a fast car might do the journey in ten minutes. He hurried out of the station, and jumped on to a cross-country bus as it moved away. Taking a ticket to Hertford, he settled down to think things out.

So Foster was prepared to pay over a thousand pounds for Anna's notebook! No doubt he never intended to hand over the money and merely hoped to trap him into a meeting, but that was not the important point. The vital thing was that fifteen hundred pounds was quite a possible price for the list, and that Foster and his mysterious organization were not only murderous but rich. Desmond became frightened as he contemplated the enormity of his enemies, and passionately resolved to collect the letter, take the money, and post the notebook to Foster with the true explanation of how he had obtained it. But he could not forget that he had killed Anna and the Jew, and knew in his heart that Foster would probably never forgive him for stumbling upon the outskirts of his vast and incredible secret. They would not spare him, even if he returned the list: there is no possible appeasement of an injured tiger. The bus, like a squat green beetle, crept on through the awakening spring.

CHAPTER IX

From Hertford desmond caught the next train to London. Although he was sure he had not been followed, and knew that it was beyond the powers even of a Foster to have posted spies for him at every railway station, he felt, all the same, as nervous and conspicuous as an honest man travelling without a ticket, and, lurking in the airless waiting-room until the train came in, bounded suddenly into a first-class carriage when it was already moving off. To his annoyance he was not alone, but shared the compartment with three officers who huddled together in earnest conversation.

"I say," said one, "why didn't the troops have any pudding last night?"

"What! Didn't have a pudding? I thought they had the same pudding we had."

"No, the sergeant told me they didn't have any pudding at all."

"I say, that's a bad show! Mustn't happen again."

"It wasn't a bad pudding we had."

"I didn't fancy it myself—I've never cared much for pudding, as a matter of fact."

"I don't know; I like a good pudding. Food's not been so bad lately."

"Didn't think much of the bacon this morning; can't stomach army bacon."

"Yes, I know; most people don't like army bacon. I fancy it myself, though. When I was at home last week they gave me some bacon, and I didn't like it as much as army bacon. I told them army bacon had a better flavour, even though it *is* streaky. They were surprised."

"I suppose there *is* more flavour to army bacon; it depends how you like it."

"That's so."

"I say, are you sure the troops had no pudding? Wants looking into. Can't have that sort of thing."

"Well, I thought they had the same pudding as we had . . . "

Desmond was happy. Here, he thought, was the solid basis of British civilization, and as long as her soldiers could ramble on about puddings; fanaticism and tyranny stood very little chance. He would like to have joined the conversation and given his own views about bacons he had experienced, but restrained himself and sank into a pleasant stupor. Not until they drew into London and the dingy whirl of Liverpool Street swept him up did he remember that his was a different life and that he was caught in another side of history.

Over a dull but grossly adequate lunch, he considered his next steps, and decided that he had been unduly pessimistic. He would go to Missenden, collect the registered packet, and post the notebook to Foster with a full explanation. Then, he would write to Mr. Poole and resign his job—which, in any event, the war might easily bring to an end in the near future—and hide somewhere in the country for three or four months. When Foster received his list and found that Desmond was doing him no more harm, he would soon abandon any attempt at pursuit, and have quite forgotten the affair by the time he emerged from hiding, for he did not seem the kind of man to risk himself and his organization in search of a futile and unnecessary vengeance. In a way, Desmond felt pleased at the prospect of losing his identity and. leaving his friends for a time; and resolved to employ his forced seclusion in writing one of the numerous books he had planned during the last ten years. Natural optimism and a brandy with his coffee brightened the prospect still further, and he left the restaurant almost convinced that his luck had held again, and that Anna's death and his subsequent troubles might really have been the most fortunate events of his career, since they had given him the means and the compulsion to throw off all his emotional and material entanglements. Threat of death had obliged him to start a new life; and, a decade hence, from the apex of his literary greatness, he would think kindly of Foster, by then no doubt lying, riddled with bullets, in the grave the violent dig for themselves, and insert each year in the *Times* an appropriate little iambic to the memory of the man who had unwittingly caused his Hegira. All that remained was to go to Missenden and collect his passport to fortune.

He rang up Baker Street and found he had several hours until the next good train. It would be dangerous to visit his usual haunts—Foster was quite capable of posting a watch on his home and (if he knew of it) his club; but a cinema or a walk in the park were equally and notably uninviting. Boredom and curiosity combined to suggest a reconnaissance of Mr. March's bookshop, and Desmond, telling himself at each station that he would alight and turn back at the next, took the Underground to Hampstead.

Mr. March traded in one of the narrow, crooked alleys off Heath Street; and Desmond, walking casually past his door, was more than ever convinced that this was not the sort of shop at which the Jew would have been a customer.

The window display was as jumbled and littered with incompatible learnings as the mind of a senile scholar. In the place of honour was a gigantic and beautiful edition of the *Novum Organum,* flanked on one side by a German treatise on volcanoes, and the other by an illustrated hand-book of military uniforms, in which pommaded and waxed-moustached officers postured like petulant peacocks before explosive panoramas in which thousands of red and white cavalry charged in perfect alignment over a rock-strewn and erupted countryside. Around these three planets surged a crowded, dusty confusion of sermons, obscure Drydens, Victorian manuals of physical training, odd volumes of the *Spectator,* garlands of play-bills, satires on forgotten vices and encomiums of equally forgotten theological virtues. It was a literary refuse dump, containing, one imagined, pearls as well as rubbish; it was the flotsam from four centuries of Grub Street.

After strolling up and down two or three times and seeing nothing in the least suspicious, Desmond opened the door, which rang with a feeble tinkle, and walked inside. The shop was much larger than had appeared from the street, and stretched like a broad littered passage into a murky dimness at the back. As he peered cautiously about him, an elderly man, presumably the owner, emerged from behind a bookshelf.

"Are you interested in any special subject?"

His voice creaked like an unoiled hinge, and as he spoke he thrust his head forward like an inquisitive bird. He was short and bent, with pale, smooth hands which he held clasped before his stomach in the obsequious gesture of an innkeeper. Yet the twist of his mouth and the glint in his little eyes made a parody of his subservience, and his clothes, which suggested those of an Edwardian buck, made the parody itself grotesque.

"No," answered Desmond, "I've no special interests— or rather, I have so many that it's useless to recite them. It would be a help though, if you had a catalogue."

The man rummaged under a pile of folios.

"Here is my latest list. If any of the items interest you I shall be in my office at the back."

He slipped away out of sight, and Desmond, turning so as not to be observed, flicked through the pages until he came to Item 87.

P. VIRGILII MARONIS OPERA. Interpretation et Notis illustravit A. Raven; contemporary vellum; Paris, 1681 : £2 10s. od. A nice copy of this edition. Some annotations in a contemporary hand on the first page of Aeneid Book II.

Desmond was puzzled, and looked at the number again. What could have interested the Jew in a Latin edition of Virgil? He re-read the entry, and his nerves jolted as he absorbed for the first time *"Illustravit A. Raven."* But this was ridiculous! How could Anna have edited a seventeenth century Virgil? Plainly it must be a coincidence of some kind; perhaps the Jew had chanced on the entry and been sufficiently amused to order the book. . . . But even as he thought of his silly explanation he knew it was absurd; there must be more behind it than that. Somehow, at the back of his mind, he associated Anna with Virgil, and tried to recollect if they had ever discussed Latin poetry. No; even in bed, when he tended to cultural chattiness, they had never—then he remembered his search through her bedroom and the cheap little Aeneid hidden so carefully beneath her expensive underclothes.

Pretending to be absorbed in the catalogue, he tried to resolve the problem. In the first place, the important thing must be the Aeneid itself, and not any particular edition of it. Secondly, he could not believe that the Jew had really wanted Item 87, for had he done so he would certainly not have wasted his time making "an enquiry" for it; and Desmond was sure, too, now he considered it, that the book described in the catalogue did not really exist—"A. Raven" was altogether too much to believe. He pulled out the card he had taken from the Jew and studied it carefully; the postmark was W.i., so it had not been posted from the bookshop; and the date was the sixteenth—the day after Anna's murder. Might it perhaps have been merely a notification of her death? Maybe: but that still failed to explain the connection between Anna, the Jew and the Aeneid. The clue probably lay in the Annotations to the beginning of Book II; in Anna's copy, he remembered suddenly, there had been a number of pencilled markings. There was nothing else to go on; his only chance, dangerous though it might be, was to trick some information out of Mr. March.

He coughed and walked noisily to the back of the shop where, in a partitioned alcove, the bookseller and a lanky, dull-skinned girl, with eyes like round pebbles behind her thick glasses, were seated at a manuscript-piled desk drinking tea out of handleless white cups.

"Mr. March," he said, "is No. 87 still in stock?"

They both looked up, teacups poised, and stared at him with the unblinking intentness of surprised parrots. Mr. March swivelled in his chair.

"No, I'm afraid it's sold."

Desmond, with the feelings of a tight-rope walker on a rotten wire, decided to bluff. He found it easier now than he had when a prisoner; in an antique bookshop he was on his own ground, and the bizarre appearance of Mr. March gave him the confidence of an actor in a pageant.

"I understand that a colleague of mine was told on the 15th that No. 87 was out of stock. Why wasn't I notified? " The two glared at him, and Mr. March answered sharply.

"That's nothing to do with me; I only send to people on my list. Who are you?"

"It *is* to do with you that I haven't been notified. And never mind who I am; I take my orders from Mr. Foster and I won't be questioned by you."

At the mention of Foster's name the man's mouth fell open, and his pallid face sagged distressingly.

"I've carried out my orders, I've done nothing wrong," he piped. "I notified everyone as I was told to. You can't say anything against me! I've always done as Mr. Foster said! My daughter knows that, she can tell you that." The girl nodded dumbly. Judging by their terror, Desmond might have been an executioner, and with a certain malicious pleasure he understood that to be Foster's servant was scarcely better than to be his enemy.

"Never mind that," he said coldly, "I'll leave Mr. Foster to deal with the matter. Just tell me this," he went on, inwardly trembling as he felt his way to the heart of the matter, "what replaces No. 87? Horace, isn't it?"

"Oh no, oh no," came from the old man, "it's 164 now, and the special code. . . ."

"Be quiet, father," said the girl in a nasal and resolute voice, "you're getting old; I think this man is an enemy."

She stood up from behind the desk and pointed a small gleaming automatic at the pit of Desmond's stomach.

"Keep your hands by your side," she said, "and don't move. Father, telephone to Belsize Park and tell them to send someone up immediately."

Muttering to himself, and glancing in equal distress at Desmond and his daughter, Mr. March picked up the receiver and fumbled at the dial. Desmond and the girl looked at each other; he with a feebly ingratiating smile that faded into fear; she with lips pressed together and eyes gleaming, her whole clumsy body rigid with joy at this triumph over one of the sex which had so persistently rejected her. The old man was still dialling the number when the bell at the door rang and heavy footsteps entered.

"Well, well," roared a hearty voice, "where's Mr. March? Having tea as usual, I expect."

"Quick!" hissed the girl, "that's Dr. Armstrong; leave the 'phone to me, and stop him coming in here!"

With a groan, Mr. March dropped the receiver, pushed past Desmond muttering an apology, and shuffled out into the shop. He still seemed perturbed, but no more so than a man caught in an awkward social situation. Either h$ had made an astonishingly rapid recovery from his previous fear, or, as Desmond suspected, he was at the age when every joy and trouble is of equally fleeting importance.

"Good afternoon, doctor," he quavered, "I was hoping you'd drop in. I've got a nice lot of medical pamphlets downstairs I wanted you to look over. There's a presentation Sydenham amongst them."

"Good, good," bellowed the doctor, "lead on Macduff! Did I tell you about the *Sceptical Chymist* I found at

Norwich? Extraordinary piece of luck! I was strolling round the market ..."

Desmond was standing by the door of the office. With a swift movement he stepped into the shop and saw Mr. March talking to a rotund, white-haired old gentleman.

"Why, good afternoon!" he said, "I do believe it's Dr. Armstrong!"

The doctor turned to look at him.

"Yes, I'm Dr. Armstrong, but I don't remember you." "I don't expect you would; I was only a boy with a broken arm when you last saw me. I expect you'll remember my father, though, Gerald Robinson?"

"Robinson, Robinson, let me see ... I can't place him exactly, but then I've met so many people. At any- rate," he went on jovially, "I'm very glad to meet you under happier circumstances. You a book collector?" "Only in a small way, I'm afraid—no

Sceptical Chymists for me, alas!"

The doctor was delighted.

"Nor for me, as a rule; it was a most remarkable good fortune. I was strolling round the market ..." Desmond edged slowly towards the door, interjecting "Really!" ... "Astonishing!" ... "Only eighteen copies known, you say?" and other appropriate remarks whenever the doctor threatened to pause in his discourse, while Mr. March stared helplessly and his daughter whispered urgently at the telephone. As he reached for the door handle, the girl advanced holding a book in her left hand to cover something in her right.

"Here's the book you asked me to find for you; perhaps you'd care to come in the office and look at it."

Desmond glanced at an imaginary watch, gave an exaggerated start and jerked open the door.

"Heavens!" he cried, "I had no idea it was so late; I'll miss my train. Good afternoon, Dr. Armstrong; good afternoon, Mr. March!"

He fled down to Heath Street, half expecting a bullet in the back, and ran towards the station. At the corner, he lurked in a doorway, watching the road from Belsize Park, and in a few minutes saw a powerful car roar up the hill and skid recklessly round towards the Heath. Remarking to a news vendor that some people nowadays didn't care how they drove, and agreeing that something ought to be done about it, he strolled with breathless casualness into the station and booked to Baker Street.

After getting his ticket to Missenden and buying a cheap suitcase and a pair of pyjamas, since it occurred to him that the post office might be shut when he arrived and he would have to stay the night, he found he had only three shillings of the Jew's money left. With a grand gesture he gave it to the porter who opened his carriage door. After all, when one is beginning a new life, one might as well leave the old with a flourish.

CHAPTER X

MINUTES OF A GENERAL MEETING OF THE
CENTRAL COMMITTEE FOR WESTERN
EUROPE

Present: A (in the Chair), B, C (representing the Eastern Section),
D, E, F, G (Secretary).
Held at: London Headquarters.
Date : 8.30 p.m. 24th inst.
*The Minutes of the previous meeting were read and approved. 1st of
the Agenda:* Special Business.

The Chairman: Since I am aware that all of you are anxious to be
kept fully informed of the situation in regard to the Raven affair,
which we discussed a week ago at our Extraordinary Meeting, I
thought it desirable to open this evening's business with a
statement of the present position.

Firstly, I am glad to be able to assure you that the murder has
had no apparent repercussions. The police are, I understand, still
conducting their investigations, but appear to have discovered
nothing about either Raven or her murderers, and have not
directed their enquiries towards any of our agents. To the best of
my knowledge the Home Office are not interested in the matter.
G, whose department it is to deal with such matters, will confirm
what I say.

G: Yes. After consulting the Aliens' Branch, the Special Duties
Department and the American Embassy, the police are treating the
matter as one of ordinary routine; and to my information have
suspended investigations for lack of evidence. Unless the authorities
are working with a most unusual subtlety, I think we can assume
that the murder was not a Secret Service affair, and that the contents
of the Contact List are not in the hands of the Home Office.

B: What of this Thane? Were our instructions in regard to him
successfully carried out?

The Chairman : Up to a point, yes. He was detained and after questioning, made certain admissions. Unfortunately, he subsequently escaped and has not yet been recaptured.

E: Good God, who is responsible for this! Was Foster in charge of the business?

The Chairman: Yes.

B : Let us hear O'Brien's report.

The Chairman: O'Brien was killed by Thane in making his escape.

Several present interjected remarks at this point which are not recorded in the minutes. The Chairman called for order.

The Chairman: Do not let us leap to hasty conclusions. I have asked Mr. Foster to be present this evening to submit us a full report.

Mr. Foster was then called, and read his report.

Mr. Foster: On the 18th instant my men seized Thane and took him to my house in Hertfordshire where he was detained until my return to England yesterday. I at once questioned him, and after interrogation he confessed to being a casual employee of the British Secret Service with the duty of watching Raven, whom he imagined to be a German spy, and claimed to have killed accidentally without the knowledge of his superiors. He did not appear to know of our organisation, and seemed astonished at his apprehension. After further questioning he alleged that O'Brien was employed by Military Intelligence, and since I had no previous knowledge of the man, who had been sent to me without my approval or consent, I was prepared to credit the allegation. By breaking a window and attracting the attention of the police, Thane succeeded in creating a diversion, and made his escape after killing O'Brien when the latter tried to prevent him. Darkness rendered pursuit difficult, and after causing the death of another of my men, he succeeded in evading recapture. This afternoon, he visited March's bookshop and attempted to obtain the code of the Contact List, but again escaped before he could be detained. I am sure that the list is in his possession and that it has not been communicated to any other person. I regret that I have no information as to his present whereabouts.

E: This is outrageous! How dare you insult us with such a confession of incompetence!

Mr. Foster: My incompetence, sir, is the outcome of your suspicions. By thrusting O'Brien upon me you made efficiency in this matter absolutely impossible. I cannot and will not continue to work for you under such conditions.

E: Will not? There, are means, Mr. Foster, that may compel you, whether you will or no.

Mr. Foster : Those are means, sir, which can be employed by more than one person in more than one direction, as you may one day discover.

E: By God, are we to endure this sort of insolence?

The Chairman: Gentlemen, gentlemen! I forbid this bickering. Mr. Foster, you forget your position; Mr. E, you forget yourself. The meeting demands an apology from you both.

E: I am sorry for the form of my remarks, but I do not withdraw their substance.

Mr. Foster: I apologise for my indiscretion.

The Chairman: Good. Let us proceed. Has anyone any questions?

D : Do you believe that Thane belongs to the Secret Service?

Mr. Foster: On the whole, no. He may have been occasionally in their employ, but I am sure that his connection with Raven was purely a personal one, that he found the Contact List by chance, and that he is now trying to sell it to the highest bidder.

G: Are we to understand that Thane killed both O'Brien and your own man single-handed?

Mr. Foster: Yes, he did. Circumstances favoured him.

B: Why, Mr. Foster, what a dangerous fellow this Thane must be! Do you think you can handle him unaided?

Mr. Foster: I think I can deal with persons more formidable than he.

E: I trust you will have no occasion to attempt it.

The Chairman: Mr. Foster. Have you now any hope of recovering the List?

Mr. Foster: Most certainly I have. Although I have not as yet traced Thane, I have certain information that may be of great value, and this, with your permission, I intend to follow up.

E: What exactly is this information?

Mr. Foster: That, sir, I would prefer not to divulge. Interference with my methods permitted Thane's escape, and I hope you will not regard me as disrespectful if I say that I shall be unable to continue my work in this matter, or any other, unless I am given a definite undertaking that I shall be left in sole and unquestioned charge, without the aid of unwanted assistance and advice.

E: Mr. Chairman! Surely you will not permit . . .

The Chairman: I am afraid, sir, that I agree with Mr. Foster. I think it is best for him to carry out his work in his own way, and I would like to thank him on your behalves for his report. I trust, Mr. Foster, that you will have better fortune in the near future, and that you will soon bring your search to a successful conclusion. You have now, as always, my complete confidence.

Mr. Foster: Thank you, sir. I shall do my best to deserve it.

Mr. Foster then left the meeting.

E: What do you mean, Mr. Chairman, by supporting that man against me? He is clearly arrogant and dangerous to an impossible degree, and should at once be removed.

B: I am afraid he will sell us to our enemies unless we silence him immediately. He has already killed O'Brien, and can no longer safely be trusted.

G: I agree in principle with the last speakers.

F: So do I. I have encountered his type before; their self-importance and ambition often end by driving them into treachery.

The Chairman: Gentlemen; I am of the same opinion as you, but this is a situation requiring tact rather than firmness. For some time past, Foster has been showing too much independence, and has, I think, come to believe that his undoubted executive talents entitle him to a dominant place in our organisation. A short while ago he made certain suggestions to me upon our general policy, and I had to remind him that he was merely an employee from whom obedience and nothing else was expected. He showed signs of resentment, and from that moment I regretfully decided that he must be removed at the earliest convenient time. Nevertheless, we must not forget that he holds, at present, a very formidable position. He knows more about the workings of our movement than does any other individual, and if he chose to betray us could do so more completely even than I could myself. He is, you see, in direct charge of our minor agents and has, I believe, recruited a bodyguard for himself from persons not known to us. It is extremely regrettable that such a position should have been allowed to arise, but the political situation in England has made our work here extremely difficult. Since Great Britain is the only major power without a powerful body of politically discontented persons from whom we could draw material, it has proved necessary to rely upon men whom I may describe as professionals to undertake the active side of our work. In raising and training a suitable organisation, Foster has shown an undoubted genius which it would be an injustice to deny. Now, however, his task is almost completed and his indispensability is almost at an end. When this unfortunate affair is cleared up, we shall have to endure him no longer.

E: Are you sure of his present loyalty?

The Chairman: Yes. I have made him certain promises, to be fulfilled upon my coming to power, that should satisfy even his ambitions, and I have personally undertaken to protect him in any circumstances, even against the rest of the Committee.

B : Surely you do not mean that seriously?

The Chairman: Naturally I do not.

G: I do not like it. Foster is a clever man, and he must suspect us as strongly as we distrust him. Unless we take him into our confidence, and convince him still further that his interests are identical with our own, he may make some attempt against us.

The Chairman : I disagree. After all, he can gain nothing of value by opposing us, and may hope for a great deal when we succeed. Even should he suspect our intentions towards him, he can have no more than a suspicion, and is enough of a gambler to take considerable risks. I repeat, too, that I have guaranteed his position, and that he reposes great confidence in me.

G: I do not like it. I wish we could remove him at once.

The Chairman: We shall do so directly he has recovered the List. As long as that is out of our hands, we remain in danger, and our quarrel with Foster must take a second place.

E: Who shall we have to take over his position?

B : Why, Thane, of course! He has got the best of him so far. *{Laughter.)*

G: It is not impossible that Thane does not exist at all, or that he is merely a puppet of Foster's. I do not think we should entirely trust Foster's reports upon him.

The Chairman: I am not unmindful of the possibilities you suggest, but their consideration must wait for a later date. Is the meeting agreed that we give Foster a free hand at present and remove him immediately the Raven affair is cleared up?

C: I disagree. I think he is the ablest man in our employ, whose services we should do very ill to lose.

D: I support the last speaker. Machiavellism is not always sound policy.

E: Neither is Christian humility.

The Chairman: I withdraw my motion and propose another: That Foster be allowed a free hand at the present time, and that his future status be decided at a later date.

This was agreed unanimously. The meeting then proceeded to consider the 2nd of the Agenda.

CHAPTER XI

As Desmond had expected, the Post Office, which, on the liberal principle that private interest is public benefit, combined the distribution of mail with the retailing of mixed groceries, was closed by the time he arrived at Missenden; so he booked a room for the night at the Labour in Vain. The inn catered principally for week-enders. The porters, though shirt-sleeved, were uniformed; the set dinner cost six-and-six; the doors were latched, gnarled, highly-polished and difficult to shut; and couples who arrived in cars were shown to double rooms before they had signed the register. It was a fine, seventeenth-century building, enjoying a fortunate situation at the intersection of two main roads, and counted itself superior to a Trust House. Solitary young men were plainly infrequent visitors there, and the surprised intonation of the receptionist when she found that Desmond was alone, so took him aback that he absent-mindedly began to sign his own name, and had to alter it to 'Thatcher' under cover of a blot.

In the lounge after dinner he surveyed his fellow guests and found them uninspiring. The usual military—a group of young Stars vieing in servile laughter at the staccato witticisms of a Crown, and an isolated, gentlemanly Chevron reading *Punch* in a corner. The usual couples— the elderly regulars doing crosswords; the young irregulars, insufferably bored with their *Tatlers* and each other's conversation, wondering how early they dared go to bed. The usual solitaries—an old lady; a sleek man like a superior commercial traveller sitting motionless behind an evening paper. This last, however, did not fit quite as well as the others, and Desmond's frayed nerves flickered to an instant of suspicion. Then he relaxed again: no one could have followed him, no one knew where he was, and in any case the man showed no sign of interest in him. He rebuked himself sternly and rang for another coffee. To develop persecution mania while one really was being persecuted would be a sure crow's-flight to lunacy.

The evening seemed interminable. Irritably he glanced through the *Aspect* he had bought to read in the train, and savoured again the astringent flavour of Bob Paget's translation from the Hindi of Taj Mhuk:

In the spring I had A cow
A wooden bhokki*
And a virgin daughter.
Oh ay oh ay
Then the rains came
And the English soldiers.
Ayee ayee
I still have my bhokki.
Oh oh oh oh.

Idly he scribbled on *Country Life* and criticised the grammar of *Beautiful Bucks.* Hopelessly he went through his pockets for literary fodder to stay the craving that would drive him, when nothing better offered, to pick up dirty scraps of yesterday's newspapers or study the advertising matter wrapped round a tube of toothpaste. Tonight he was lucky; he had kept Mr. March's catalogue and remembered the old man's mumble about the "code." What was it he had said?—"Oh, no, it's 164 now, and the special code... Without much expectation, he turned to item 164.

FOSTER (Rev. Andrew). A Short Commentary upon the Second Chapter of Ephesians, shabby cloth, London, 1889. 8s. 6d.

His heart gave a kick of excitement. First Anna editing Vergil, now Foster commenting on Ephesians—this was too much to be merely coincidental. In both cases the names of members of the mysterious organisation; in both cases the mention of definite parts of easily accessible texts. If the entries indicated codes, as

* *Little talisman.*

Mr. March's indiscretion irresistibly suggested, they must depend upon the books themselves and not upon any particular copies of them. Perhaps the bookshop was a post office of the gang, and the catalogue might conceal general instructions on matters other than ciphers. He began carefully to study each entry but soon realised the futility of the task, since beyond his two slender clues he had nothing at all to go on. He returned to Item 87—"Some Annotations on the first page of Aeneid Book II. . ." When he had collected the registered letter he would get an Aeneid and, before returning the notebook to Foster, see what a few hours' work would do to explain the impossible underworld from which he had just escaped. He lay back in his chair, dozing and imagining heroic alternatives to his conduct in the last week, until it was past twelve, and time for bed. The lounge seemed quite empty, but as he turned the bend of the stair he noticed that the sleek man still sat motionless in his comer, staring into the fire.

Promptly at nine the next morning he waited outside the post office. The man he had noticed the previous night in the lounge apparently also had business there, for as Desmond pushed open the door he drove up in a smart Bentley, jumped out leaving the engine running, and thrust rudely into the shop ahead of him.

"'Morning," he said. "Have you a Registered letter for the name of Tisket? "

Desmond gasped, and gaped blankly, while the postmistress picked up his fortune and pushed it under the bars; then stepped forward and knocked the man's outstretched hands aside.

"Look here," he shouted, "I'm Tisket and this is *my* package!"

The man paled and jerked his head towards the door, then seemed to think better of it, and stuck out his chin aggressively.

"This is impossible; the man's lying. He registered in the hotel as 'Thatcher,' and I've never seen him before in my life. I'm a personal friend of Mr. Tisket's and he asked me himself to collect this letter for him. I've a note from him to prove it."

He took a paper from his pocket and flourished it rapidly. This was too much for the post mistress, and clasping the letter to her beige jumper she petered rapidly to the back of the shop.

"Arthur!" she called. "Arthur! Do come here! Two gentlemen are making trouble over a letter and I don't know what to do!"

There was an angry grunting from the lower bowel of the shop, and a little stubbly man came unwillingly forward, wiping his breakfast from his mouth with the back of a hairy forearm.

"Now then," he said heavily, "what's all this?"

The disturbance had given Desmond time to collect himself. Foster must have found the receipt for the registered letter in his pocket-book, and sent this man down to enquire after Tisket in the hope of tracing his escaped prisoner. Finding no one of that name in the neighbourhood, the man had presumably decided to see if the letter was still in the post office, in the hope that it might reveal something usefully informative. Obviously he did not know who Desmond was, but had taken the precaution of studying the hotel register and discovered that he was not Tisket. Desmond shuddered momentarily at this fresh glimpse of his enemies' thoroughness, but encouraged by the man's first swift flash of fear and inspired by the thought of the money, which spurred him as strongly as ideals do certain others, he determined to be, for once, as resolute as his opponent. Before Arthur had finished speaking, he interrupted angrily.

"My name is Tisket; Thatcher is the *nom de plume* under which I write in the press. I know nothing at all about this person, and can only assume that he is attempting to steal my letter, which contains a large sum of money, as you'll see if you care to open it."

The other seemed taken aback, then threw a paper on the counter.

"The man's a liar. I posted the letter myself at Leicester Square Post Office and here's the receipt to prove it." Desmond saw that his guess had been correct—it was the genuine receipt: "Tisket, Missenden P.O." He was inspired.

"All right. If you're a friend of Tisket's and posted the letter yourself, tell me what his Christian name is. It's written on the package."

Arthur, who during this dialogue had been ruminating like a shell-shocked sheep, decided it was time to intervene.

"'Ere, 'ere," he said, "we can't 'ave this. Agnes, go and get the policeman."

"There's no need for that," cried Desmond desperately, "make him say what Tisket's Christian name is!"

"Blast your insolence!" said the man with obviously simulated anger, "I'll do nothing of the sort. I demand to be given my letter!"

His hand began to slip towards his hip pocket, as the post mistress, her eyes popping, made for the doorway still clasping the registered packet. With a decision that surprised himself, Desmond snatched the letter from her hand, gave Foster's man a clumsy punch in the face that sent him sprawling across a pile of biscuit tins, and ran out into the street. As the woman screeched and Arthur gave a puzzled roar, two soldiers on the opposite side of the road turned towards the shop, and someone pushed up a window. Desmond jumped into the car, shoved in the clutch and fumbled wildly with the gears. As he began to move off, his competitor for the letter, sleek no longer, dashed from the shop and jumped on to the running board. From the seat beside him, Desmond snatched up a convenient spanner, obviously left there for just such a contingency as this, and knocked off his assailant with two back-handed swipes. Then his foot found the accelerator and the Bentley swerved hyperbolically down the broad street. In a few minutes he was clear away.

After driving for a quarter of an hour, he turned down an unfrequented lane, abandoned the car, and set off across country. As he walked he opened the letter and pocketed the money, glancing as he did so at the diary.

It consisted entirely of figures, none of them, he noted with interest, higher than twenty-six, not separated into words, but running on in solid blocks. The only indication of an individual word was the title.

"Eleven letters," he thought, "the same number as there are in 'Contact List'!" He felt full of elation, and as he walked briskly through the orderly fields of Buckinghamshire, he hummed peculiar psalms of his own composing and saluted with ridiculous greetings the solemn and sophisticated sheep.

An hour's walk brought him to the main road, and a passing bus carried him on to Aylesbury. Over a brandy in the first pub, he considered what to do next. It was, he saw with relief, all very simple. He had the money, no-one knew where he was, and he was free from all personal obligations. He would write a letter of resignation to Mr. Poole, and a note of false explanation to his bank, arrange with the post office to forward his letters, and retreat into literary rustication until poverty or conscription put a term to his retirement. It would be practically impossible for Foster to trace him, and when he received back his precious list he would never take the trouble.

First, however, he would have to go to London to see to the closing of his flat and to fetch his clothes. It seemed fairly certain that Foster had set a watch upon the house, and the best solution was to ask a friend to do the packing for him and then meet him with the luggage—or better, since he might be followed, to leave it in his name at some Left Luggage office. To select a suitable emissary was not so easy, but after a moment's reflection he saw that his old friend Shadwell was the ideal choice. Secretive, intriguing, ready to go to any inconvenience to crawl into an acquaintance's secrets, he would eagerly perform such an errand if sworn to secrecy and told, say, that Desmond was hiding from detectives set on him by his wife. Of course he could not for long keep such an anecdote to himself however earnestly he had promised discretion, but that, Desmond saw, was all the better. At one stroke it would infuriate his wife should she come to hear of it, make Shadwell his willing assistant in future errands of a similar nature, and provide a satisfactory explanation of his sudden disappearance. The least investigation, of course, would easily disprove the story, but he knew from past experience that so long as an imputed motive was sexual, sordid and slightly ridiculous, one's friends would do their utmost to believe it.

Now he must post the diary back to Foster; and as he strolled towards the station he weighed it speculatively in his hand. Surely just one attempt to decipher it would do no harm . . . ? He walked round the broad Square, telling himself that unless he could buy a Vergil before he passed a post office, he would try no more to prove its dangerous secret, but send it back to its rightful owner. He reached a post office without passing a bookshop of any sort; then saw one a few doors ahead. Telling himself that his inconsistency was really free-will, and inquisitiveness contempt for superstition, he went in. Yes, they had an Aeneid—a second-hand school edition.. No, he didn't object to ink-stains and dogs-ears. Yes, it was a fine day and he didn't want anything further. Good morning.

He walked on, studying his purchase, which had plainly helped to instil the Classic Platitudes into a good many thick schoolboy heads. A. Thompson, IIIb, had written his mis-translations above every line of the first pages, then abruptly tired; Edward Pritchard, Upper Fourth, had expressed his uninteresting personality by writing his name a dozen times on the title-page; and several other owners had competed to immortalize their signatures and classes. Unable to resist so many precedents, Desmond unscrewed the Jew's fountain pen, and wrote "D. Thane" in a large round hand, adding as an afterthought "Upper Middle." He was still smiling to himself, pleased by this childish conceit, when he reached the railway station.

Shadwell, when he phoned him at Marylebone, was out and would not be back before evening; so once again, as on the previous day, he found himself in cafeless London with nowhere he dared or cared to go. The afternoon, warm and bright, had the feeling of early summer, and once more Hampstead seemed the best and pleasantest place to pass the time. There in the urban rusticity of the Heath, he would contemplate the City lying in its valley below, and make a determined attempt to decipher Anna's diary. With a Woolworth's notebook and a resolve to shun trouble and Mr. March's bookshop, he took an extravagant taxi to Highgate Hill.

The Heath was unusually crowded for the early afternoon, and soon, to his delight, he heard the distant baying of a fair. This was better than work—a work, moreover, for which he still felt a slight, superstitious distaste—and, buttoning the diary securely in his hip pocket, he set out over the slope to the swarming hollow where the wheels spun, the crowds surged round the booths, and steam syncopation bellowed tirelessly. Swept up into the giggling, gaping, guffawing swelter of briefly and bravely uninhibited Londoners, he would be beyond the reach of Foster, of war, even of individuality.

Try everything once. Swing the heavy hammer and join in the friendly jeers when the first stroke quite misses the peg; chuck cork-like balls at nailed and weighted coconuts, rejoicing in the general amazement when one, miraculously loosened, falls an unwanted trophy; score a bull and a box of chocolates by cunningly aiming at outers; vainly, at twopence a time, match skill and subtlety against remotely controlled race-horses; hopefully hand out sixpence to watch Red Indian Tortures, but lack the stomach to see the World's Most Revolting Fat Lady. Try everything once at least. Take an afternoon off.

With his shoes full of dust and an undesired alarm clock clutched stickily in his hand, Desmond let himself be cast up from the crowd on to a paper-strewn but comparatively open ridge above it; and sitting down to rest for a while before exploring the other half of the fair on the opposite side of the Heath, he gave himself up to a pleasant nostalgia. When he was younger, how often had he and some brilliant friend strode for hours across these wooded hills, profoundly juggling with the universe and shyly confessing to each other's genius; how often, .from some convenient mound, had they prophesied the imminent downfall of the city which stretched beneath them; speaking, no doubt, with a Marxian wordiness but feeling the unexpressed spirit of the major prophets. How often, too, had he dragged some young woman for miles around Ken Wood and bored her with four hours of political anthropology, as a prelude to an attempt at a quite commonplace seduction. Dear old days! Stupid old days, he hastily corrected himself, and realised with angry alarm that he must be already approaching the age when one is sentimental over everything in the past simply because it has disappeared.

He pulled himself abruptly from introspection and got up, almost stumbling over a recumbent couple who had mysteriously appeared behind him. Although it could not have been much past four o'clock, the horizon was already littered with silent interlocked pairs, lying motionlessly twined together like some huge, slow deep-sea slug. Presumably passion impelled them, though it was possible that many of the couples were intolerably bored and knew of no way to say so, but beyond an occasional tentative stroking of foreheads, there was no appearance of it; they were less like embracing lovers than dying arctic explorers clasped together for warmth. It seemed incredible that so many people should shamelessly go so far without going farther. In no other time and country, Desmond thought, could there have been so much licence and so little lust, so little convention and so much restraint.

Filled with noble disgust, he strode on, carefully ignoring an attractive girl in green trousers who was walking in the same direction a few paces to his left. He had occasionally, in the dear old days, tried to pick up on the Heath, but with so little success that he had sworn never again to make the degrading attempt. Yet now, he assured himself, taking a quick glance left, he was altogether different and more confident, easily able to make and handle such base encounters. He took another look, and received what was almost certainly an encouraging smile. With immediate resolution, like a man who has tossed a coin to decide his course and then does exactly the opposite, he turned away and made sternly off. After ten paces he regretted his austere decision, after fifteen he approved again, after twenty he turned round to look for the girl, but she was already out of sight. With blazing revelation he knew what he had really wanted to do all the time. This was a holiday, prey was abundant, and he was out on the hunt.

As soon as he began to cruise in search of quarry he felt, inevitably, that the chance he had missed was the best of the day, and that he would not again encounter a subject so young, attractive and available. With a scowl of synthetic embitterment he regarded the numerous impossibilities; the already attached beauties, the laughingly linked trios, the desirable inaccessibles. Surely, with a war on, there should be a considerable feminine surplus? But no; men—and predatory men at that—were almost in a majority, and it was hard to believe that at that very moment over two million potential competitors were being drilled and dosed with bromide in armed and segregated monasteries.

A good technique, he had been told, was to approach a couple, since even the timorously respectable, finding strength in union, were unlikely to rebuff an attack by a smaller force. This, unfortunately, he could not bring himself to attempt, for although he was quite prepared to degrade himself by gambolling round one prospective victim, he refused to do so before a giggling audience. It must be one or nothing. All the singles, however, were in some way unsatisfactory. She was hideous, and so was she. That one over there looked nice—no, on closer view she was unbearably silly and probably noisy as well; while that admirable specimen down by the tree was obviously waiting for someone. "What a monster I must be!" he thought, as he eagerly scanned every figure that approached. "No woman is safe from my intentions; a fellow couldn't trust his sister alone with my mind. Only the law and my good taste divide me from Caligula." But as he rejected possibility after possibility, he knew perfectly well that his motive was not a proud discrimination, but shyness and self-conceit.

Determinedly he reasoned with himself. Repulse was no injury, and welcome no obligation; the titters of those youths on the bench could mean nothing to such a man as he; while he knew, as every expert from Lord Chesterfield onwards had known, that even the most undesired advances are taken as a compliment by the women who coldly reject them.

All in vain. It was clear, he told himself as he sat resignedly down on the grass, that he was not in his right milieu; fresh air and open spaces obviously put him off. He glanced regretfully towards a pretty and aloof young woman—an obvious impossibility—and saw with malicious pleasure that a squalid and greasy youth was nerving himself to address her. As she passed him the youth sidled up to her.

"Hallo," he heard him say, "are you going my way, baby?"

To Desmond's disgusted amazement the girl simpered. "Ooh, I don't speak to strangers."

"Aw, don't high hat me, sweetie," grinned the youth in a feeble Americanese, and walked on beside her. Within a hundred yards they were arm-in-arm.

Desmond was furious. Was he to be the only failure on the whole bloody heath? Was there anyone with four limbs, a tongue and a member who could fail to get off on a public holiday? With the desperate resolution of Mettius leaping into the gulf he swore to try the next chance he encountered, or for ever after at Hampstead to hold his peace. With a firm step he climbed the slippery grass bank that led up to the Spaniards Road, and took up his position.

To his left, nothing but couples. To the right, couples, trios and a single. But what a single! Eyes like moons, pimples like stars, and teeth that had competed with each other to be the foremost, the whole surmounted by a little round white paper hat of the kind he had seen vended at the fair, inscribed "Come Up and See Me Sometime," and obviously imbued with an all-too-ready eagerness to welcome the most diffident advances. Oath or no, this was too much: he was not going to cut off his nose (and put out his eyes) to save his face. Hastily he crossed the road, and saw on the other side the girl in green trousers who had first attracted his attention. Fate had obviously intended them for each other.

He drew level with her and was disconcerted to be greeted

with a welcoming smile. Surely she couldn't be?

"Excuse me," he began doubtfully, "have you by any chance got the time?"

(Yes, if you've got the money.)

"I should think you ought to know it. Last time I saw you you were carrying a clock."

He was a little taken aback.

"Oh, yes, I did have one once, but I threw it away for causing alarm and despondency."

She laughed. "I don't believe you remember me. I almost spoke to you over by the pond, but you looked so stern, in spite of your clock, that I hadn't got the courage."

Did she really believe she knew him, or was this a new variation of the old technique? As he looked at her he had an unpleasant feeling that he recognised her face, and that they had really met somewhere before. This must be dealt with at once.

"As a matter of fact," he said firmly, "I'm afraid I don't remember you. The truth is, that whenever I see a person with a really intelligent face" (always praise a person for qualities they haven't got: those they do possess they'll know about already and take any comment upon as a proper and expected tribute), "I simply have to speak to them—they're so very uncommon. Much as I should like to have met you before, I'm afraid I haven't had the good fortune."

She seemed pleased but unconvinced.

"I'm sure we've met; we were introduced last month at the Howards' party, although you didn't take much notice of me then, in spite of my intelligent face. Aren't you Desmond Thane?"

He remembered her now, a very smart young person in Mayfair black, looking far older and more sophisticated than the bareheaded girl walking beside him. For an instant he thought of admitting his identity; then his habitual secrecy, accentuated still further by his experiences of the last week, got the better of him.

"Oh, that explains it," he cried with false enthusiasm, "I'm Thane's cousin, you see, and this isn't the first time I've been mistaken for him—there's a very striking family resemblance, because of our genes or something of the kind. It's all in Mendel, I expect, if you bother to read him. I'm sorry, actually, that I'm not Thane: if I had been I certainly wouldn't have forgotten you."

The girl was disappointed.

"Oh, what a pity! I did hope you were him. It would have been such fun if I'd found him."

"'Found him'?" said Desmond. "What do you mean? Is he lost?"

"Why, haven't you heard? He's lost his memory and disappeared."

Desmond was horrified. This must be the doing of Mr. Poole, unable to believe that anyone would leave his job while fully in possession of his senses.

"Good heavens, has he really? How did you find out?"

"Oh, he vanished nearly a week ago and there's been a bit about it in most of the papers. When I saw you on the heath I felt sure you were him, wandering about rather lost, looking for your personality. You *are* sure you know who you are, aren't you? Oh, well ..." she sighed regretfully.

Desmond began to see that the situation might have its advantages. Loss of memory would not only explain his disappearance and absolve him from describing his whereabouts during the time he was away; it would also provide him with an excellent excuse for taking a secluded holiday, perhaps even, if he could get a doctor's certificate, on full pay at the firm's expense. He could recover his memory somewhere safely out of London, and on some medical grounds—the necessity of avoiding excitement or something of the sort—he could easily contrive to avoid going back to his flat or office at all until Foster was tired of looking for him.

"Well, well," he said cheerily, "poor old Thane, I hope nothing happens to him! And now, since we're practically old friends, what about having some tea?"

Without waiting for an answer, he took her by the arm and turned on his best conversation. He was at the very top of his form.

Soon after six his new acquaintance had to leave him, and his regret at her departure was mingled with relief that he was at last alone and able to consider his position. Over tea he had remembered with a shock his telephone call to Shadwell, but could not be certain whether or no he had left his name with the woman who had answered the phone. Shadwell, who invariably read every word of three daily papers, was sure to have heard of his disappearance, and be full of subtle and slanderous theories about its cause; a message from the missing man would stir his tireless curiosity to a running flux. As things were now, the man's help would be an embarrassment and was best dispensed with; but should he know that Desmond had telephoned it was essential to appease him with some seeming confidence, before he embroidered his news and spread it about his enormous circle of acquaintances.

Stopping in the street, Desmond thought carefully whether he had left his name. First he decided that he had, and opened a door of a call-box to phone Shadwell with some hasty explanation; then, seized with fresh doubts, walked a few paces away, only to return as he veered again to his original opinion. Passers-by looked at him curiously, and he suddenly noticed a man watching him with a sidelong glance from behind an evening paper. With a dart of fear he noticed that he was very near March's bookshop, and, hastily crossing the road, walked rapidly away. At the corner he glanced back, .and saw that the man who had watched him was strolling casually behind, still pretending to be absorbed in the news; his hands, clasped round the edge of his paper, had the thick, hairy fingers of a wrestler. Desmond began to feel panic, and, crossing the road again, set off at a fast walk that soon became almost a run. A hundred yards farther on he looked back, and saw that the man, his paper tucked under his arm now, was still behind him, only a little nearer.

His knees began to weaken, and he looked vainly round for a taxi, but none was in sight. A short way ahead hung the blue lamp of a police station—surely even Foster's men would not dare to do anything there? He slowed down and stopped opposite the steps, his fists clenched in his pockets and his mouth ready for a shout. His pursuer slowed up also, and stopped in front of him.

"I'm a police officer," he said, "may I see your Identity Card?" Desmond hesitated incredulously, his heart hurrying, then saw two constables push out of the swing door and nod to the man as they passed. Almost sick with relief, he pretended to search through his pockets.

"I'm afraid I haven't got it with me."

"Then perhaps you wouldn't mind stepping into the station."

Still uncomfortably weak and breathless he followed the officer up the steep white steps.

Inside he grew alarmed again, as the plain-clothes man, telling him to wait on a bench by the wall, had a long whispered conversation with the station sergeant, in the course of which both men glanced repeatedly from him to something lying on the desk. Could they be going to arrest him for the theft of the car?—but the owner, a criminal himself, would never dare charge him. Or was it to do with his absconding from the inn without paying his bill?—but they couldn't have traced him. Or was it to do with Anna? He felt his armpits and the back of his knees grow cold with sweat.

At last the sergeant beckoned him over.

"I understand you haven't got your identity card with you. Would you mind telling me your name and address?"

Desmond hesitated. If he gave a false name they would soon discover it, and if he told the truth it might somehow give him away—or was that absurd? Unable to think coherently, he tried to gain time.

"Am I bound to tell you my name? I mean, do I legally have to, or needn't I?"

He stumbled stupidly, and felt a fool. The two policemen looked at him calmly. The sergeant said:

"Is your name Thane?"

Christ! So it must be Anna!

"No," he said. "Oh no."

The constable (obviously a promising officer) took the Vergil that protruded from his pocket, opened it, and silently showed his superior the ridiculous "D. Thane." "Good work, Robbins," said the sergeant. The plainclothes man simpered.

"I spotted him at once. I never forget a face."

Desmond ran his hands through his hair and said nothing. The sergeant pushed forward a paper that lay before him.

"Does this mean anything to you?"

Desmond looked down and saw a small but very recognisable photograph of himself. Underneath was written:

MISSING FROM HIS HOME BELIEVED SUFFERING FROM LOSS OF MEMORY Mr. Desmond Thane, a journalist employed by International Features Ltd., last seen on the evening of . . .

There followed a brief and accurate description, including even the clothes he was wearing. He was flooded with relief. So that was all: the police, he suddenly realised, must have been looking for him for days. This was, he saw swiftly, the best thing that could have happened, since it would enable him finally to prove the genuineness of his amnesia, and enable him to recover his memory under proper medical supervision instead of doing so privately in a distant village. The sergeant was speaking again.

"If you remember who you are now, we'll see you get home safely. There's nothing to worry about."

Wasn't there indeed! To be carefully taken under police protection to the very place where Foster was probably waiting for him might be dramatic irony but had nothing else to recommend it. He looked up slowly and tried to speak as if he were slightly dazed.

"This photo and description seem to fit me, so I suppose I'm the same person—quite a nice name that, Desmond Thane. But I don't know who I am or where I've come from; I don't even know where I am now. I know that you're a policeman and that this country is called England but that's about all. I'm very tired."

He sank down on to a bench, frowning worriedly at his feet, and heard the sergeant push back his chair and hurry out of the room. A heavy hand patted him on the shoulder.

"How about a nice cup of tea?" said the policeman.

At first Desmond found his new role more a relief than an effort. Beneath his superficial cheerfulness, the experiences of the past week had left him by no means unaffected, and despite a mental veneer of callous amusement at his own misfortunes, he was worried, frightened and terribly tired. To relax concentration and let attention slide from its knife-edge of keenness, was almost too easy, and the glazed eye and monosyllabic answer that he deliberately assumed for the first few minutes soon ceased to be wholly feigned. In the last days he had crowded the emotions of years, and the dark, cool, public-lavatory light of the police-station was irresistibly soothing. He was shocked to find himself half asleep, then mildly shocked again that he made no attempt to conceal it. He felt as a general might feel when he himself became a casualty—at heart relieved to be freed from all further responsibility.

He observed the proceedings of the next few hours with the detached interest of a third party. The shy friendliness of the policemen, the unoptimistic questioning of the inspector. The search of his pockets and the sergeant's whistle as he found the bundle of notes—at this point h$ recollected enough of the world to ask in a dazed but firm manner for a receipt, and to insist upon keeping the Vergil and the diary—seemed to have a purely literary quality; to lack the noise and sharp edge of happenings in the real world. By the time the police doctor saw him he was as comatose as could be wished, and submitted without comment to taps on the knees, lights shone in the eye and the casual punchings and proddings reserved for the seedy criminal. To all questions he only replied:

"I don't know who I am. I found myself in the street a short time ago and didn't know where I was. I tried to hide what had happened when the police questioned me because I didn't want to be bothered, and I knew there'd be a fuss if I said I didn't know who I was. I feel very tired, but I expect I'll be all right to-morrow."

This must have been the right line to take, for when the doctor stood up, he snapped his spectacle case shut with the decisive assurance of the expert whose judgment has once more proved to be correct. As he walked off with the inspector, Desmond heard him say:

"Clear case of amnesia; I'll have him taken to the hospital at once. A few days' rest should put him right, though other symptoms sometimes develop. Oh, by the way," he added, "what are his means?"

They were going out of the door now, and Desmond only caught:

". . . journalist . . . large sum of money on him. ..."

"Excellent!" came the strident medical voice. "I'll arrange for a private ward."

The door shut, and he was left alone with the cold dregs of his nice cup of tea.

CHAPTER XII

The next few hours passed in a dreamy confusion. He heard the station sergeant telephoning about him, but was unable to catch what he said, and thought it wiser to show no curiosity. He was inspected a second time by a doctor, questioned perfunctorily and taken off by car to a red brick neo-Georgian hospital ten minutes' drive away. Here he was re-examined by a sprightly young man in a white coat, while two others lounged on enamel- topped tables, swinging grey-flannelled legs, and a fourth, in a corner, did something deft and nasty to an ulcer that an old man timidly proffered him. Then he was handed over to a matron and taken down long blue-lit passages to a little, white, high-ceilinged room with a bathroom leading off it.

"Now, Mr. Thane," said the matron brightly, "we'll have a nice bath, get straight into bed and not worry ourselves till the morning!"

She bustled past him and turned on a stream of water so hot that steam spurted up to the ceiling. Desmond, slightly shocked by the ambiguity of her invitation, and reflecting that such injunctions against worry would probably drive a genuine patient to hysteria, complied as meekly as a newly admitted convict. Just before he lay down he remembered Anna's notebook, and with a vague instinct of caution, tucked it carefully inside the lining of his bolster. Then he went to sleep.

He woke in the morning full of high spirits, and only with difficulty restrained himself from getting up and dressing. He had intended to impress his amnesia on the nurse, who began to harry him into cleanliness at about half-past six, by affecting a forgetfulness of how to shave, or asking, with pathetic wonder, what was the use of that funny thing hanging on the chain in the wash-basin. But she looked so brisk and full of practical common sense, that he thought better of it, and resolved to try his deceptions only, so far as possible, upon men of science. He had his opportunity a few hours later when he was visited by a little pale, ferret-faced man who introduced himself as Dr. Vescott, the Hospital psychologist.

Dr. Vescott, who belonged to the abrupt and shocking rather than to the suave and insinuating school of. psychoanalysis (a division more important, in practice, than that between Freudian and Jungist) assaulted at once.

"So you've lost your memory, Mr. Thane. Why?"

He paused tensely like a cat who has sighted an approaching moth. Desmond, who had expected the chattier approach favoured by the amateurs of his own acquaintance, was taken aback.

"I don't know."

The doctor leant forward and spoke deliberately.

"You only forget because your unconscious mind wants you to forget. Now, what kind of thing might you have wished to put out of your mind? Don't ponder; answer at once, even if your answer doesn't seem sensible."

Desmond answered at random.

"My name, I suppose."

Dr. Vescott was interested.

"They've told you that your name is Thane?"

"Yes."

"Do you believe it?"

"Intellectually, yes. But I feel that I might just as well be you or anyone else."

"What does the name Thane suggest to you? Just let your mind relax and say anything that occurs to you." Nothing at all occurred to Desmond. At length, under the doctor's encouraging eye, he felt he could keep silence no longer, and answered wildly.

"Chamber-pots."

The doctor, torn between his text-books and his common sense, stared suspiciously, and Desmond hastily called on his conscious to redress the mistake of his Id.

"I think I can see how the association arose," he went on

hurriedly. "Thane—Anglo-Saxon prince—big pot— chamber-pot. That must have been it."

The psychologist nodded warily.

"Yes, that might be so. Now, Mr. Thane, I understand that your memories extend only to yesterday afternoon?" "Yes. I find that I know things—I know, for instance, that I'm British, and I think I know which are the best London restaurants; but my personal life seems to have begun yesterday; so far as I'm aware this bed is the first I've ever slept in."

"Did you dream at all last night?"

The opportunity was too much to resist and Desmond let himself go.

"As a matter of fact I did, but I can't make very much of it. All I remember is that I was walking up a flight of stairs and came into a garden full of lilies and cucumbers. Then, when I looked closer, I saw that they were knives with jewelled hilts set in curious wedge-shaped patterns, like cuneiform characters. Suddenly there was an airraid warning and I looked up to see an enormous Zeppelin with huge round bombs hanging underneath it like clusters of grapes. I knew that my uncle was up there and that unless I shot him down he would behead me or cut me out of his will—I'm not sure which."

The analyst's expression was inhospitable, and Desmond, feeling he had gone too far, hastily tried to temper his imagination with the authentic nonsense of a jumbled nightmare he had actually experienced.

"Oh, yes," he continued. "There was a lot more, so muddled that I can't properly recall it, about a terribly important railway journey in which I kept having to change at Gloucester whatever route I tried to take. I never seemed to get any farther."

Dr. Vescott sat silent, drumming absently with his fingers, until Desmond, afraid that he might have betrayed himself, became a little anxious. Then: "With what do you associate Gloucester, Mr. Thane? " The question jerked so suddenly from his thin lips that Desmond was confused.

"Why, that's the place that Dr. Foster went to." Directly he spoke, depression swept over him in a wave, and he felt like a man who wakes from a dream of fortune to the cold morning of his execution. His mockery of the doctor no longer amused him; he was consumed with irritation and self-distaste.

"And what does Dr. Foster suggest to you?" "Absolutely nothing; only the nursery rhyme about him."

Dr. Vescott looked at him for a minute or two without speaking, then stood up.

"I think that will do for this morning, Mr. Thane; I'll come and see you again tomorrow. And meanwhile," he added, as he went out, "there's no need to worry about Dr. Foster."

Desmond was left with the unhappy suspicion that Dr. Vescott was a far acuter psychologist than he had at first imagined. As he sat looking at the closed door, and went over in his mind the details of the interview, he felt himself beginning to blush.

When he had recovered a little from his sense of embarrassment, he resolved to make his postponed attempt to decode the notebook, and asked the nurse to fetch him writing materials. This desire, however, must have seemed as significant as a hunger striker's request for a glass of water, since she immediately hurried out and returned with the house physician.

"So you want writing materials, Mr. Thane? What do you want to write?"

"I shan't really know till I start. I just feel that I want to put down words on paper."

"You have no idea what you want to say?"

"I think perhaps I have. I feel that if I have a pen in my hand I may be able to write down more about myself than I can remember at the moment. I was going to try and write my autobiography."

"An excellent idea; Nurse will bring you a writing pad and pencil. And by the way," he added casually as he left, "even if what you write doesn't please you, save it for Dr. Vescott; he'll be most interested to see it."

So Dr. Vescott wanted to be a literary critic, did he? Well, he should have as good a selection of style as falls to the lot of most reviewers. Partly to amuse himself and partly to justify his request for paper, he began to scribble abortive reminiscences directly he was left alone.

"I was born in the Vicarage of N— in the year 19—. My mother had died some years before my birth, and since my father was too busy working on his texts and his parishioners to pay much attention to a small boy, I was left in the care of Hannah, the Vicar's housekeeper, a sour-visaged woman, whose favourite occupations were reading Ruskin and counting the prunes in the blue-painted tin in the kitchen, lest fat Martha, the cook, had been pilfering them to give to her worthless relations. My father's visits to the nursery were rare but delightful. Once, I remember, he found me playing trains with his calf-bound edition of the Early Fathers. I expected a rebuke, but he merely took up the volume behind the engine and shook his head gravely.

"'This is wrongly placed, my boy. Origen was never tender and quite unfitted for coupling.'

"It was that evening I learnt that Hannah drank. . . ."

At the foot of this nonsense he scribbled in a wild hand: "Was this boy I? Who knows? " and began on the next sheet.

"Danny Thane slouched against the hoarding at the corner of Corporation Street, scowling at the trams that clattered past, and rubbing the five greasy halfpence in his trouser pocket. If it were sixpence he could have a tart, if fivepence a swig of meth. in half a pint of South African red port; but, however often he counted it, it was still only twopence halfpenny. He spat neatly between his cracked patent leather shoes, and scratched a yellow pimple off his upper lip, feeling as he did so the half-healed scar made by Jaimie's broken bottle.

"'Ah's guid enough to broach ma faither's heid,' he thought bitterly, 'an' ah willna work nae more nah ah's sixteen. Ah'll wait till dark, an' cut Mister Macpherson's face wi' ma new weapon.'

"He ran his finger lovingly along the razor Annie had given

him, and thought with slow pleasure of how she had greeted when he lugged out Gerry from under the bed and drew the steel over his contorted face. Thaat had been fine, thaat had..."

He regarded his work admiringly. "That should keep Dr. Vescott quiet for a bit," he thought. "I've betrayed enough psychoses to float a clinic." He put the papers ostentatiously on the side table, and turned to his serious business.

At first sight the undertaking was extremely formidable. On the title page of the diary was written simply:

26. 26. 26. 26. 18. 26. 25. 7. 17. 14. 5

The rest of the leaf was blank. The following pages were a mass of figures, beginning with a small block like an initial paragraph, and then continuing in lines of a regular length as though they were verse or a list of contents. The whole diary consisted of similar lists, save for the last three pages in which the figures ran on in long sections like pieces of continuous prose. Nowhere was there a single letter, and, as he had noticed earlier, none of the numbers were higher than twenty-six.

He turned back to the title—yes, as he had already observed, there were eleven figures, and he must assume, for a start, that they represented the eleven letters of "Contact List." But how could one explain 26. 26. 26. 26? No word in any language of which he had heard could repeat the same letter four times in succession, nor was there in "Contact List" any letter repeated five times. It was clear that unless the code was based upon some anagrammatic or arithmetic system he could never hope to solve, it could not depend on the direct substitution of certain numbers for certain letters. 26, at any rate, couldn't always stand for the same thing.

Now for the other clue—"Some Annotations upon the first page of Aeneid Book II." Without great expectations he read to himself the first lines of Vergil's famed, but in his own opinion somewhat over-rated, trumpetings:

"Conticuere omnes, intentique ora tenebant. Inde toro pater

Aeneas sic orsus ab alto: 'Infandum, Regina, jubes renovare dolorem, Trojanas ut opes et lamentabile regnum Eruerint Danai; quaeque ipse miserrima vidi, Et quorum pars magna fui . . . ' "

"All attended and intently held their mouths; then thus spake paternal Aeneas from his lofty couch." Not much help there, apparently. Perhaps if he read it aloud— "Conticuere omnes, intentique ora tenebant ..."

All at once he heard it; the first four and the sixth letters of the first word were the same as those of "contact," and the whole five were represented by the number 26. Excitement seized him, and it was some moments before he could calm himself sufficiently to consider coolly this remarkable coincidence. Since, upon his assumption, the figures represented "contact list," and the Latin was key to the figures; then the figures must represent the relation between the Latin and the concealed English, and 26. 26. 26. 26. 18. 26. must show how CONTIC became CONTAC. The numbers, obviously, stood not for particular letters but for their position in some special order—such -as, he thought suddenly, the alphabet. If one put the alphabet in a circle and counted round from a letter, the CONT of the English were twenty-six letters from the CONT of the Latin, and so the 18 should mean that the A of English was that number from the I of the Latin. Eagerly he began to count, but was so excited that he had to add up the numbers on his fingers before he could get them right. Yes, it was correct: A was the eighteenth letter from I, and the concluding T of "contact" was the twenty-fifth letter from U. Each letter one wished to write, in fact, was represented by the number between it and the equivalent letter in the Latin text. It was a very simple code but in its way a perfect one, for unless he knew of the key passage, the decipherer, whatever his under-standing of letter frequencies or numerical tricks, would be practically helpless. Without troubling to confirm the four letters of "list," Desmond hastened to test his discovery upon the preamble to the book itself, and after a few mistakes from a nervous inability to count correctly, read:

AGENTS OF THE FIRST GRADE
OPERATING IN GREAT BRITAIN.

He was filled with a greater sense of triumph than he ever remembered experiencing, and would readily have burnt incense to a statue of himself. Instead, he was content to give the nurse who brought in his lunch a smile of such heavenly benevolence, that she must have thought, not for the first time, that another of the patients had developed mental symptoms.

Three hours later, his eyes strained with peering at Anna's tiny figures, he closed the books, carefully thrust them back inside the bolster, and tried to see his incredible discovery in its true proportions.

At first the diary had revealed nothing sensational. It consisted, as he had suspected, largely of lists, and for an hour or more he had struggled through boring and meaningless columns of names, most of them quite unknown to him. The majority suggested the business middle class and had prosperous-sounding addresses in industrial cities, but a good number bore army or airforce rank, some boasted obscure titles, and a few he thought he recognised as those of journalists and minor writers. They might have been the patrons of a Midland Charity, or the shareholders of some slightly suspicious new company. At last, impatiently, he had turned to the three pages of text at the end, and learnt the general outlines of a fantastic international conspiracy.

But, after all, why should it be wholly fantastic? What was intrinsically impossible in a union of all the oppositions to supplant all their rulers? Their interests, it was true, were doubtless finally incompatible, yet so were those of the different partners in the Axis; the fact that at the moment alliance could lend common strength to individual weakness was reason enough for the most improbable partnership. Were the interests of the enemies of Hitler and the enemies of Stalin any more incompatible than those of the men themselves? Or was their alliance with American isolationists and Fascist-minded British business men anything in the least unexpected? The surprising point was not that such groups should have interests temporarily in common, but that they should have taken so long to recognise them; the plans of I.O., as it so honestly called itself, were no more megalomaniac than those of the Nazi International.

As for the prospects of a successful coup in this country; events in Norway and elsewhere should have proved a sufficient precedent, while even this partial list of I.O.'s English agents showed that their supporters included prominent members of the classes that control the levers of power. But these people were merely members of the organisation, even though Foster himself was included in their number; and had, apparently, no executive power. Who sat on the "Central Committee" so often respectfully mentioned? Desmond had a terrifying vision of treachery everywhere, sitting invisible at Cabinet meetings and Trade Union Councils, on the boards of great companies and in the workshops of key technicians. But today, as never since the Renaissance, was the great age of treachery, and traitors of one colour or another —men too weak to be rulers, too strong to be ruled— gnawed and burrowed under every power in the world. All over the earth the great gleaming structures of the absolute states were secretly rotten; beneath the facade of the powerful governments lurked, under any of a dozen labels, eating rust and the death-watch beetle. Even I.O. itself was no doubt in dread of its own internal enemies. No-one was safe any longer, no-one at all.

Now that he knew exactly what was pursuing him, Desmond felt more alarmed than before but somehow less afraid. The nightmare quality had vanished; he was freed from the tiny but growing suspicions of his own sanity that had begun of late to creep to the back of his mind. It was only now they had gone, he saw, that he had dared to admit their existence. It was not to be wondered that with such a book in his possession I.O. had pursued him, for he held, he slowly realised, the means of destroying a great part of their organisation, and of sending them to prison in hundreds. Tomorrow he would recover his memory and go immediately to Scotland Yard.

No sooner had he formed his decision than his enthusiasm faded. What was to be gained by such a course? So far as he knew they had as yet done nothing illegal save in his own case; while he had committed a murder and a manslaughter which would have to be disclosed to substantiate his story. Even should the police let him go for confessing, which was highly unlikely, he would still be in serious danger; for his enemies, scotched but not destroyed, would probably kill him as an example to other informers. Even if they left him alone he would never feel safe, but spend the rest of his life afraid of each casual stranger. And in any case, what did he care for the preservation of his own government? It seemed most improbable that I.O.'s attempt would succeed, but even should it do so, would he himself be any the worse off? Almost certainly not. The best thing he could do was to hold to his original intention of returning the book to Foster, and so make an end of the business.

But this alternative pleased him no better than the first. For a moment he possessed power; never again in his life would he stand so near the movement of history. If he tamely let his chance go he would never cease to regret it; the very least he should do was to turn it to some material profit. Suppose he sent Foster a page, as proof of possession, and offered the remainder for sale? It should be worth ten thousand pounds at least—no, twenty. He could demand that the sum be paid into his bank; then hide, as he had previously resolved, until they had ceased to trouble about him. Such a sum would probably seem quite a small one to them, an annoying but unimportant charge to be paid for Anna's foolishness. There was a risk, of course, but the possible profit was worth it. If he took the chance, the worst that could happen was death; if he refused it, he might still be killed, but whether his life was long or short he would spend the rest of it in futile self-condemnation. His brain continued busily to weigh the advantages of this course or that, but he knew that his decision was already taken. He had gone so far that there was no turning back; he was on a slope that must be run to the bottom and it was better to choose the more spectacular route. He was still alternating between fears of death and dreams of affluence when the nurse opened the door.

"Here's a visitor for you!" she said, and Shadwell walked delicately in.

Desmond suppressed his annoyance and gaped blankly at him. "Who are you?"

Shadwell laid his hat and neatly rolled umbrella on the floor, sat carefully down on a chair directly facing the patient, pulled up his beautifully creased trousers and ignored Desmond's question.

"They told me you 'phoned yesterday afternoon; I'm sorry I wasn't in. I came round to see you as soon as I had time. What have you been doing lately?"

Desmond, irritated and baffled by this insolent disregard for the solemnity of the occasion, found it hard to keep calm.

"I don't know what you mean," he replied with forced amazement, "so far as I know I've never seen you before."

Shadwell gazed up at the ceiling and hummed a bar or two from some minor composer, but gave no other answer. Desmond was unable to keep silent.

"Even if you are a friend of mine, how did you know I was here?"

Shadwell smiled.

"I phoned Mr. Poole this morning to ask him if you were back, and he told me where to find you. He said he was coming to see you himself this afternoon, even though it's Australian dispatch-day tomorrow."

"What absolute nonsense ..." began Desmond indignantly, then stopped in confusion. "I mean all these names make absolute nonsense to me ..." He stumbled hopelessly and gave up the attempt. Shadwell glanced at his watch.

"A most remarkable recovery," he exclaimed, "the faculties wholly restored in two minutes forty-five seconds!

I must be a natural healer."

"I'm sick of all this nonsense," muttered Desmond weakly, "I shall ring for the nurse."

"Oh no you won't, so stop being ridiculous. I know perfectly well that you haven't lost your memory, nor are you the kind of person likely to do so; so let's drop the pretence." His voice lost its acidity and became insinuating. "If you'll tell me why you're doing it, I won't give you away. You know you can trust me."

He waited expectantly, and Desmond sighed. Shadwell. was too acute to be so clumsily put off, but also too twisted and scandalmongering to be trusted with the dangerous truth—which in any case, Desmond saw, he would certainly disbelieve. He must be given some explanation and made a partner in some secret, for preference a ludicrous and salacious one, or he would undoubtedly repeat his discovery of Desmond's fraud and entangle him in an inextricable network of perjury and false pretences that might, for all he knew, end in a prosecution for causing a public mischief. It was useless to persist in his amnesia; he must confess, and try to put a good face on it.

"Blast your quick mind, Shadwell," he said with assumed admiration, "I knew you'd find me out. The truth is that I'm in a very difficult position, and I want you to promise me that you won't repeat anything that I tell you, as it would get me into serious trouble."

Shadwell, that mental voyeur, moistened his lips eagerly.

"Yes, yes, I promise. I won't say a word whatever you tell me."

Desmond hesitated. What *was* he going to tell him? Dismissing an unhelpful thought that women were fortunate, since in such predicaments they could always avoid questioning by pretending they had had an illegal operation, he caught inspiration by the tail and let it drag him where it would.

"Well," he began, "it's an absurd and almost incredible story, and I expect you won't believe it. But remember that I'm in a strange and ridiculous situation, and surprising effects often have surprising causes."

This little preamble had given him time to think, and he was soon in full flow.

"For some time past I've been having an affaire with Mrs. Pink, the wife of one of my Directors. She's a rather revolting sort of woman, I suppose, if you look at her coldly; fat, rich, sweaty, amorous and nearly fifty, but I confess that her favours, provided that she offered them at decent intervals, had a certain snobbish appeal for me, like a liaison with a member of the Royal Family. There was, too, a slightly sporting attraction about the business, and my encounters with her, though by ordinary standards not precisely enjoyable, had almost the fearful excitement of a destroyer creeping up in the darkness to torpedo a sleeping battleship.

"Well, as you may imagine, meetings with her were very difficult; for her husband—a terrifying, bald capitalist of the worst type—was pretty jealous, and knew enough about money to see how extraordinarily attractive his wife must be to whole armies of undesirable young men. He did, though, sometimes leave town for the night, I imagine to razz about a bit himself, and directly he was safely away, Mrs. Pink used to summon me to spend an energetic evening at their huge chandeliered and candelabraed house on Highgate Hill.

"One afternoon, about a week ago, I got my usual summons, and that night made my usual furtive entry by an unlocked side door. Mrs. Pink received me with gigantic girlish pleasure in the Venetian hall, stood me a bottle of Mr. Pink's best Margaux in the Louis Quatorze boudoir, and, like a muscular nymph who has captured an absent-minded satyr, dragged me sportively into her Style Pompadour bedroom.

"After we had been wrapped in a nightmare of ecstasy for what seemed like hours, there was a rap on the door.

"'Ah madame,' hissed the voice of Mrs. Pink's French maid, 'le maitre est revenu; vite, vite! Ah, le pauvre jeune monsieur!'

"Noting her kindly solicitude for me and resolving to thank

her appropriately in the future, I leapt from the sky-blue silk sheets and plunged into the depths of Mrs. P.'s wardrobe, while she frantically thrust my clothing after me, and Mr. Pink's heavy footsteps clumped up the stairs. In the darkness I dressed as best I could.

"'Oh God,' I cried, 'you've forgotten my trousers!'

"With a surprising agility, Mrs. Pink darted across the room, snatched them from behind the dressing-table, and, with great presence of mind, flung them into the linen-basket as her husband entered.

"'Good evening, my dear,' I heard him roar unpleasantly, 'you've gone to bed early?'

"'Oh, Arthur, I was so lonely after you'd gone to the country, I thought I'd lie down and think about you, as you wouldn't let me come with you.'

"Mr. Pink's voice softened.

"'Agnes,' he said, 'I'm a brute. As soon as I left the house I thought I ought to have taken you; I was half way to the club when I remembered this was our wedding anniversary, so I phoned up to the inn where we spent the first night of our honeymoon thirty years ago and booked the very room we had then. Hurry up and dress, my dear. I have the Daimler waiting outside.'

"'Oh, ducky, wouldn't it be nicer if you went there first, and I came afterwards in the Rolls and met you as if by chance?'

"'No, it wouldn't,' replied Mr. Pink, suddenly assuming the voice with which he cut salaries and discharged aged employees, 'you'll dress now, and come with me at once.' "I heard the bed creak as he plumped down his fourteen stone. He must have looked more determined even than he sounded, for his wife offered no further argument, and they went out together shortly afterwards.

"As soon as I heard the front door slam, I slipped out of the wardrobe, only to dart back again as steps came down the passage. For an interminable time I could hear a maddeningly conscientious maid tidying up the room, before she at last went away, and I could come out. Softly I switched on the bedside lamp, on tiptoe I crept to the clothes-basket, only to find it had disappeared; the maid must have taken it with her.

"I don't know how long I stood there biting my nails in despair. ..."

Shadwell coughed and held up his hand.

"Please," he said, "why didn't you ring for the French maid? She apparently knew all about it, and would probably have helped you."

"I didn't remember the French for 'trousers,' and didn't want to get involved in another misunderstanding. Now where was I?"

"You were biting your nails."

"Oh yes—I don't know how long I stood there biting my nails in despair. A search of the room proved what I already knew: that Mrs. Pink was not a trouser-wearing modern girl, nor even a riding woman. Her husband undoubtedly possessed at least seventy pairs of trousers, but I had no idea where his room lay, and the house was too infested with servants and secretaries for me to explore in my present state. As time passed I became more and more anxious. The Pinks had a daughter and two sons living in the house, all of whom might be expected home when the better night clubs closed, or even considerably earlier, if they learnt their parents were away. If I escaped now there was still hope of a roving taxi, and until the moon rose, the black-out might conceal my unusual dress. Regretting passionately that I had no overcoat, I slipped out into the passage, and after several alarms that must have taken years off my life, slid out by the side door on the road that runs behind the Heath.

"The moon was already rising and the street was horrifyingly light. No taxis were in sight, but there were footsteps in the distance from both directions, and despite the shadow of the house, concealment was nearly impossible. In desperation I rushed across the road and took cover in a cluster of bushes at the edge of the Heath. . . ."

"Excuse me," smirked Shadwell, "but, to the best of my recollection, all the Highgate side of the Heath is lined with railings. How did you get over them?"

"I really forget. I was in such a state of frenzy that ordinary considerations meant nothing to me. But I must have got over them somehow, mustn't I?"

"Naturally. You've always managed to get over most things, haven't you? But please continue."

"Certainly. As I crouched in the bushes wondering what to do next, a man walked past me on the path that led over to Hampstead. He was alone and looked undersized; and the sight of his trousers was too much for my fears and my moral sense. Like some ghastly troll pursuing a Scandinavian traveller, I bounded after him and catching him up, seized him by the arm.

"'Off with your trousers,' I snarled.

"'Oh, sir,' he whimpered, 'I'm not that kind of man!'

"I changed my grip to throw him to the ground, but he suddenly shook me free and ran off. I chased him, but he drew ahead and vanished into a coppice. I paused, and was about to follow him when a policeman loomed up beside me.

"''Ere,' he said, 'what's all this?'

"'Well,' I panted defensively, 'what is it?'

"'It's indecent exposure, that's what it is,' he replied; and after lending me his great-coat, took me off to the station.

"After a night in the cells, I was brought up before the magistrate, a wrinkled old man who looked as if he had been badly folded, and appeared to possess all the characteristics of an owl, except its feathers and its wisdom. He was in an ill-temper, and sifter he had sentenced a deaf- mute to three months' hard labour for touching the handle of a parked car, I began to feel very apprehensive.

"Then it was my turn, and, wearing a pair of policeman's trousers, I was hustled into the Dock.

"'Is your name John Smith?' croaked the Bench, 'of no fixed abode?'

"'I'm afraid it is, sir.'

"'Are you guilty or not guilty?'

"'Not guilty, sir.'

"'Guilty, eh? I'm glad you plead guilty, it's the manly thing to do and will save the time of the Court.' He turned to the Clerk. 'Has he any previous convictions for exposure?'

"'The answer is in the negative, your worship,' replied the clerk wittily, and one of the prisoners awaiting hearing burst into such a peal of sycophantic laughter that he was sent down to the cells for contempt of court.

"With a buzz like an alarm clock about to go off, the Magistrate pronounced sentence.

"'You have pleaded guilty to a very grave and disgusting offence for which, when I first sat on this Bench, you would have been sentenced to Transportation. In the present degenerate state of the Law, however, I regret that I can only sentence you to—ahem . . . ' He held a whispered conversation with the clerk in which I imagined I caught the words, 'What, no treadmill?', then coughed asthmatically and continued.

"'I suppose you would cast the blame for your behaviour upon evil companions or the cinematograph film, but I have had some experience of both and believe that their bad influence is much over-rated. You have made one of London's lungs into a cess-pool, and the least I can do is to fine you £10 and £10 costs. Next case.'

"'How long have I got to pay?'

"The Bench blinked at me.

"'Pay now or go to prison for one month. Next case.' "I was taken below and left to reflect on my unhappy position. I had less than on me and no cheque-book, while to confide in a friend might easily lead to a disclosure of the whole disastrous story. Eventually, I wrote a note to Mrs. Pink in which I simply said, 'Look in the linen-basket,' headed it with the address of the police station, and persuaded a policeman to post it for me. Then they took me off to Brixton in a van.

"Yesterday morning they told me that a lady had paid my fine, and let me go. Directly I was free, I telephoned Mrs. Pink and learnt that she had just returned to London and that I was supposed to be suffering from loss of memory. I rang you up to say I'd recovered, but thought better of it and decided to make my amnesia more convincing by keeping it up for a few days longer, in case anyone at the office should be suspicious. That's the whole story."

Shadwell sighed and shook his head.

"How much of this fantasia am I expected to believe?"

Desmond grinned at him.

"Oh just parts of it here and there. It's an accommodating sort of tale: you can accept or reject just what you like."

The other began to speak, then checked himself; and Desmond could see his tortuous mind working rapidly. Shadwell's gift of detecting the springs of simple actions and uncovering the lies that creep into the sincerest confidences made him, up to a point, a person very difficult to deceive, and enabled him easily to penetrate the ordinary social evasions. Not for a moment had Desmond imagined that he would believe even the outlines of his ridiculous story, but had intended it to appear the gilding of some sordid escapade he was too self-conscious to confess. 'Desmond,' he could imagine Shadwell thinking, 'must certainly have some exceedingly strong motive to make him engage in this preposterous mummery. As it stands, the story he told me is patently nonsense; a fact he made no attempt to conceal, but, indeed, emphasised by his manner of telling it. Nevertheless, there is probably something in it, and a man of my acumen should not find it hard to discover precisely what. He has clearly got himself implicated in a predicament so squalid and embarrassing that he dare not explain it to his friends or his employer. Perhaps he really has been in prison under an assumed name; perhaps he is trying to confess that he was caught in some indecent behaviour on Hampstead Heath, lacked the ready money to pay his fine, and couldn't write a cheque for fear of his name being exposed. He's so vain of his own dignity that he might go even to this grotesque length rather than have to admit such a degradation.'

At last Shadwell spoke; he was plainly feeling his way.

"I think I believe a good deal of your story."

Desmond pretended to be taken a little aback.

"Do you really? How much of it?"

"I have my doubts about Mrs. Pink."

('He's biting!' thought Desmond.) •

"Fancy that! You'll be disbelieving in my penal servitude next."

"I don't know about that. As a matter of fact, I believe the whole of your story in principle; I merely suspect that you've been displaying it to me through a purple-tinted magnifying glass. Have you ever written scenarios for historical films?"

('He's bit!' thought Desmond.)

"No, why? Or is that an unnecessary question?" "Unnecessary, I think?"

Desmond said nothing. Shadwell, wearing the illusive half-smile he had practised for so many years, straightened his tie and leisurely heaved himself up.

"I'm afraid I must be going now; I shan't give you away or repeat what you told me." Almost imperceptibly he stressed the "told." "I suppose you'll recover in a day or two? Let's dine together some day next week; how does Thursday suit you? Excellent."

He entered the date in a green morocco engagement book, and opened the door.

"Oh, by the way, there's another visitor waiting downstairs—I persuaded the doctor to let me come up first." "Mr. Whitby, I presume?"

"No, your wife."

Shadwell invariably made a good exit.

CHAPTER XIII

This was going to be a damned nuisance. His reasons for marrying Vera, like those for climbing a steep cliff, had seemed clear enough to begin with; but as the going became worse, the goal more unobtainable and the chances of safe retreat slighter, his initial enthusiasm had waned rapidly, until he came to curse the holiday spirit that had made him desert the safe flats of his previous contentment. The things about Vera that had at first attracted him—the clever little meals cooked in casseroles, the continental perfumes and trans-atlantic unguents—soon ceased to seem delightfully feminine, and became merely infuriating. Worse, he had quite misjudged Vera's character, and had imagined that because she was weak-willed and emotional she would be very easily influenced. In this, as he soon found, he was dreadfully mistaken. Her ideas, like those of most stupid people, were absolutely unshakable because they were part of her feelings and so beyond the reach of reason; and after yielding readily to his storms of angry argument, her former attitudes, as resilient as bell-buoys, would pop up again directly the pressure was relaxed.

After eight years of precarious mutual tolerance, Vera had found him unbearable; and Desmond, in an access of spite against his wealthy and sunburnt successor, had refused to consent to a divorce unless she agreed to be the guilty party. After a scene lasting three days and three hundred cliches, she had accepted; but her new lover, who valued his career at the Bar more than he did his passions, backed apologetically out leaving no evidence behind him. Desmond was suitably punished for this piece of malicious jealousy, for Vera, suddenly realising the unique advantages of combining marriage with independence, had blandly refused to act on the hotel bills and signed statements with which he began to bombard her directly he came to his senses. Vainly he threatened to have detectives set to watch her, but knew all the time it was useless; he had himself admitted too many indiscretions to expect discretion from a judge.

And now that curiosity, affection or some ulterior motive had urged her to come and see him, he felt distinctly uneasy. After their last meeting, which, called to discuss an advance on her allowance, had ended in a four- day reconciliation and a pound a week increase, he had determined to keep out of her way in future, since neither his nerves or his pocket would have stood a repetition. This, in fact, was no time to recover his memory; for should they become even temporarily reconciled—a thing he knew was not at all improbable—she would certainly ruin his plans however carefully he guarded them. Composing his features to an expression of forbidding blankness, proof, he hoped, against even Vera's volatility, he ruffled his hair, buttoned up his pyjama jacket wrongly, and sagged deeply down into his bed; an unprepossessing picture of a drab and undesirable amnesiac.

Vera was exactly as she had always been, and Desmond's faint hopes that she might play an Ophelia to his Hamlet ('O what a noble mind is here o'er-thrown! ' etc. etc.) were immediately extinguished.

"Why, Des., what have you been doing? Don't tell me that you've really lost your memory? What a scream!"

"Yes, I have lost my memory," he said with dignity, "and though they tell me you're my wife I haven't the slightest recollection of you. How did you know I was here?" he added a little anxiously.

"My dear, you're quite a sensation! Hitler was quiet yesterday, so you've got a little paragraph in all the papers! And what *were* you doing at Hampstead? But never mind that now—are you *sure* you don't recognise me?" "Absolutely certain."

"Well, really! What do you think of me now you've seen me?" She postured like a mannequin in the middle of the room, patting her smart hat with an affected gesture. Desmond, by now convinced that he was really ill, was furious at her light-heartedness, and tried to change the subject while he still kept his temper.

"Charming, charming," he said, "but as you're apparently my wife, perhaps you'll tell me something about myself?"

"Oh, you work on a terrible Press Agency—I expect you lost

your memory to forget about it. And would you believe it, my dear, I'm doing First Aid now with a most *frightful* lot of women! Always talking about their dreadful boyfriends and wanting to apply a tourniquet on the neck to stop nose-bleeding! My dear, I don't know what kind of a hospital this is; they were terribly rude when I rang them up. They said ... "

Desmond, disgusted by this familiar self-preoccupation, and alarmed that she made no reference to their separation, thought it was time to discover the reason for her visit.

"It's no use your coming here," he muttered, "I don't remember you at all. I must stay by myself until I do." "You needn't worry, Des.," she said brightly, "we didn't always get along very well in the past, though you won't remember that, but I'm going to look after you now and ask the doctor to let me take you home!" She smiled down at him with benign resolution.

Desmond recoiled; this was worse than he had feared. He guessed her viewpoint easily enough; to be tied to an active and disagreeable husband was one thing, to nurse an interesting invalid back to sanity, quite distinctly another, since for a short time at least there was nothing she would enjoy more than practising psycho-therapy on him, and showing off her peculiar pet to her numerous flock of acquaintants. If he suddenly recovered his memory and told her to go away, she would immediately suspect a fraud and denounce him to the hospital, while he could not refuse to move on grounds of ill-health without keeping up his deception for longer than he intended. The simplest method of escape was to put her off the idea by developing unpleasant symptoms, and since she was very fastidious this should not be a difficult matter.

With a sidelong leer he leant towards her and mumbled hoarsely in her ear.

"So you're my wife, are you? We're married to each other, eh? Well, since we're a respectable couple, it'd be quite all right if ... "

He gave an unpleasant cackle and pinched her thigh lasciviously. She jumped up and moved away.

"Really, Des., this is hardly the time and place for that sort of behaviour! For goodness sake be sensible!"

With what he hoped was a loathsome laugh he returned to the attack.

"Come on, darling, don't be so standoffish. The hospital's got eight hundred beds—let's use one of them for something besides dying in."

"Don't be so disgusting! Besides, someone might come

She sat down on the end of the bed, just out of reach. To his dismay he saw that she was enjoying the situation, was even a little excited by his surprising display of lechery. For her familiar and respectable husband to reveal a grossness she was otherwise too well-bred either to encounter or to endure, offered her a new and subtle sensation; and it seemed only too probable that far from departing in disgust she might at any moment yield to his pretended importunities. With maniacal swiftness he changed his attitude.

"What!" he cried histrionically, "do you tempt me to betray my beloved wife? Get thee to a nunnery—or perhaps a monastery might be more in your line."

Vera gaped angrily at him.

"What on earth are you talking about?"

"It's as plain as a seed-cake! You say I have a wife, yet I lust after you, a perfect stranger to me. You may be married to me in law, but I don't remember it or regard you as my wife, so if I go and live with you it'll be spiritual adultery. I know what it is! My wife wants to leave me, and she's sent you here to tempt me so she can get a divorce. But I won't fall into the trap, oh no, no, no, no, no!"

He wagged his head like a mechanical figure, and glared at her so furiously that she got up and backed away.

"You're mad!" she said.

He sighed drearily. "It's all the fault of race and education. Why, the less Degrees an Angle has, the more acute he is. I've got more than ninety, so you can imagine how obtuse I must be!"

"You're mad!" she repeated.

He groaned, then began to laugh.

"There are more cracks in my comprehension," he tittered, "than there are nits in the head of a blind beggar. How can poor folk keep their heads from spinning when the world whirls round so fast!"

He stopped abruptly as the door opened, and the nurse ushered in a grey-suited and slightly embarrassed Mr. Poole.

"Here's another visitor for you, Mr. Thane." She turned her beaming face on Mr. Poole. "Now remember, you mustn't stay long; I only let you up now because you said you had to hurry back. Mind you don't excite the patient."

She left them, and Mr. Poole looked uncertainly at Vera.

"Er, I don't think I've met your wife."

"She says she's my wife, but don't you believe it," interjected Desmond morosely, "it's all part of a vast international plot. I'm bloody well sick of plots," he cried violently;- "even the simple peasant thinks of nothing but having one of his own."

Vera had had enough.

"You're crazy!" she said viciously. "I always knew you'd go off your head in the end." She swept past Mr. Poole like a sports car passing a family Austin, and slammed the door behind her. There was an unhappy silence. Mr. Poole looked so ludicrously like a worried lawyer trapped in a chorus girl's dressing-room that Desmond had to say something to stifle his laughter. He started up dramatically.

"I know who you are! You're my father. Hallo, Dad, glad to see you!" He stuck out his hand in the manly but moving fashion made familiar by American films, and tried, unsuccessfully, to fill his eyes with tears. Mr. Poole recoiled as if stung by a wasp.

"Really, Thane, do pull yourself together. I'm not your father!"

"What! You aren't my father, after all?"

"No, of course I'm nothing of the sort," explained Mr. Poole indignantly. "I'm no relation at all to you, except in the way of business."

Desmond flung himself back in the bed and covered his face with his hands.

"Oh, mother, mother," he groaned, "why didn't you confess to me? I'd have understood and forgiven your pardonable weakness. Who would I have been to cast the first stone! "

Mr. Poole's voice rose to a desperate squeak.

"Thane! Do try and collect yourself. I'm no relation of yours and I'm nothing to do with your mother. Now, you must listen to me. I'm Poole of International Features and you're Desmond Thane, my assistant. Do you understand? "

Desmond sat slowly up.

"Poole—the name's familiar. . . . Yes," he exclaimed brightly. "I've heard of you, I think I've met you, but that was ten years ago and you were a coastal resort then. You were wavy and sandy in those days but now you're dark and straight. What *have* you been doing to yourself! "

He cackled stupidly for some moments and Mr. Poole stared at him suspiciously.

"You're not well, Thane," he said at last, "but I feel there is more in this than meets the eye. Are you quite positive that you don't remember who you are?"

"I don't know, I really don't. I sometimes make guesses, but they're always wrong. Why, only a few minutes ago I thought I was Desmond Thane!"

He burst into renewed laughter that at length expired in little, painful chuckles. Mr. Poole picked up his hat and spoke decisively.

"I don't think you're getting proper treatment here; I'll speak to my own doctor about you. I have to go now, but if there's anything you want me to do, I'll try my best to help you. Or perhaps there's someone you'd like me to send to see you?"

Desmond was suddenly ashamed of having mocked this silly, kindly little man who meant so well but did so foolishly; and had to choke back an impulse to apologise and tell the whole story. Instead he said:

"They tell me I'm your assistant on a Press Agency, so I suppose my being ill must have caused you a good deal of inconvenience. I'm sorry."

Mr. Poole brightened like a child unexpectedly praised, and smiled at him.

"Don't you worry about that. Thane; we'll carry on somehow until you come back. Are you sure there's nothing you want me to do?"

"Nothing—or, if you prefer it, everything."

Mr. Poole found no answer to this, but held out his hand, drew it back, held it out again, coughed, picked up his stick, coughed again, opened the door, mumbled, shuffled, fumbled and left at length with a jerk. It was a flattering performance; he might have been taking leave of his Directors.

After his visitor's departure, Desmond felt a little worried by his own behaviour. He had certainly gained his purpose of frightening Vera away, but if, as was very likely, she and Mr. Poole had told the doctor he was seriously unbalanced, it might prove difficult to stage a recovery at once rapid and convincing. When Dr. Vescott came on his next visit, he would, he decided, evince a marked improvement, drop all his foolish jokes, and show a complete recovery on the following morning. As a beginning, he tore up his autobiographies and threw them in the waste paper basket, doing the same, in an access of caution, to his translation from the notebook. The diary itself he left securely hidden in his bolster. For more than two hours he lay undisturbed, and had begun to smell with pleasant expectation the supper of the patients in the adjoining ward, when the door opened on the house physician and the matron. The latter bore his clothes over her arm, and both had the gravity of a deputation.

"Well, Mr. Thane," began the doctor, "I've been in touch with your brother, and he's arranged for you to be moved from here to a private nursing home, where you can be under the care of your own physician. If you'll dress now, you can be taken there this evening." Desmond looked at him suspiciously, fearing a trap. Had Shadwell been talking? He scanned their faces anxiously, but saw no falsity.

"I've got no brother," he said at last. "I don't know what you're talking about. I've got no old physician, either," and for once he was speaking the truth.

The Matron was soothing.

"Never you mind that, Mr. Thane, we know you don't remember things yet. Just you dress now, and don't trouble yourself."

Desmond grew uneasy.

"But I'm quite comfortable here, thank you; I don't want to go to any nursing home. As a matter of fact, I feel much better already."

"Now, Mr. Thane," said the house-physician firmly, "you'd better get dressed, there's a good fellow."

His tone was subtly different from that which he had used at their first interview, and Desmond became alarmed.

"I'm quite happy here, thanks, and if you don't mind. I'll stay where I am. If you want my bed or anything of that sort, you're at liberty to discharge me any time you like. I'm beginning to remember a bit about myself, and I'm quite certain I haven't a brother."

The doctor shrugged his shoulders and glanced back through the half-open door.

"Perhaps .you had better come in, Dr. Wainwright," he called, and stepped aside to admit a soft-footed, black- coated medical figure.

"Hallo, Desmond, don't you remember me?" said Foster.

With a stifled shriek, Desmond leapt out of bed and seized the house-physician by the arm.

"He isn't a doctor!" he shouted. "He isn't a doctor! I know him! He's an impostor, a criminal who wants to kidnap me!"

No-one, terrifyingly, seemed in the least surprised by this outburst, and Foster walked gently towards him.

"Now, Desmond," he said soothingly, "surely we aren't going to have all that again? Surely we've finished with all that years ago? You're just coming for a quiet rest in my house, and I'll see that no-one kidnaps you. You know you can trust me; I'm your old friend Dr. Wainwright, and I'll see that you come to no harm. You mustn't get excited, or it'll take you longer to get better."

He spoke softly and slowly as one might to a nervous horse. Desmond turned to the doctor and tried to keep his voice steady.

"For God's sake," he said, "do believe me! I was only pretending to have lost my memory; I really know perfectly well who I am, and I can assure you that I have no brother. This man belongs to a gang that, for reasons which would take too long to explain, want to kill me, and his whole story is a trick to take me away. Look up his credentials, and you'll find I'm speaking the truth."

Foster sighed, and addressed the house-physician.

"As you see, doctor, an advanced case. I believe Sir Frederick told you in his letter that he had to be certified in 1933 after a prosecution for assault; but his brother and myself always believed that the trouble was mainly psychological, and after lengthy treatment I secured his release two years ago. I then believed him entirely cured, although it is only fair to say that Sir Frederick, with his greater experience, expressed certain doubts, but directly his brother told me of this loss of memory I recognised it as one of his former symptoms, and feared the worst. Now ..."

He made a regretful gesture, then continued briskly. "How long has he been in this state?"

The other thought.

"Apart from his amnesia he was comparatively normal upon admittance, but his wife and his employer, who visited him this afternoon, found him highly excited and suffering from delusions."

Foster nodded sagely.

"As I expected. On the previous occasion I mentioned he at first simulated loss of memory to conceal the onset of his delusions."

"Perhaps also as a conscious endeavour to explain the unconscious urge towards the division of personality?" Foster nodded approvingly.

"An interesting supposition. I believe that Sir Frederick himself holds a similar viewpoint."

Desmond, who had been listening to his little dialogue with paralysed amazement, interrupted furiously.

"Don't let yourself be duped by this man! I tell you he's an impostor and a criminal! I tell you . . ."

The house-physician spoke patiently.

"Now, Mr. Thane, you must calm yourself. You don't think I'm a criminal, do you? Well, I assure you that Dr. Wainwright is a distinguished physician, with the highest recommendation from Sir Frederick Jameson, an old friend of mine, and one of the governors of this Hospital." He tapped a folded paper he held in his hand.

"Any letter he's given you is a forgery!" cried Desmond hopelessly. "I tell you I'm as sane as you are; you can put me to any test you like."

The house-physician shrugged his shoulders and addressed himself to Foster.

"You are quite right, Dr. Wainwright; a case of his kind cannot be properly treated here. He will obviously be better at a private home under special observation." Aware that it was his last chance, Desmond tried again.

"If you won't believe me," he pleaded, "for God's sake send for Dr. Vescott, and let me talk to him. If he says I'm mad, I'll go without any more fuss, but/ I beg you let me see him, just for five minutes."

The house-physician was cold.

"If you want any medical opinion I am quite competent to give it to you myself."

"I know you are, doctor, I know you are, but Dr. Vescott is a specialist and in charge of my case. You can't let me go without seeing him."

The other's expression became still colder.

"I'm afraid that any responsibility there may be must rest with me alone. I can see no reason to seek the assistance of Dr. Vescott in this matter."

He moved away, and Foster came forward.

"It's no use behaving in this way, Desmond," he said kindly but a little sharply, "you're only wasting time. You've nothing to fear from coming along with me; you remember how comfortable you were last time." He laid a fatherly hand on Desmond's shoulder and his lips twitched almost imperceptibly. Desmond knocked him violently aside and backed into a corner.

"One step nearer," he shouted, "and I'll ..."

With astonishing speed the doctor and the Matron flung him down on to the bed and held him expertly so that he could not move. Foster bent over him and felt his pulse.

"A hypodermic?" he interrogated of no-one in particular.

"If you could hold him for a moment, doctor . . ."

Foster took his arm from the Matron and she hurried out, returning in a few minutes with instruments on a tray. <

"You're making a serious mistake," said Desmond weakly, but offered no further resistance as the needle was thrust into his arm. For a minute or two they held him firmly, then stood up.

As he lay there, a numbing warmth creeping through his whole body, he saw the scene as though from an immense distance. The Matron staring at him curiously, the young doctor whispering deferentially to Foster, who stood smiling as suavely as the sleek specialist in the Underground Railway advertisements. Then the Matron began swiftly and efficiently to push him into his clothes, and it occurred to him dreamily that perhaps he really was mad and that his recent experiences (how hazy they seemed now) were merely a neurotic's nightmare. He was still wondering who was right when Foster and the doctor helped him to his feet, and led him out of the room and down interminable passages, until they came to. the open air and a big, dark car fitted up inside like an ambulance. He was glad to lie down on one of the two bunks, for by now he was very sleepy and could scarcely hear Foster and the house-physician exchanging professional courtesies. Then the door shut and he felt the car move off. With a last immense effort he opened his eyes, and saw Foster leaning over him. Slowly and deliberately, Foster winked.

CHAPTER XIV

A darkness, a noise, a confusion of voices and people. The Jew endlessly running on the edge of a floodlit precipice, Anna asking interminable questions in a tiny, stifling room, her diary become a gigantic cumbersome parcel that must be carried to a vital train at a distant and changing terminus. The long, dusty road travelled a dozen times and each time the parcel mislaid; the traffic block, the wrong turning, the forgotten destination, the feet that will not walk, the hands that cannot hold, the ever more monstrous diary—all these at last smoothly overcome. Then the last run down the platform achieved with the ease of a skater, and the door of a first-class carriage yielding to a touch. All at once heat and darkness and Foster leaning from every window, Foster pursuing him out of the station, down the hill, back through the sweltering street, and into a little alley the breadth of a coffin. A pushing for room, and a great wind blowing the buildings over and over, whirling Foster, the diary, and a cloud of bricks up and away like a shrubbery stripped by a tempest. In all the chaos he alone stood firm, then the brick-storm caught him too and swept him after the rest, over and over to nothing. . . .

Gently Desmond opened his eyes and stared at a flat white ceiling, indifferently trying to piece his nightmare together and wondering why it had made his spirit so heavy. Today or tomorrow, he thought, after a time, he would leave the hospital, and . . .

"Well," said Foster's voice from just behind him, "where have you hidden it?"

Instantly but without shock he remembered; and for a moment felt his stomach turn as though he were in a falling lift. Then all emotion left him and he was unnaturally calm. Without moving his head he asked the delaying question, although he already knew its futility.

"What do you mean?"

"The Contact List."

"I haven't got it—I threw it away."

Foster sighed.

"Are you still going to be obstinate? You know what I shall have to do if you are?"

Desmond knew.

"All right," he said, "I left it in my pillow at the hospital; I expect it'll still be there if you care to go and fetch it. It hasn't done me much good; I hope you'll get more profit from it."

"Thank you. I shall send for it in the morning. I hope for your sake that you are speaking the truth."

A chair creaked as he got up, his soft footsteps moved across the room, the door opened and shut. Not for some minutes after his departure did Desmond find the will to sit up and look about him. Without surprise he found that he was back in the room from which he had escaped three days ago. The bed was the same, the chair and blazing light were the same, the only difference was the boarding up of the window he had broken. He lay back on the bed and counted the minutes ticking slowly past. After a while the door opened again and someone shuffled into the room.

"Here we are again," said the fat man.

Everything was the same.

For some time there was silence broken only by Fat's nervous fidgeting, then unexpectedly he burst out with the breathless abruptness of the shy man overcome with a longing to be talkative.

"I'm glad you killed the Jew!"

Desmond, too downcast to be interested, replied with automatic politeness:

"Oh, really, why?"

"Always arseing about, he was. Always do this or go there or do that—never left off even when there wasn't a job on. Always arseing about, he was: always bossing about or sucking up to Mr. Foster. But Mr. Foster saw through him all right; he wouldn't have put up with much more of him. It was time he got knocked off. How did you do him, Mr. Thane? Did he make a noise?"

He wriggled to the edge of his chair and leant forward expectantly, podgy hands on knees, his little eyes sparkling. Desmond, wanting only to be let alone, tried to make the man go on chattering.

"Oh, there wasn't much to it. Tell me some more about him. Have you picked up his body?"

The other, the wall of his shyness broken, was unquenchably voluble.

"You wouldn't believe the time we had with him, you simply wouldn't believe it! I went and found him after you telephoned Mr. Foster, and when it was dark we all went out and picked him up. He was so heavy with the water he'd soaked in we had a fine business getting him into the car, and a nasty mess he made of the cushions when we got him there. On the way home some soldiers stopped us, and Frank wanted to start shooting, but Mr. Foster stopped him and talked to them and it was all right. We threw him into the old well in the garden, and when we were just tipping him over, a frog jumped out of his mouth, and Frank let out a yell and Mr. Foster hit him. I'd have laughed if I'd dared, but I've never seen Mr. Foster in such a temper. Something must have upset him." He giggled quietly to himself, rocking backwards and forwards. Desmond, who at first had scarcely listened to him, began to take more interest and, as the effects of the injection wore off, looked hopefully for a chance to make use of his guard's unexpected friendliness.

"It must have been fun," he said warmly. "I wish I'd been there," and stood carelessly up.

The move was premature. In an instant Fat had his knife out, and his smile cut off as if an invisible hand had slapped his face.

"Now, Mr. Thane," he said, and with thumb and index finger spun the knife dexterously until the blade seemed a cylinder of silver. Ostentatiously Desmond stretched his arms, yawned, scratched the back of his neck and sat down again, cursing himself for being too precipitate. After a moment the man slipped the weapon back into his breast pocket and let his hands hang down by the side of his chair, but he kept his eyes glassily fixed on Desmond's and showed no sign of continuing his reminiscences. The atmosphere had chilled.

Desmond tried to dissipate the tension, and fumbled tentatively for a conversational opening.

"I suppose your work is very interesting as a rule?" No answer. He struggled on.

"I expect Mr. Foster is rather a difficult man to work for. Is he often in the country?"

No answer. He tried another approach.

"Don't you think that a man as clever as Mr. Foster should belong to the Central Committee?"

Fat stiffened.

"What do you know about the Central Committee?" "A good deal. As a matter of fact I used to have a fairly close connection with it."

He could see the man regarding him with an odd mixture of venom, suspicion and respect. It was clear that this plump, cruel little creature could have no important place in the organisation and would know little or nothing of the Committee's proceedings—he had plainly been inferior to the Jew who had himself been no more than one of Foster's agents—yet he knew of its existence, and seemed from his expression to hold it in considerable awe. Desmond felt his way carefully forward.

"I've a friend on the Committee, actually. There'll be trouble for someone when he hears of the way I've been treated."

The fat man narrowed his eyes till they were scarcely visible, and picked at his lip with a thick, black-nailed finger. As Desmond looked at him he saw that beneath his petty nastiness and superficial oddities, he was a vicious, dangerous creature, completely merciless and probably a little mad. With the Jew, even with Foster, Desmond had felt on common ground and known fundamentally that their minds worked in the same way as his own. With this man it was different, and he gradually grew terrified. Then Fat spoke, and seemed once more just a dangerous but stupid little man.

"Why didn't you tell that to Mr. Foster the other night? " "Because if he'd known who l am he'd have killed me at once. He and the Committee, you see, don't always get along very well. But," he added hastily, "of course you wouldn't know anything about that—almost nobody does."

"Oh, yes l do," sniggered Fat cunningly. "l know a lot more than anyone thinks!" He hesitated, then vanity got the better of him. "l know Mr. Foster doesn't always tell the Committee the truth. l heard him phoning them and saying you killed the lrishman." He wagged his head violently.

Desmond felt he was on the edge of opportunity, if only he knew how to take it. His pretence of a connection with the mysterious Committee could easily be riddled by anyone with cool sense and a capacity for logic, but to the fat man, a half crazy being inhabiting a world of tortuous intrigues of which his cloudy brain must grasp barely the outlines, was obviously incapable of cold analysis. Cruelty and deceit were his only realities; he was Foster's dog with a secret itch to bite his master. Doubt cast into his brain would spread out ripples to its farthest limits and take effect long after it had been first dropped. Acutely conscious that nothing he did now could increase his peril, Desmond continued:

"Oh yes, he's always lying to them. He'll be found out one day; if anything happens to me he'll be found out. The Committee never spare anyone, and never forgive." There was a pause.

"The Committee know what Mr. Foster does," said Fat at last, "they leave everything to Mr. Foster." "That's what he says. But if anything happens to me someone will be punished for it; you needn't have any doubts about that."

"They can't touch Mr. Foster," said Fat, decidedly; "no one can touch him."

"No, they probably can't touch—him."

He fell silent and lay back staring at the ceiling. He was determined for once not to spoil his chances by going too far or too fast. Fat had ceased fidgeting, and sat for a little without a movement. Then he said,

"Mr. Foster's going to have you killed when he's got the book he wants. He told me so."

Desmond felt slightly sick and with a great effort kept his voice level,

"I know; and when the Committee hear of it someone else will be killed."

"They wouldn't dare touch Mr. Foster."

"Perhaps not, but he isn't the only one mixed up in this business." He paused. "The Jew's gone already."

"They wouldn't dare touch Mr. Foster," repeated the fat man for the third time, "they leave everything to him. Why, he's seeing them this very evening to make his report."

"Someone else will be killed," repeated Desmond, "someone else will be killed."

There was a longer silence than before, then the fat man slipped out, locking the door behind him.

Desmond lay still, trying to weigh the possible consequences of what he had said. In the grotesque underworld of Foster and his friends suspicion must flourish like a mushroom in a cellar, sprouting and profilating until ordinary sense was lost beneath its shadow. The fat man, he felt sure, would not repeat what he had said to Foster— he was far more likely to attribute to him some statement he had never uttered—but distort it in terms of his own mania and store it up for some future and unpredictable reckoning. Foster himself, it seemed, deceived his superiors — unless indeed his lie about O'Brien's death was Fat's own invention or misunderstanding. Perhaps Foster really was acting against his Committee's instructions; perhaps by trying to promote dissension amongst his enemies he had made his own destruction certain. He ceased speculating and tried to think of anything apart from his present circumstances. But all the time his brain beat to the endless repetition of "Someone else will be killed, someone else will be killed."

... and when he recovered consciousness informed me that the Contact List was concealed in his room at the hospital. I am sure that he is speaking the truth, and have arranged for the collection of the list to-morrow morning.

(This concluded Mr. Foster's report.)

The Chairman: Thank you. I am sure I express the feelings of the whole Committee when I congratulate you upon your excellent work in recovering the List.

Mr. Foster: I am glad that my efforts have met with your approval, and hope that they may continue to deserve it in the future.

G: I suppose Thane is still at your house?

Mr. Foster: Yes. I shall keep him there until the List is actually in my hands, in case he has not spoken the truth, although, as I have said, I am sure that this is not the case.

G: And then ?

Mr. Foster: Then, naturally, I shall have to dispose of him; he has learnt too much to be safely left at large, and may actually have been an enemy of our organisation, although I have found nothing to prove that he knew very much about us. The details of his disposal you can safely leave to my discretion. And now, gentlemen, with your permission I shall leave you. I have, as you know, other of your business to attend to.

E: One moment. We have heard so much about this Thane and been told such a great deal about his elusiveness and obstinacy, that I for one should like to question him myself. Perhaps you would arrange to have him brought to London before you remove him, as I think you put it.

Mr. Foster: I do not see that any useful purpose would be achieved by such an interview. I have already told you all that is known about him, and I do not think anything important could be added to it. The sooner he is out of the way the better. Might I ask what exactly you hoped to learn from him?

E: I should like to hear him tell us how he killed O'Brien.

Mr. Foster: What do you imply by that?

E: I imply nothing; I merely express a curiosity that I share with others. I should like, I repeat, to hear his account of O'Brien's unfortunate death.

F: We should also like to hear from his own lips some further details of his relations with Raven.

B: And of his providential escape from your house.

Mr. Foster: Do you insinuate that I have been lying to you?

E: Oh no, only that your reports may occasionally have been incomplete.

Mr. Foster: If you are dissatisfied with me, you are at liberty to ask for my resignation.

E: I do not think we should be willing to do that. You are not a man with whom we shall readily dispense.

Mr. Foster: I accept your assurance at its full weight.

The Chairman: I beg you, Mr. Foster, not to misunderstand my colleague: all of us here—and I myself in particular—have the greatest confidence in you, and place the fullest reliance upon your reports. I must remind you, however, that the Meeting has expressed a desire to see your prisoner, and must therefore ask you to arrange for him to be brought here to-morrow. I am sure you will understand that our request in no way implies a criticism.

Mr. Foster: I do indeed understand your feelings, and naturally accept any suggestion of yours, Mr. Chairman. If you wish I will telephone to my agent at once and instruct him to bring Thane to London.

The Chairman: Thank you, I think that will be best. You will find a telephone in the next room.

(Mr. Foster then left the Meeting.)

E: Excuse me, gentlemen, I also have to telephone.

(E then left.)

F: It is plain that Foster is exceeding his position. I consider . . .
The Chairman: I think we had better suspend discussion on this matter until a later stage of the Meeting.

(A short while afterwards E returned to the Meeting, and was followed in a few moments by Mr. Foster.)

Mr. Foster: I have spoken to my assistant, and he will bring Thane here to-morrow. I have warned him to show the utmost vigilance against any further attempt at escape.
E: A very proper instruction.
The Chairman : Good; we will not detain you any further. You will, of course, be present here to-morrow.

(Mr. Foster then left.)

The Chairman: Well?
E: I went to the lobby without being observed by Foster, and listened in to his conversation on the extension. Here is a verbatim record of what was said:

"This is Foster speaking. Get rid of our guest immediately and dispose of him in the usual manner. Take care that he leaves no traces behind him. If you should be questioned, say you had to do so for your own safety. Do you understand?
Who's going to ask me about it, Mr. Foster?
That's no concern of yours; your business is to obey my instructions. Now remember, even if the Committee question you, you did it while he was attempting to escape.
But, Mr. Foster . . .
You understand me; see that you make no mistakes. Good night."

That is all. I think it is conclusive.

The Chairman : I think it is.

B: This is clear treachery. We must deal with Foster immediately.

The Chairman: There is still, I must remind you, need for caution; we cannot be finally rid of Foster until we have taken over his work and dealt with his assistants. For a few days longer he may still be dangerous, and for that time we can do nothing conclusive.

G: What about Thane?

The Chairman : We must see him, of course, and discover why Foster is so anxious to prevent the interview. E, you had better telephone to this agent of his and order him to bring his prisoner here to-morrow. See that he makes no mistake about it, and warn him that if any accident happens he will be held responsible. You might also tell him not to repeat this to Foster.

B : The poor fellow will find himself in a fine dilemma. *E:* I will make it clear to him which horn he had better choose.

(E then left)

G: But what will Foster think when he sees Thane arrive here safely? Will it not put him on his guard?

The Chairman : He is already aware of our feelings, but, I suspect, contemptuous of our power over him. Thane's unexpected appearance will show him that we know more than he thinks, and that even his own assistants obey us rather than him. It will give him a severe fright, and once frightened he may make some rash move that will render our eventual task the simpler.

(E returned to the Meeting)

E: I have tried to phone to Standon, but there is an air-raid warning in the district, and the Exchange are refusing long-distance calls; I have asked them to ring me directly the line is clear.

F: Unless you get through soon I am afraid you may be too late.

E: I am afraid so. . . .

The telephone ringing in the empty depths of the house woke Desmond from an uneasy doze, and he heard the hurried pad of footsteps down the passage as the fat man ran to answer it. The conversation was a brief one, for scarcely a minute after the ringing had ceased he heard the conclusive tinkle as the receiver was replaced, and the steps, slow and deliberate now, of his gaoler coming up the stairs. Fat stood in the doorway without entering and beckoned to him with his head.

"Come along downstairs," he said; and Desmond knew, as surely as though a freshly dug grave had opened at his feet, that now he was going to be killed.

He felt cold and as weak as a convalescent. Several times during the past days he had imagined some similar moment, and always believed that at the last, knowing that all was lost anyway, he would find an access of physical fury, and, heroic in the defence of his own life, fling himself upon his executioners. Instead, drained of all energy, he found himself incapable of any effort, and understood, as he had never done before, why victims of incurable diseases never murder their enemies, nor condemned men rush at their firing squads. His sole impulse was somehow to gain a little time, and his one resolve, co-mixed of pride and a reading of the fat man's psychology, to conceal any sign of fear. Squatting up on the bed, with his back against the wall, and clasping his hands together to hide their trembling, he spoke as casually as he was able, enunciating each word as carefully as though it were in a foreign language.

"I presume that means you have orders to kill me? " The man shuffled his feet.

"You come along downstairs with me."

(I suppose I'm too heavy for him to carry downstairs afterwards. Besides, it might make a mess of the room.)

"If you do this you won't last much longer yourself. I suppose you realise that?"

For a moment Fat seemed to hesitate, then he spoke sharply:

"Come along downstairs."

(I mustn't make him angry, thought Desmond; if I provoke him he'll do me in on the spot, and cheat me of five minutes' more life.)

"All right, as you wish."

He got up and walked carefully to the door. Some Chinese sage, he remembered, had said that although when we walk we use only the ground the soles of our feet actually cover, we could not move a foot were the earth we do not use cut away from around us; but as he crossed the room he felt as though he was stepping from rock to rock over a vast emptiness where one false pace might tip him over a precipice. With exaggerated care he made his way past Fat and went slowly down the passage to the head of the stairs.

With a shock like a knife-thrust came the howl of an airraid siren. It must have been very near the house, for the peak of each wail seemed to shake the air itself, and each fall, as it drew breath for the next long yell, seemed to suck at the pit of the stomach. It was like the noise of some vast, injured animal, and Desmond, shaken for a moment into neglect of his own situation, told himself that it was the agonised, continent-wide death-cry of a self-destroyed economic system as it heard the approach of the vultures it itself had created. His fancies were abruptly dissipated as Fat tugged at his arm.

"That's the siren!" he said, unnecessarily. "Come on quick, there's going to be a raid! "

He gripped him urgently by the elbow and began to push him downstairs. With delighted astonishment, Desmond saw that the man was seriously frightened.

"Have you had many raids here?" he asked as they stumbled on to the landing.

"No, no, this is the first. Come on and get away from that window."

Without wasting more words, he dragged him down to the hall, and hesitated doubtfully. Then he switched off the light, opened the front door and began to lead him out into the garden.

Desmond hung back.

"Where are we going?"

It was a clear night, and dozens of searchlights, some of them very near, so lit up the sky that he could see the other's face contort.

"You're going where the Yid went; into the well!"

With a series of double crashes like pairs of doors being rapidly slammed, an anti-aircraft battery opened fire on the other side of the hill. The fat man slammed the door and jumped back into the darkness of the hall.

"Bombs!" he said. "Big ones!"

"Yes," answered Desmond as more guns opened up, "lots of them! "

"Get in here, we'll be safer from blast," urged Fat, and pushed him into a little arched cupboard under the stairs. High overhead they could hear the sound of engines.

Desmond began to understand the man's exaggerated anxiety. For years the public, especially the readers of the cheaper papers, had been fed with tales of the horrid devastation brought by air attack; had been shown news films of flaming buildings in Barcelona, and photographs of truck-loads of bodies rumbling through the streets of Shanghai, with the result that a gigantic apprehension had arisen unsurpassed since the inroads of the Tartars. Men like Fat, with much imagination and little logic, could visualise clearly enough the flying metal that slashed limbs from trunks, the falling masonry that crushed heads to pulp, yet never absorbed the smallness of all recorded casualties, understood the limited number of bombs it was possible to drop, nor appreciated the restricted deadliness even of the greatest explosives. Indeed, how could they be expected to do so, when all the experts, from Cabinet Ministers downwards, were revelling in rhetorical Jeremiads that quite drowned in their clangour the small voices of reason and statistics? After a few real raids, of course, the most pessimistic would lose much of their agitation even though their physical fear increased, for the true cause of their panic was not so much actual danger as the awful prestige of a new and much advertised form of warfare. For many people, the first serious raid must have been almost a relief.

In Fat's case, such an attitude was still further accentuated. Almost unbalanced in many respects, he was a mental coward, afraid of anything he had not experienced or could not understand. He was quite probably a physical hero and, with Foster to order him, might resist impossible human odds. An air-raid was different; it was something he had only encountered in skilfully-written scare stories for a dozen pre-war years. The guns banged again, and Desmond heard him draw in his breath with a hiss. Yet he was not afraid to crouch in the dark with a prisoner of twice his strength who knew he was going to be killed; whereas Desmond, who prayed for a bomb to bring down the house on top of them, dared not, for fear of a knife in the stomach, jump on the craven little murderer who shivered a few feet away from him. All he could do was to try and keep Fat's fears at the flood.

"That was a near one!" he whispered as all the guns fired together, "they must be after the arms factory up the line."

"Arms factory? I haven't heard of any arms factory."

"Oh yes, there's a munitions works a couple of miles from here, but you wouldn't notice it unless you knew about it, it's so well camouflaged. If they hit that, the whole village will come down."

"It's a long way off," mumbled Fat, "we're all right here."

"Oh no, we aren't, I know too much about air-raids to think that. I was in Spain in the civil war and I've seen what bombs can do. I helped to dig people out once from a cafe that had got a direct hit. The tea-urn had been blown right through one man, and tea and blood and dust were all mixed together and dripped on my neck as I bent over a leg. It was terrible. ..."

Planes were overhead again and the guns continued to fire. Under cover of the noise, Desmond tried to shift his position, but a powerful light was dazzlingly flashed on to his face.

"You keep still," muttered a voice from the blackness behind the torch; "don't you try and make a dash for it."

The explosions increased again, and the light trembled a little but the voice went on, "I know what your game is, and you'd better not try it."

The torch snapped out. Desmond began to speak, then sighed and ceased. There seemed nothing more to be said. They sat in silence as the gunfire died away; Desmond apathetically aware of a cramp creeping up his thighs, the fat man snuffling quietly to himself. After a while the phone began to ring, and Fat crawled agilely out, bolting the door behind him, and leaving his prisoner hunched miserably in the darkness. The conversation seemed to be a long one, for it was quite a quarter of an hour before he opened the door and shone his torch down on Desmond.

"Your friend must have heard about you, Mr. Thane," he said rapidly, "the Committee have told me to"bring you up to see them to-morrow. I hope ..."

A huge jet of sound sprang up outside and swept away the rest of his speech. It was the All Clear.

CHAPTER XV

Once more the car with frosted windows, the swift drive to an unknown destination. For all his ingratiating grins and newly-found eagerness to oblige, the fat man, before he climbed into the driving seat, had bound both Desmond's hands with a Boy Scout's competent ingenuity, and left him, safely trussed in the back, to the company of his own thoughts.

Fat's attitude had changed a good deal after his victim's unexpected reprieve, for he assumed that it must be the work of Desmond's mysterious friend, and realised with some apprehension that if this was the case his prisoner might prove sufficiently influential not only to escape but also to take vengeance for past ill-treatment. When Desmond recovered from his first shock of relief, he had encouraged his captor's fears, and in the twenty-four hours between the air-raid and his present journey had gathered a number of clues as to what might lie ahead of him.

Foster, it seemed, had not only ordered his immediate death but had also told Fat to misrepresent it to the Committee; and the Committee had not only reprieved him, but had also told Fat to conceal this fact from Foster. That there was some split in the organisation was clear enough; his own place in the quarrel was more difficult to see. Was the Committee merely curious to see the cause of all their trouble, or had the message perhaps come from some rival group who believed he still held the List, or did they merely mean to kill him in some other place because the events of his first imprisonment— the policeman's visit, the shooting on the line—had made it dangerous to leave his body down at Standon? Resolutely he thrust speculation from his mind; for he already felt close to the edge of a breakdown, and knew that if he drove his thoughts many more times over the same hard ruts he might lose control altogether. Settling down into a corner as comfortably as his bonds permitted, he composed himself to the mental and physical numbness that can, for the cowardly, take the place of endurance.

The car swerved, slowed smoothly and stopped; a sliding door rattled to behind it. From the smell of petrol, Desmond guessed they were in a garage, and when Fat opened the door and gestured him out he could see in the dimness—the place was lit only by a single blue bulb —the shape of another car painted in Army camouflage. He followed the man up a flight of whitewashed steps, along a short passage and into a little, plainly-furnished annexe. Fat untied his hands and nodded him to be seated, while he himself, hands in pockets, leant constrainedly against the wall. Desmond saw that the trip must be an important occasion for him, for he had exchanged his baggy blue suit for heavy, profusely-striped trousers and a smart black jacket, and brilliantined his thick hair so lavishly that when he shifted his head he left a dark patch of grease on the pale distempered wall. They were both unnaturally silent and inclined to fidget, straining their ears for any sound from outside, like patients in a doctor's waiting-room. Another door, which Desmond had not noticed, opened a few inches.

"Good evening, Cartwright," said a dry, precise, slightly nasal voice, "I am glad to see you have arrived promptly. Have you had any trouble?"

Fat jumped to his feet and stood at a sort of knock- kneed attention.

"Oh no, sir, thank you. Everything has gone fine! I've done just what you told me, sir; I haven't heard from Mr. Foster, sir, but when I do I'll say just what you told me. I'll ..."

"Then that will do," the voice cut in coldly, "I shall discuss that with you later. In the meantime, blindfold that man and wait with him until he is sent for. After that you are to go to the usual address and wait there until we get in touch with you."

The door closed softly, and Fat, fumbling in his pockets, produced a highly-coloured silk handkerchief. As he drew it over his eyes Desmond noticed a squat electric clock ticking above the mantelpiece; it was half-past nine. Fat, breathing heavily down his neck, made a good job of tying the bandage, then sank down in a chair beside him. They waited.

The door must have opened again, although. Desmond had not heard it, for the same dry voice spoke suddenly from behind him.

"Cartwright," it said, "take him to the door of the Board-Room, and leave him there. At once."

The fat man jerked up and caught Desmond by the wrist.

"Come on," he whispered urgently, "get a move on," and towed him along behind him. Desmond tried to memorise the way he was being taken, but soon lost all idea of direction in the turns of stairways and passages. Abruptly the other stopped, so that he stumbled into his back, and he heard Foster's voice exclaim furiously.

"What are you doing here! Why haven't you ..."

Then he checked himself, and there was silence save for the fat man's footsteps scuttling away over the carpet. Desmond stood helplessly, turning his bandaged eyes this way and that, until a hand tapped him lightly on the shoulder.

"This way, please," said a quiet voice, "the Committee is ready to see you."

Desmond let himself be led forward and pushed gently down into a wooden armchair. He sensed that he was in a large room, and the continuous subdued rustle in front and on each side of him implied the presence of a good number of people. Already he felt he knew a little about the gathering he had been brought to face. The thick softness of the carpet, the faint, warm scent of cigar smoke, the silky smoothness of the chair-arms beneath his hands all suggested wealth, and the silent attention of the group that must be regarding him spelt purpose.

He licked his lips and waited, until Foster's voice came smoothly from one side.

"Well, Thane," it said, "you can take off the bandage now."

His tone was almost genial, and Desmond felt a tremor of doubt as he struggled with the knots behind his head. All at once he was aware of a change in the room; the faint rustling had stopped, there was an utter and unnatural silence. With sudden clarity he understood and clasped his hands firmly in front of him.

"Thanks, Mr. Foster, but I prefer to remain blindfold. I have learnt enough of your organisation by now to know the value of ignorance. If I see the faces of the Committee, they'll certainly kill me; if I don't, they may believe my story and let me go."

He stopped, and after an instant the rustling; began again. His heart ceased to leap and his breath came more easily as, with the special sensibility gained by long experience of difficult superiors, he knew beyond doubt that he had made an excellent first impression. With a preliminary cough, an elderly voice, pedantic and a little asthmatic, addressed him from directly in front.

"You are quite correct in the first part of your statement, but I fear you may be mistaken in the second." There was a snorting laugh from the far side of the room, but the voice wheezed imperturbably on. "You have been brought here not because of your activities against our organisation, for your efforts in that direction have proved wholly ineffective, but in order to give us a fuller explanation of your motives and conduct than you have already made to Mr. Foster. You will therefore describe in detail your relations with Anna Raven, your motives for killing her, your reason for taking the Contact List and"—he paused as if with some hidden significance—"your experiences since you have been in the hands of Mr. Foster."

Before Desmond could reply, Foster interjected brusquely. "Mr. Chairman, I protest most strongly against this ridiculous waste of the Committee's time. This man has already given me the fullest possible account of his activities, which I have passed on to you exactly as I received it. I suggest that he be removed at once and that we proceed to serious business."

The nasal voice that had summoned Desmond to the meeting laughed shortly, "This is not the first time you have made such a suggestion, is it, Mr. Foster, though previously it has not been given before so large a company?"

There was an oppressive silence. When Foster answered his

voice was unusually harsh, and less assured than Desmond had ever heard it.

"I resent your insinuations although I don't properly understand them. If you insist on insulting me by asking this man to repeat what I have already told you, I shall have to leave the meeting."

Another voice broke in, speaking with a lisping, foreign intonation.

"Before you leave us, Mr. Foster, I should like to ask our prisoner one question in your presence. Thane," he said softly, "why did you kill O'Brien?"

With the accumulated venom of the past week impelling him, Desmond answered in the most casual tone he could assume.

"Oh, I didn't touch him, Foster had it done. He told the fat man to stab him; the Jew tried to stop them, and I made my escape in the confusion. I've no idea why he did it; but if he hadn't, I should never have got away."

"That's a lie!" said Foster savagely, and Desmond heard a chair pushed back as if someone had sprung to his feet. The elderly voice they had addressed as Mr. Chairman intervened calmly.

"Take your hand out of your pocket, Foster, and please be seated. This matter will have to be thoroughly investigated, not made the subject of a brawl. I must ask you to respect the order of the Meeting."

When Foster answered, his tone was once more calm and arrogant.

"I am sorry, gentlemen, if I lost my temper at this person's lies, but I have heard so many of them in recent days that I have quite lost patience with him. I am sorry if I have shown any disrespect to the Meeting, but I must repeat that I shall feel obliged to leave if this public interrogation is to continue." He paused questioningly, then continued decisively, "Very good, gentlemen, so be it.

Should it become necessary, you will find me easily enough. Good night." His footsteps went firmly across the room, stayed for an interrogative moment at the door, then went out and faded off into silence.

His departure seemed to lift a pressure from the room, and there was a momentary shuffling of papers and shifting of chairs, stayed by the sharp tap of a hammer.

"Well, gentlemen," said the Chairman, "I think we see our way clear. I shall take the necessary steps within the next few days; until then we can turn to other business. As for Thane," he spoke in a different tone as if he had just recollected his presence, "I suppose we had better hear his story. Please begin."

Desmond, a trifle perturbed by this sudden lapse of interest in him, began at once with a simple, direct and almost entirely honest version of his adventures. Besides a certain characteristic exaggeration of his own acuteness, and a much distorted account of O'Brien's death, he kept to the truth, and found an astonishing pleasure in at last escaping from the strain of maintaining falsehood. When at length he was finished, he could feel that his audience believed him, and leant back with the satisfied confidence that his troubles were nearly over.

The Chairman gave a little cough.

"Thank you, that will be all."

A hand touched him on the shoulder and quietly urged him out of his chair. After two paces he stopped and swung round, seized by a horrid realisation of what the man's words implied. For the first time in his dealings with members of the gang he had not been questioned or threatened, but simply dismissed with the courteous finality of an examiner rejecting a failed candidate. They had heard him, believed him, and crossed him out; beyond the door to which they were politely leading him lay swift and inescapable death.

"Look!" he asked desperately, "you haven't finished with me, have you? You are going to let me go, aren't you?" He strained forward hopefully.

"Take him out," said the Chairman briefly. "Next on the Agenda."

The grip on his arm tightened, but he shook himself free.

"Mr. Chairman," he cried, "there's no need to kill me like this! I don't know anything and I won't repeat anything; I couldn't do you any harm even if I wanted to." Someone ran up behind, caught his arms in a halfnelson and began to pull him backwards. "Just listen to me," he shouted, "you'll make a mistake if you kill me, I can be very useful to you!"

A feminine voice spoke from the back of the room.

"I think we might hear him for a moment, Mr. Chairman. He might possibly be of some value to us."

"As you wish." The Chairman raised his voice slightly. "Let him go, but wait outside within call; you may be needed later."

The hands released him, and someone guided him back to the chair. Too agitated to remain seated, he stood up and leant on the high back as he spoke, addressing himself sometimes to the Chairman and sometimes in the direction of the woman's voice. He made no attempt to hide his fear, for an instinctive cunning told him that in an organisation such as this, fearfulness of one's superiors was the beginning and end of wisdom.

"Listen," he began eagerly, "it's not in your interest to kill me. No doubt you could get rid of my body fairly easily, but that wouldn't by any means be the end of the business. Once already I've been reported missing from loss of memory; my second disappearance from hospital will make me, even in war-time, a national front-page sensation. Just think of it in ordinary terms. Desmond Thane, a respectable journalist of excellent personal character, suddenly disappears and is discovered some days later suffering from loss of memory. He is taken to hospital, where he is visited by a number of his friends, but the next day is carried off by a strange doctor, acting, so he claims, on the instructions of the patient's brother. After a day or two, more of Thane's friends call to see him, are told what has happened, and given the address of his nursing home. Upon enquiry, this proves to be nonexistent; and it is also found that he has no brother, that he had never been under mental treatment and that the doctor who removed him is not in the medical register. Then the sensation breaks with a vengeance. Huge photos of Thane and the hospitals description of Foster are splashed in all the cheap papers and seen by millions of people all over the country. You may not know it, but when I escaped from Standon I spent the night with two people living a short way away, who would certainly recognise my likeness and so bring the hunt to Foster's immediate neighbourhood. He must be well-known down there, and his appearance is distinctive enough to be obvious even from a police description. Besides, a policeman actually saw me in his house under circumstances sufficiently striking to have made me the object of village gossip for several days afterwards. Beyond a doubt, they'd soon get hold of Foster or some of his men, and do you think for a moment that they'd keep their mouths shut? No, they'd tell all they knew at once, and your game would be well and truly up. You ought to have killed me when you had me the first time; now you've left it too late, and your only safe course is to let me go before the investigation starts."

He paused for breath, and from the stillness of the room knew that he was holding his audience. Much encouraged, he continued persuasively.

"That's one side of the question; now consider the other. If you let me go I can probably be extremely valuable to you. I don't know what form your activities take, but I am sure that I have attributes that might be useful to them. I have a good public character and a respectable position in society. I live by myself, and for years past have given no-one any account of my movements; I am quickwitted and ready for nearly anything; I think I have little personal or social conscience. Above all, I am a murderer; and since no-one but you knows of my connection with Anna Raven, I am completely at your mercy. Nobody could make a better or safer employee, and I am perfectly willing to come in on anything you do. Of course you don't trust me, but I daren't do anything against you as long as I live. Only if I meet with death at your hands can I become a danger to you."

Carefully feeling his way round to the front of the chair he sat down and folded his arms. For some minutes there was a sibilant whispering, too faint to overhear, then the Chairman spoke deliberately.

"I quite agree with much of what you have said, but there is one weakness in your argument of which you are no doubt very much aware. Although we know you are Raven's murderer we have absolutely no legal proof of it, since your telegram to her, the only link between you, was taken from her flat on the night of her death and has never been seen by the police. We have, in fact, no hold over you at all."

He ceased, and Desmond anxiously speculated as to the motives of this unnatural honesty. Slowly and emphatically he continued.

"We will agree to your proposition and take you into our service upon the condition that you supply sufficient evidence to convict yourself of Raven's murder in a court of law."

"But how can I? What do you mean?"

"You will, this evening, write a series of letters to Raven, dated in sequence from your first acquaintance with her until a few days before her death. They will trace the course of a violent passion for her, show an increasing suspicion and jealousy, accuse her of infidelities and finally threaten in the plainest terms to kill her. They will be simply written so that the most obtuse juryman will realise all their implications. Although neither you nor the police are aware of it, Raven owned a week-end cottage under another name, which she frequently visited and which has remained shut up since her death. When you have written the letters they will be tied together and put in a desk at the cottage, together with other personal papers. Should your services become in any way unsatisfactory, we can arrange for enquiries to be made about purchasing this cottage, the true name of the late owner to be disclosed, an entry forced, her papers and letters read, and information laid before the police. I do not think that any argument however specious, or any allegations however sweeping would enable you to escape ' the consequences. That is the decision of the- Committee."

"But what shall I say? How shall I ..."

Another voice cut in sharply.

"You are a writer, you need no advice from us in such a matter. Do what you are told and do it quickly, or else take the consequences."

A hammer tapped on the table.

"Take him away," said the Chairman, "provide him with writing materials. Next on the Agenda."

He was caught by the arm, hustled out of the door, and through another. A hand snatched the bandage from his eyes, and when he accustomed himself to the glare of light he saw that he was in a small room with a chair, a table and a mahogany writing-desk furnished with ink, blotting-paper and a fountain-pen. After a while, the door opened a few inches and someone threw a flat packet neatly on to the table. A voice spoke from the darkness outside.

"You'll find several different writing papers in that package; see that you vary the kind you use. Write about a dozen letters in all, and date them at irregular intervals, starting from a week after you first met Raven and continuing until three days before her death. Head them all with your London address, and sign all except the first three with your Christian name. The first two had better be friendly but a little formal, the next six amorous, and the remaining four increasingly jealous and finally threatening. The last must definitely threaten to kill her —you might actually mention strangling, but say also that you have a pistol. What precise words you use is your own affair, but see that you play no tricks. You may think of inserting some explanation in code, or perhaps of altering your normal handwriting, but by God you'd better not try it. If we detect one conscious fault in what you write, you'll be taken away and beaten until you die. Do you understand?"

"I understand."

"Right; get to work and see that what you write is good. You'll be given four hours, then I'll come back and collect what you've done. And remember, no tricks, no reservations, and no incompetence, real or assumed. Now start."

Desmond was left alone to the execution of his own condemnation. Perversely, he felt almost happy, and his captor's threats left his confidence quite unshaken. Parody was his particular forte, and he was sure that, inadequate as sincere letters would actually have been, those he was now going to compose would prove perfect examples of their type. He took up the package and examined the notepapers they had given him, artistically choosing the best quality paper for his introductory letter and reserving a cheap, garish blue for the scrawled and ominous climax. Then he settled down at the desk with the business-like satisfaction of a candidate faced with a question on his special subject. He knew he was going to make an excellent job of it.

Hours later he stood up, stretched himself, and wandered round the room. His fingers were stiff with cramp, his brain fuddled with tiredness, but he was filled with the pure pleasure of the successful artist. He had, at first, played with the idea of attempting to invalidate the letters and double-cross the Committee by consistently mis-spelling the name of some familiar acquaintance, or by slipping in references to political events a week before they took place; but soon decided that such a method would be altogether too dangerous. Instead, he had tried to safeguard himself in the only possible way, by so exaggerating the character he had to represent that no-one who knew him would believe he had meant it seriously. But when he remembered the kind of letter that is actually quoted in law-courts, and imagined the joy with which his friends would welcome such a ludicrous insight into his superior soul, he knew that no exaggeration he dared risk would seem absurd to a judge, a juryman or even to his own circle. There was nothing to do but give himself up to his worst creative abilities.

The results were impressive. In their own unpleasant fashion his Letters to Anna (he already saw them in capitals) were perfect; should he ever come up for trial any Sunday newspaper would offer thousands for them. They contained everything. Warm, sweet sentiment, hot-handed passion, embarrassing religious introspections, painful endearments, and hackneyed blood and thunder were all represented in rich platitudinal flower; from the whole stinking nosegay of bogus sexual emotion, not one nauseous blossom was missing.

For some time he paced up and down, savouring his best phrases, until the door opened its familiar crack and the familiar voice addressed him.

"Have you finished? Good. Give me the letters, and wait quietly."

A hand took the bundle he proffered, and the door shut. Time passed slowly, and it might have been hours or only a few minutes before the door opened again.

"Turn round facing the wall; you are going to be blindfolded."

Desmond turned obediently and let a handkerchief be pulled over his eyes. He heard a chair scrape as the invisible speaker seated himself at the table. Then:

"I am going to ask you certain questions; answer them briefly and accurately. What is your full name and the exact date of your birth? "

"Why do you want to know?"

"Answer my questions and don't waste time."

"My full name is Desmond Andrew Thane. I was born on the fourteenth of August, 1908."

"What precisely is your present employment? How much are you paid; does it reserve you from military service? How long have you held the position?"

Wearily Desmond answered, but the questions went on and on. The name of his bank and the exact state of his account, the names and addresses and professions of his relations and principal friends, the full details of his education, the number of photographs of himself he believed to be extant, the places in which he had lived, and the towns he had visited were all made the subject of long and intensive enquiry, but still the interrogation continued. Desmond lied as much as he dared—denied that he belonged to a Club, suppressed the existence of a few distant relatives—but most of the questions were too direct to be avoided, and when at last the dry voice paused and the questioner pushed back his chair, he knew he had been forced to supply an almost complete dossier covering every side of his life, and that from now onwards a voluntary disappearance would prove almost impossible. He was very tired, and it took an effort to shake himself awake and realise he was being addressed.

"The letters and your answers to my questions seem satisfactory," the man was saying, "and it has therefore been decided to release you for the present. You will return to your previous employment immediately, and we will notify the hospital that you have now recovered. I regret that your wallet and other belongings which were taken from you at Standon cannot be immediately returned to you; they will be sent as soon as possible.

Meanwhile, here is a pound which will be deducted from the sum in your notecase."

A cold hand thrust a folded note between his fingers. The speaker continued.

"You will, of course, make no reference to anything you have experienced during the past week, nor will you change your address or leave London. You may be under observation, and any suspicious behaviour on your part will be immediately dealt with in ways which you can imagine. That is all."

"But I say," said Desmond, "isn't there anything else? Haven't I got to do something for you?"

"When there are orders for you you will receive them; you need not fear that we shall forget you. Membership of this organisation is usually for life. Now follow me." He took Desmond by the wrist, and guided him through a maze of stairs and passages to a flight of stone steps which felt like those that led out to the garage. At the bottom he was pushed into a car, the door slammed, and he was rapidly driven off. Cautiously edging along the seat, he found, as he expected, that he was alone, but dared not remove the bandage. After driving for about twenty minutes, the car stopped and someone opened the door.

"Get out," he said, and waited while Desmond groped his way down to what felt like a pavement.

"You can take off the handkerchief now and go home," said the voice, "you'll be hearing from us." The car started up and moved off. When Desmond tore off the blindfold, he saw that he stood outside the door of his own house.

It was soon after dawn, and though the pavement was still sunk in darkness, the tops of the tallest buildings were already tipped with light. As he felt for his keys, he remembered that they were still at Standon, and, not unpleasantly resigned to a walk and an early breakfast, strolled slowly along the shuttered and silent streets. He was safe at last and free from the threat of death, but he felt no relief. Twist his mind as he would, he could see no way of escape. Plausibly he argued that they intended only to frighten him, and that he would never hear from the Committee again; hopefully he pretended that the work he might have to do would be easy and profitable; vainly he tried to expel the memory of those fatal letters. It was useless. Although, like Lazarus, he had marvellously returned to his own familiar world, he remained oppressively aware that he dwelt there only on sufferance; at any moment, in the height of any felicity, he might be pulled back to the dark and pitiless underworld.

It was now quite light, and as he looked down the long channel of Gower Street, he could see the patterns of green on the rounded hills of Hampstead. There was a cold breeze from the corner of Russell Square, and shivering a little he quickened his pace. But his thoughts went with him and could not be shaken aside. The porters cleaning the steps had the faces of spies, the spacious streets were a prison, the houses traps. Whatever happened, something was wholly lost; he would never, he knew, feel quite the same again.

CHAPTER XVI

Nothing happened, to his surprise, almost to his chagrin, Desmond found that few of his acquaintances had heard of his amnesia or even noticed his absence. Those who had done so, readily accepted his weak explanation that the whole story had been due to Mr. Poole's precipitance when he failed to arrive at work, and after laughing heartily at this remarkable mischance, eagerly returned to the pleasanter occupation of talking about themselves. Shadwell, of course, continued to drop mysterious hints, but this was so familiar a feature of his conversation that no-one appeared to pay much attention to him. Even his return to International Features was easier than he had expected. Mr. Poole welcomed him with unnatural heartiness, and at first made a great number of extraordinarily casual visits to his room, but, beyond that, showed no change of attitude towards him, and was soon, indeed, making little jokes about his tendency to absent-mindedness. The truth, Desmond slowly realised, was that his employer's infuriating inability to appreciate what anyone else was doing or saying had at last proved itself useful; the obstinate cataract through which he had so often regarded Desmond's ideas had also succeeded in blinding him to his eccentricities; so that, on his familiar principle that what he did not understand therefore did not exist, Mr. Poole had succeeded in forgetting precisely what his assistant had said to him in the hospital. And so Desmond's life went on exactly as before. For all he could point to, nothing whatever might have happened.

But to Desmond himself everything was appallingly different. As the days passed, his terrors, instead of decreasing, grew; while the dangers he had experienced preoccupied his imagination more and more, until he was unable to understand how ever he could have taken them lightly. He was, of course, in the common state of psychological after-shock, in which one pays, by subsequent breakdown, for coolness in actual danger; and would, in the normal course, have recovered very rapidly. But now, unhappily, he knew that the threat was not over but merely suspended; and he started with shocking doubt at every rap on the door or ring of the telephone. If he could have taken a holiday, he might have recovered his balance, but his promise to the Committee bound him, and he dared not make the venture. He became obsessed with the feeling that he was being spied upon, and spent hours in the early morning peering from his windows for hidden watchers. Repeatedly he told himself that his fears were fancies, or that even were they justified, there was nothing that he could do about them; it was useless. By the end of a week he had come to the crisis; he knew that either he would wake from his mental fever and laugh at himself, or else go to pieces altogether.

That evening he dined at the Radical Club. Ever since he had told the questioner from the Committee that he belonged to no Club, he had seen its substantial palladian halls as his only safe refuge, the one place where his enemies would not be watching him; and whenever his mania became too great to be borne, he had, with immense precautions and by a circuitous route, slipped off there to spend a few precious hours of normality. He knew, of course, that if the Committee really had any interest in him, they could easily have discovered about his membership, and reach him there as surely as anywhere else. But this made no difference to his feelings, for when he was at work or at home pure reason had little effect on him, while when he was in the Club, his neurosis was equally powerless. He had, in fact, devised his own false universe, in which ordinary common sense played no part.

The Radical's sombre lounges proved that night as soothing as he had expected. He drew a perennial satisfaction from the clusters of preoccupied baldness that sat in bunched posies round the smoking-room fireplaces, or exchanged important gossip in the alcoves of the domed hall; and never ceased to enjoy the small oddities of the place; the solemn official buried in his *Daily Mirror,* the white-headed old gentleman who unashamedly sat on five papers lest other members should have them before him. Securely fortified behind a corner-table in the diningroom, he ate his dinner with more relish than he had his lunch, and though he still harboured his fears, they at least no longer obsessed him. Suddenly a familiar tone pierced through the bubble.

"No, that won't do at all. Take it away and bring me something else."

It was the rusty and unmistakable voice of the Chairman of the Committee.

Desmond dropped his fork and checked an impulse to jump up. As quickly and cautiously as a startled hedgehog, he peered about the room to find the speaker, but all the faces were unfamiliar. Then he remembered that he had never seen the Chairman; and, fixing his eyes on his plate, he strained to catch the fatal voice. Yes, there it was again: ". . . always making mistakes. Something ought to be done about it."

The petulant old voice grumbled on, and Desmond's glance moved sideways from table to table towards the source of the sound. The speaker, shockingly, was only a few feet away, though his back was turned; and Desmond, directly he felt he could trust himself to get up without making a clatter, slipped away round the other side, leaving his meal Unfinished. From the door he stared across at the author of his ruin, and saw a wizened, vulturine little elderly man, his large head sparsely straggled with greying hairs, his skin, even at such a distance, bunched and creased, his fingers tapping nervously as he talked. From where he stood, Desmond could not hear what he said, but saw that, although the thrust of the Chairman's head suggested an aggressive harangue, his face continually twitched into an ingratiating smile.

Desmond beckoned to a waiter.

"Who's that man over at the table in the corner? Look, the one by the right-hand window, talking to a man with white hair?"

"That's Sir Joseph Harton, sir."

"Is he a Member? Who's the man with him?"

"Oh yes, sir, Sir Joseph is one of our oldest members, though he doesn't come here very often in the evenings. The other gentleman is a guest, and I don't know his name, though I expect I could find out if you wished it." "No, no, never mind that. Thank you," replied Desmond quickly, and hurried out of the building.

Outside in the street he was seized by an overwhelming anger. The Chairman (for now, in his mind, he bulked larger even than Foster) had broken into his easy life, imprisoned and tortured his body, hounded his mind until he was all but crazy, and now had invaded his last and only privacy. In his rage he quite forgot that his own crime had caused his misery; and blindly blamed it all on the Chairman, who was, in a way, no more than his well-deserved Fury. Not knowing quite what he intended, he ran back into the Club.

Inside, he hesitated; then with a return to sense, went up to the library and took down the current *Who's Who*. Sir Joseph Harton, Bart., had quite an impressive entry.

M.P. for South Trenton, 1921-9, and from 1931; Undersecretary of State for India 1927-8 ; Deputy-Chairman of Committees 1935-6; President Midland Conservative Association 1935-7 indicated an active political career; while *Director Harton, Ware and Trustlove, Ltd., Director Malayan Lead Corporation, Director Steamboat Engineering Company, Director Simpson Andrews Bank* indicated very considerable wealth. Besides all this, Sir Joseph had found time to be *President of the Northern Mine-Owners' Alliance, President and Founder of the All-British League, Vice-President of the Wiltshire Antiquarian Society, and Visitor of St. Joseph's Hospital, East Hartlepools.*

Superficially, a full and successful career, yet, thought Desmond, a record of relative failure. Sir Joseph was eighth Baronet, educated at Winchester, Trinity, Dresden and the Sorbonne, and so, presumably, had inherited his money; yet with all the opportunities so favourable a beginning represented, the man had accomplished little of importance, and snatched a fleeting Under-Secretaryship as his highest reward. But the voice

Desmond had heard at his interrogation, the face he had just seen twitching at the corner table, were not those of one who would be contented with small rewards, but betrayed a mind lusting for predominance, and suggested a man to whom all but the highest was worth very little. At the foot of the paragraph was *Author: The Path of the Philosopher King* (1927).

Intrigued, and jealously annoyed that his enemy should invade letters as well as business and politics, Desmond, not very hopefully, looked up "Harton" in the catalogue, and found, to his surprise, that a copy of the book was in the library. It was, he discovered at last, at the top of a high, dusty shelf; a thin, privately-printed volume, inscribed in a small jagged hand "With the Author's Compliments to the Radical Club," and had, Desmond noticed spitefully, none of its pages opened. Brutally tearing the leaves apart with his thumb, he sat down and began to read.

He had looked forward to meeting some natural literary incompetence, but had never expected to find such a bad book as this. Ill-phrased, flat with platitude and riddled with cliches, possessing all the faults of popular journalism without its saving lucidity, the book was an appalling anthology of technical and stylistic error, and would have been quite unreadable however original its subject. Yet though the manner was atrocious, the matter was still worse, and even the obscurity of the writing could not conceal the emptiness of what was written. Half-digested Plato, misunderstood Hobbes, a vulgarisation of Nietzsche and a misreading of the minor Freudians were applied to a sketchy outline of anthropology and world-history to prove that enlightened autocracy was the aim of all society, and that human progress was about to culminate in the sudden apotheosis of the rational tyrant. How this philosopher-king was to arise, the book did not clearly explain, but sly comments on current events and coy references to the Ruler's necessary characteristics made it clear that he might, not impossibly, be found in the author himself.

Desmond lay back in his chair and laughed; the monster he

had dreaded was nothing but a megalomaniac ass, no more to be feared than were all his stupid peers who expressed their ludicrous self-conceits in Bloomsbury coteries, obscure political parties, or in the lonely silences of their Kensington flats. Sir Joseph Harton was no more than empty wind, blowing hither and thither and meaning nothing. With a swift glance to make sure that the library was empty, he tossed the book neatly across the room into the open grate.

After a while, doubt crawled back to his mind. Harton was an intellectual nullity, but did that finally dispose of him? Often before, Desmond remembered, he had contemptuously dismissed as fools men who, though incapable of abstraction or self-analysis, were quickly and formidably intelligent. History, too, gave the same warning. How did the critical reviewers regard the first edition of *Mein Kampf*? Or, a grander instance, what did the cultured Byzantines think of the Koran? The literary-minded always forget that power belongs to those of another kind, that men most incapable of reason are often the most competent in practice, and that it is not the Professors of Economics who make fortunes on the Stock Exchange. Sir Joseph was crazed with vanity, but he was extraordinarily dangerous, although his cleverness was not of the kind that could express itself in words. Desmond knew he could outargue the Chairman on every page of his book, yet here he had been cowering in terror because the man was in the same building. He remembered that in his schooldays his superior wits had never finally saved him from the bully; for only in a very limited sense is knowledge effective power.

He got up, picked the book from the fireplace, and put it back on its shelf. His mockery of the Chairman had flickered out; his anger, for a time damped down, began to mount again. He went heavily downstairs and sat waiting, exactly for what he did not know, in the shadow at the side of the hall.

After about half an hour, the door of the smoking-room opened, and, in the rectangle of light it revealed, he saw the figure of Sir Joseph Harton. He walked like an old man, carefully lest he slip on the polished floor, and Desmond suddenly recollected that *Who's Who* had not given his date of birth. He paused just in front of him without turning his head, and went down the steps towards the cloakrooms. In a minute or two Desmond followed him.

At the door of the washroom he paused and stood quietly watching. Sir Joseph washed his hands slowly and very thoroughly, soaping them again and again, and brushing separately each immaculate nail. Carefully he dried his hands, using two towels; carefully he combed and parted his scanty hair. Then he turned to go, and saw Desmond standing before him.

Desmond had expected some dramatic denouement, but the Chairman plainly did not recognise him; fear and the blindfolding must have altered his appearance at the interview more than he realised.

"Excuse me, sir," he said and made to go past him. Desmond stretched an arm to each side and barred his way.

"Good evening, Sir Joseph," he replied breathlessly. "Don't you recognise me?"

For a second the other seemed astonished, then astonishment flashed into knowledge, and knowledge into fear. He opened his mouth either to speak or to shout for help, and Desmond, without thought or plan, leapt forward, caught him by the throat and rushed him into one of the bathrooms that opened off the lobby. He knew he intended to kill him.

Bolting the door behind him, he pushed the Chairman up against the wall.

"Now," he whispered pointlessly, "what about it?" The Chairman did not answer a word, but opened his pale blue eyes very wide and stared straight into Desmond's. For the first time in his life, no doubt, he had come against violence. The organisation of which he was head killed and maimed, but that happened out of sight and meant no more to the Committee than coal-cutting does to mine-owners, Desmond could sense his agonised new awareness of the physical powers of the body. As he leant there against the wall he felt broad hands round his neck and could see the little dark bristles in Desmond's chin. For an instant he knew that man is an animal, and that all the casual talk of "removal," "purging," "unavoidable casualties," really meant that bones were breaking, flesh pulping, and organs being torn apart. The hands tightened round his throat, and he understood that beside death all power and ambition were nothing.

Desmond waited for him to speak, and knew that his first word would free his passion and let him press the thin, palpitating throat, until Chairman, Baronet, M.P. and Company Director were no more than a lifeless, mass of carbon, calcium and water. He dug in his thumbs still harder, and Sir Joseph made no resistance, but gave a little gasp and shut his eyes.

"Well," he repeated harshly, "what about it?"

The Chairman said nothing, but leant there with his eyes shut and his mouth open, a ludicrous parody of a small child expecting a sweet. His body felt as fragile as a mummy's, and Desmond saw he would give him no trouble. 'Now for it,' he thought, 'one, two, three, and away he goes! ' He drew back a little to get better leverage, and saw the Chairman's hands hanging limply at his sides, palms open, as though he were already dead. 'Come on,' he said to himself, but did nothing. ' Get it over! ' his will commanded, but his hands relaxed. With as great a relief as if he himself had been reprieved, he knew he was going to let his enemy escape. Suddenly he gave Sir Joseph a little sharp flick on the cheek.

"All right, Mr. Chairman," he said, irritably, seating himself on the edge of the bath, "you can relax now; I'm going to let you go."

Slowly and cautiously, like some old tortoise peering from its shell, Sir Joseph opened his eyes and studied his assailant. For a time neither of them spoke; then the Chairman said:

"I don't think we mentioned your remuneration the other day. If you cared, I could give you an advance until the matter is decided."

His hand moved uncertainly to his breast pocket, but he never took his eyes off Desmond's.

With a sudden access of pride that surprised himself Desmond answered brusquely.

"Do what you like; I don't want your money, so you can keep your hand off your cheque-book. If you get out of here alive it won't be by paying your way."

This silenced the Chairman for a while, and Desmond sat still, enjoying his controlled but obvious terror. At last Sir Joseph tried again.

"Foster has been removed," he said placatingly; "he was largely responsible for your unfortunate treatment, but he is out of the way now and won't bother you again." Desmond was interested.

"Have you killed him, then?"

The other seemed distressed by such bluntness.

"I gave orders this afternoon that he should be prevented from making further mistakes, and I think my instructions will be acted upon. But now that he has been removed," he went on rapidly, "we shall have no more need of your services, and I will have your letters returned to you at once. The whole affair was a mistake of Foster's, and I had little to do with it."

He looked hopefully towards the door, and Desmond laughed.

"You must be losing your grip; you offered me an advance of salary a few minutes ago." Suddenly he grew furious. "You stupid, near-senile beast," he shouted, "you ought to have been killed long ago! You and your kind are all the same, all of you hide your vices behind words and your crimes behind cliches. If I kill a personal enemy, it's murder; if you do the same, you've 'removed' him; if a gang of you in charge of a nation quarrels with another gang, it's war or even a crusade! You think you can buy or bully everyone. First you torture me and mean to kill me, then you offer me money to save your own life. I, God help me, am too feeble-minded to finish you off now, though I know you'll be after me in the morning. Oh, for Christ's sake get out before I change my mind and break your neck!"

Sir Joseph had wisely kept silent during this incoherent farrago, and, after a momentary hesitation, darted from the room. At the foot of the stairs Desmond overtook him and caught him by the collar.

"And another thing," he said, "I've read your book and it's lousy. I haven't laughed so much for a long time. I know you can't help being illiterate, but you ought to keep it quieter!"

Pushing the Chairman aside, he ran upstairs and plunged out of the Club. As he hastened recklessly through the blacked-out streets behind Pall Mall, he talked angrily to himself.

"I'm a bloody fool! I get this man in my power and what do I do? I don't kill him, I don't even black his eye, I refuse his money. All I do is be rude about his book! "

He suddenly began to laugh so uncontrollably that he tripped over a kerb and saved himself from falling by clutching a lamp-post. Clinging there in the darkness, with the muted roar of the traffic in Piccadilly to accompany him, he laughed and laughed until his stomach ached and he feared he would never stop.

Two hours later, seated in his favourite chair beneath the pleasant light of a reading lamp, he admitted to himself that it was all up. However subtly he reasoned, he could not avoid the inescapable facts that he had threatened the Committee beyond all mercy, that no story he could possibly invent would enable him to ask for police protection, and that to stay here waiting for the Chairman to take his revenge would be more than his nerves could stand. With an unquenched flicker of his old anarchic spitefulness, he had wired to Foster at Standon, saying simply: SIR JOSEPH HAS ARRANGED A HOLIDAY FOR YOU IN A HOT CLIMATE GIVE HIM ONE FIRST, but by now he hardly cared if it were received or not. Perhaps Foster was already dead, perhaps he would never get the telegram or misunderstand it if he did. Perhaps, on the other hand, and Desmond thought this most likely, he would receive the warning, circumvent his doom, and in some way take his revenge.

As for himself, he knew the course he must take.

EPILOGUE

Escape, if it be wholehearted, is often surprisingly simple. A mendacious declaration to Mr. Poole of his irresistible impulse to fight for Human Rights; a request, granted with offensive readiness, for a letter stating that he was not indispensable; and a lunch-hour disappearance, leaving no address. The Recruiting Centre, kindly to volunteers, had examined, accepted and dispatched him with a speed and efficiency that subsequent experience of military procedure made seem almost incredible; and although a few of his friends had learnt of his surprising intention, he had successfully concealed not only his future unit, but even the branch of the Forces to which it belonged. The whole enlistment had taken less than two days, and now, hearing from no-one and corresponding with none, his old life had vanished as completely as if he were dead. Known only by a number, embedded amongst ten thousand others in an anonymous camp in a censored and distant county, he felt as safe from the Committee as though he were in prison or in the midst of the Kalahari Desert.

He caught occasional echoes from the outside world. Once, six weeks or so after he arrived at the camp, Desmond saw in a crumpled newspaper two days old, a paragraph stating briefly that Sir Joseph Harton, for seventeen years Conservative M.P. for South Trenton, had collapsed while leaving the House and died at his home in Eaton Square a few hours later. When he received his pay at the end of the week, he had telephoned Foster's number at Standon, only to be told by the Exchange that the line had been out of service for almost six weeks. For a few days afterwards he speculated, as well as one can speculate in a small wooden hut amidst forty other people, as to whether Sir Joseph had killed Foster and died naturally, or whether Foster had escaped and killed Sir Joseph; and wondered, sometimes, whether the death of the Chairman had broken up the Committee. But there was always brass to be cleaned, or fatigues to be done, or darts to be played with a dozen different accents, and he did not bother himself unduly about such questions.

He had begun to see that whatever happened or might happen, the Committee and all its legal and illegal kind were probably finished. The control of power by a few, the state of affairs in which important individuals could struggle amongst themselves for rule over millions, was probably over for good, or at least in a final decline, whatever the length and outcome of the war. The 'Committee, with its gangsters and tortures; the oligarchic governments, with their sound-proof cellars and roomy prisons, were already imperceptibly crumbling, and the present conflict, with its shaking up and shaking down of a thousand old institutions, would very likely end such anachronisms for good, in the double sense of the word.

Desmond himself was already forgetting his old identity, and since he knew that his future would be different from his past, he let his mind hibernate until the cold spell was over. Occasionally he thought of Anna, and more often, strangely, of the Jew, but found that they moved his feelings to an ever lesser extent. For what, after all, were two small murders in the midst of so much slaughter?

Made in the USA
Middletown, DE
22 August 2024